Alloa finds a thief. She denounces him, discovering too late that he has stolen her heart. Alloa travels to Europe and once more the paths of the two cross, but this time fate holds them together in a bond of danger. Torn between duty and yearning, Alloa finds that she must make a decision which could turn her dreams to nightmares. With the strength born of a truthful heart she makes her choice and learns that fortune has not released her from the bond she thought forgotten.

Also in Pyramid Books

by

BARBARA CARTLAND

THE THIEF
OF LOVE

by

Barbara Cartland

▲PYRAMID BOOKS   •   NEW YORK

THE THIEF OF LOVE

A PYRAMID BOOK

First Published by Herbert Jenkins Ltd.
© Barbara McCorquodale 1957
First Sphere Books edition, 1967

First Pyramid edition published January 1974
All Rights Reserved

ISBN 0-515-03272-7

Printed in the United States of America

Pyramid Books are published by Pyramid Communications, Inc. Its trademarks, consisting of the word "Pyramid" and the portrayal of a pyramid, are registered in the United States Patent Office.

Pyramid Communications, Inc., 919 Third Avenue, New York, N.Y. 10022

This Book is Dedicated to my Sons, Ian and Glen In Memory of Biarritz in April 1956.

THE THIEF
OF LOVE

Chapter One

As her hands were full Alloa was glad to see that the door of the suite was half open.

She sidled through it into the *entresol* and walked through another open door into the bedroom.

It was only as she was putting down on the bed the freshly ironed clothes which she was carrying that she realised that a man was standing by the dressing-table.

He must have been aware of her at the same moment as she noticed him, for he turned and she saw, with a sudden shock of surprise, that he was holding in his hands the little diamond encircled miniature which usually stood beside Lou's gold-topped scent bottles.

With a throb almost of fear Alloa realised what he was. For a moment they only stared at each other.

Tall, dark, and good looking in a rather raffish way, the man was definitely not English.

"What are you doing in this room?" Alloa asked.

She realised almost with a sense of satisfaction that her voice did not betray the sudden agitation within her breast and the fact that her knees were trembling.

There was a perceptible pause before the stranger answered:

"You must forgive me if I am trespassing."

"Put that miniature down at once," Alloa said.

He glanced down at it with an air almost of astonishment that it should be in his hands. Then obediently he set it down on the table.

"You are a thief!" Alloa said accusingly. "I am going to ring the bell and hand you over to the hotel attendants."

She looked around a little wildly for the bell and realised that it was on the other side of the bed where she could not reach it.

"I promise you I have stolen nothing," the stranger said smoothly.

Alloa thought that for a moment there was a faint smile at the corner of his lips.

She guessed that he was laughing at her helplessness, knowing that she was at some distance from the bell and that although she stood between him and the door she would prove a very small and insignificant obstacle should he wish to escape.

But because she was frightened she would not allow herself to be intimidated.

"You may not have taken anything yet," she said. "But you will have great difficulty in explaining why you are in this room and what you are doing here, especially as you were holding that miniature when I came in."

She remembered, as she spoke, how she had said to Lou Derange only yesterday:

"That miniature is far too valuable to leave lying about."

Lou had laughed at her.

"You can trust all the staff here," she said. "Besides, they are not to know the diamonds are real. Personally, I enjoy looking at myself framed in such opulence. Encircled in diamonds! What more could any girl want?"

There was just a hint of bitterness behind Lou's joking, but Alloa ignored it and laughed as was expected of her.

Now she thought how right she had been. Such valuable things should not be left lying about in a hotel.

"I think you are being unduly harsh with me," the stranger said. "May I confess that, seeing the door open, it was only curiosity that brought me into this room?"

He smiled as he spoke and the smile transformed his face, making him not only immeasurably more handsome but almost irresistibly attractive.

'He is a crook all right,' Alloa thought to herself. 'Only a crook would contrive to be so charming in such a very difficult situation.'

"My father has often said that curiosity is the first step towards temptation," she said severely.

"Your father must be a very wise man."

"He is a Minister of the Church of Scotland," Alloa said.

Feeling that in some way her father's calling gave her an authority which was otherwise lacking.

The stranger smiled again.

"In which case he would doubtless add, in this instance, 'to err is human, to forgive divine'. Are you going to forgive me?"

"If I did my duty," Alloa replied, "I should report your presence here immediately. Oh, I know you are thinking that you could escape before I could reach the bell, but there is nothing to stop me from screaming. There are always waiters and chambermaids on duty on this floor. They would hear me and come running. You wouldn't get very far."

"I can see that I am completely in your hands," the stranger said meekly. "But I am not attempting to escape. Instead I am throwing myself on your mercy and asking you to give me another chance."

"Then you admit you have done wrong?" Alloa said quickly. "That you are a thief?"

"You can hardly expect me to admit anything so incriminating," he replied. "That would be very indiscreet on my part and would, in fact, saddle you with

11

a very uncomfortable responsibility. Suppose I turned out to be a desperate dangerous criminal!

"If in a week's time you saw my photograph in the papers as being wanted for murder or arson, then you would never forgive yourself for having let me go.

"No! I promise you that my presence here is due, as I have already said, entirely to curiosity."

"You wanted to see what the suite was like?" Alloa asked.

"Shall I say I wanted to see the suite in which the attractive Miss Lou Derange was staying?" the stranger answered.

"How have you heard about her?" Alloa enquired.

The stranger smiled again.

"Dare I confess it? I read the gossip columns!"

"Oh, of course!"

Alloa looked almost relieved. There had been many paragraphs about Lou and her great fortune and the parties which had been given for her and her mother since they arrived in England.

"And so, you see," the stranger went on, "as I was passing down the corridor and saw the door of the suite open, I decided to look inside. Reprehensible, I must admit, but not criminal."

"Then why were you holding that miniature in your hand?" Alloa asked accusingly.

"Because I had an idea that the portrait might be of Miss Derange. Am I right?"

"Yes . . . yes, it is," Alloa admitted.

He seemed to have an answer for everything, and yet that made her even more suspicious of him.

"What do you do? I mean . . . what is your job?" she enquired.

"Oh, I do a lot of different things from time to time," he answered evasively.

12

"And you are working here in this hotel at the moment?"

"I am here for the moment," he admitted.

"Why don't you get a proper job?" she asked. "There are plenty going. Young men are wanted in industry, in shops and offices—in fact anyone can get work if they want it. Why don't you seek employment in something in which you can be really interested and stick to it?"

"Do you really think I should do that?" the stranger asked.

"Yes, I do," Alloa replied. "It seems such a waste, such a pity that a man like you should be . . ." She was just going to say the word thief then corrected herself. ". . . should have a wrong attitude towards society."

"You think that is why I am behaving in this manner?"

"And isn't it?" Alloa asked. "You are young, you are healthy, you are well-spoken; and yet, as you admit, you are drifting from one thing to another. That is not the way to be successful."

"Do I want success?"

"Of course you do," Alloa said severely. "Everyone wants to be a success, everyone wants to make money, or, more important, to make something of their life."

"And if I tell you that I am doing what I enjoy doing, that I haven't any ambitions?"

"But that is just what you mustn't think," Alloa said. "You see, one is not put into the world just to enjoy oneself, but to make the very best of one's talents, whatever they may be, and in that way to be a good citizen."

"You almost convince me," he said slowly.

His voice was serious, but the corners of his mouth betrayed him.

"You are laughing at me!" Alloa exclaimed. "I suppose I am a fool to think I can alter you when you are already set in your ways, when you have already found it easier and more amusing to make money by crooked means than by honest ones.

"Well, if you won't be saved from yourself, I suppose nothing that I can say will make any difference."

"No, please, you are not to speak like that," the stranger pleaded. "I wasn't laughing at you. I was thinking how sweet you looked as you tried to point out the futility of my behaviour. You are very young to be a reformer, and perhaps I am too old to be reformed."

"No one is ever too old," Alloa replied. "I have seen my father convert men who were over sixty and they have become absolutely reformed characters."

"I expect that was because they were too old to enjoy the pleasures of youth," the stranger smiled.

Alloa gave a little gesture of hopelessness and irritation.

"It is easy to sneer," she said. "But sooner or later you will find out that you are making a fool of yourself. There is no real happiness in wrong doing."

"Are you sure of that? Perhaps you have never done anything wrong."

"If I did I should be sorry, and I should try at once to make amends."

"Yes, I am sure you would do that," the stranger said. "And perhaps because you are so persuasive I will try, too, to make amends for the faults I have committed in the past."

"Will you really?"

Alloa's little face lit up.

"Yes, really," he said.

It was difficult for her to tell whether he was speaking the truth or not. And yet there was something in his dark eyes that told her that he was.

"I believe you," she said. "Try, please try really hard to go straight. I promise you in the end that you will never regret it."

"Shall I say that I will give it a trial for your sake?" the stranger replied.

"Not for my sake but for your own," Alloa answered. "There is so much good in you, I am certain of that. You have only got to give it a chance to come out. You have only got to resist the wickedness which you now find attractive and then you will feel quite different—a different man."

"You are very persuasive," he said. "Did you learn such eloquence from your father?"

"I am not trying to be eloquent," Alloa said simply; "it is just what I believe, what I am absolutely convinced is the truth."

"And there is nothing more convincing than sincerity," the stranger said a little drily.

"You will try to get a decent job?" Alloa pleaded. "I wish I could help you, but I don't know many people in London. You see, I have been here only six months. If we were in Scotland, my father would help you. He has helped lots of young men to start a new life. You should see some of the letters he gets from them.

"They are so grateful because they are happy, because they are no longer afraid of the police or of being found out.

"That, they say, is the worst thing of all—the being scared of every step on the stairs, of thinking that round every corner someone may be waiting who may denounce you."

"I won't be afraid of those things any more," the stranger said. "And I think perhaps I can manage to find employment without your help, though it is a nice thought to think that you might give it to me."

"It would be very difficult for me," Alloa said,

"knowing nothing about you. But if you are certain you can manage to find something . . ."

"I shall manage," the stranger said. "But I shall always be grateful to you because you concerned yourself with me, not knowing what I am really like."

"I am sure you are good at heart, even if you are . . ." Again Alloa stopped and looked embarrassed.

". . . a thief," the stranger finished. "For that is how you think of me."

"I am sorry about that, but I won't think hardly of you in future," Alloa said earnestly. "Not now that you have promised me you will reform and will try and find yourself a proper job—a real job. You have promised, haven't you?"

The stranger nodded.

"Yes, I promise."

"And you will remember how dangerous it is to be curious?" Alloa said. "If anyone else had come in here instead of me, you might at this moment be under arrest."

She glanced over her shoulder.

"It might easily have been Mrs. Derange's maid, or even one of the hotel servants."

The stranger nodded.

"It was a risk I ought never to have run."

"No, indeed," Alloa said. "But not, remember, because it was dangerous to you, but because it was wrong."

"Yes, yes, I see that," he said softly.

Again she fancied there was a touch of laughter in his voice, but his eyes, watching her, were very solemn.

"But now you had better go," Alloa said. "It would not do for anyone to find you here and I could not explain your presence."

"You would not lie?" he said.

"No, of course not," Alloa said quickly, and added:

16

"Not unless it was absolutely necessary—a white lie to save you from being arrested."

"A white lie," he repeated the words softly. "I would like you to tell a white lie on my behalf, but perhaps that is asking too much. Thank you for being so kind to me. Thank you for showing me the wrongs of the past."

He walked towards her as he spoke and before Alloa was quite aware of what he was going to do he had taken her hand and raised it to his lips.

She looked down at his shining dark head.

Then once again she was looking up at him, realising, now he was closer, how tall he was and how there was some almost indescribable pride,—or was it arrogance?—about the way he held himself and in the carriage of his head.

"I hope that life will treat you lightly," he said quietly. "And that you will never find it difficult to be positive about what is right and what is wrong. Black and white sometimes become almost indefinably mixed."

Alloa did not know what to say to this and she was still feeling shy because he had kissed her hand.

"I want to know your name," he said. "Are you a friend of Miss Derange?"

"No, not a friend," Alloa said. "I am Mrs. Derange's secretary and, well, sort of companion to her daughter."

She glanced down as she spoke at the pile of underclothes that she had been ironing and thought that her jobs were so varied that it was difficult to put them into any particular category.

"And your name?"

Alloa smiled.

"It sounds strange," she said, "but my name is Derange, too—Alloa Derange. Alloa because I was born in the mining village of that name, and Derange because

17

my father belongs to the British branch of the same French family from which Miss Derange's father claimed his ancestry. We had never met. It was quite by chance I heard that this job was going."

"Alloa Derange. It's a charming name. I shall not forget it."

"If it is not the wrong thing for me to ask, what is yours?" Alloa enquired.

"Why do you want to know?"

She thought his voice was unexpectedly sharp.

"Oh, please," Alloa said quickly, "you mustn't think that I have asked that to make indiscreet enquiries about you or to give you away once you have left this room. I wouldn't think of doing a thing like that."

"No, I am sure you wouldn't. I believe you. I was only curious."

"It was because . . ." she said, colouring a little, "I thought perhaps I could pray for you. It is difficult to pray for someone if you do not know his name."

"My friends call me Dix," he said. "And, pray for me. I should like to be sure of your prayers."

For a moment he looked down into her eyes and Alloa had a strange impression that he was looking down into her very soul. And then, almost silently, so swiftly that she hardly saw him go, he was gone and she was alone in the empty room.

She drew a deep breath and then walked across to the dressing-table to pick up the diamond-studded miniature from where he had put it down and place it in its usual position.

Lou Derange's pretty face, with her dark, winged eyebrows, had been exquisitely painted on the oval ivory; but Alloa knew that it was the glittering brilliants encircling the frame which had made the stranger notice it the very moment he had come into the room.

She gave a little sigh.

It was a pity that someone so good-looking, so charming, should be living what her father would call a life of corruption. And yet, how many people there must be in the world who preferred the easy way of making money to the more difficult one of earning it by honest work.

Alloa sighed again and looked at herself in the mirror. Had he really listened to her?

Had she really done some good; altered him in any way from his set purpose? She felt suddenly despondent and strangely depressed.

Why, indeed, should he have paid any heed to what she said? She looked so ridiculously young, she told herself. She was twenty, nearly twenty-one, but she hadn't seemed to change since she was a little girl in the school-room.

Her fair hair fell straight on either side of her little pointed face and then curled up at the ends just a few inches from her shoulders.

Her eyes were very blue and, though her lashes were dark and she had plucked her eyebrows to look sophisticated, there was still, she thought despondently, an almost childish look about her.

Who was likely to take her seriously? Especially a man of his age, a man who undoubtedly had a wide and varied experience of women.

"Oh, God, help him! Please help him."

She whispered the prayer, then turned away from the sight of her lips moving in the reflection in the mirror.

Dix! It was a strange name, meaning ten in French. She supposed he must be a Frenchman, and yet it was hard to tell.

His English was faultless, but there was just that very faint accent. Perhaps he was Spanish, or even Italian.

She had no way of telling, and now she wished she had asked him.

Alloa gave herself a little shake. Why did she keep thinking about the man? She had let him go. She had said she would pray for him.

Once a day, at night when she went to bed, would be enough. She had many people for whom she prayed; he could be added to them without intruding himself upon her thoughts at other times.

Resolutely she crossed the room and started to put away the beautiful underclothes of satin and lace that she had ironed so diligently in her own room.

There had been no mention of her maiding Lou Derange when she had been engaged.

"I need a secretary," Mrs. Derange had said, "while I am in Europe. I had to leave my own at home to look after the house and all my social engagements. I thought it would be easy to pick one up in London, but the agency tells me that they are quite hard to find."

"It is a busy time of the year," Alloa had answered. "I am only giving up my position at the end of the week because the firm for which I have been working is moving to Manchester."

"And you don't want to go with them. I can understand that," Mrs. Derange said.

She looked down at the slip of paper which she held in her hand.

"Well, it seems as if it was meant for you to come to us. I couldn't believe my eyes when I saw your name. 'Look, Lou,' I said to my daughter. 'This girl has got the same name as our own. Do you think it's a mistake or is it genuine?' "

"I can understand that you thought it very strange," Alloa said.

"Strange is the right word," Mrs. Derange agreed. "It isn't as if our name's a common one. As my husband explained to me over and over again before he died, all the Deranges in America are direct descendants of the original *de Rangé* who was sent by Louis XIV with various other noblemen to populate Canada.

"He had a title of course and I have always believed that my husband was entitled to call himself *Comte*, but he wouldn't listen to me.

" 'I am an American, Susie,' he used to say. 'And I don't hold with titles. Just straight democracy is good enough for me.' But now we're in Europe and I intend to visit the head of our family. Lou should know her French relations."

"And who is the head of the family?" Alloa asked.

"You don't know?" Mrs. Derange asked. "Isn't your father interested in his antecedents?"

"I am afraid he isn't," Alloa answered. "He always thinks of himself as a Scot. He is back in Sutherland now, where his father and his grandfather lived, and to him that is home."

"Well, I have taken the trouble to trace the family back to its very beginning," Mrs. Derange said with satisfaction. "And the head of the family is the *Duc de Rangé-Pougy*. You can see, of course, how the *de* got added to the name in the New World and became Derange.

"That was understandable; but there is no doubt at all that we are all direct descendants of the *de Rangé* family, who go back in a direct line to Charlemagne.

"I have been in touch with the *Duchesse*, the *Duc's* mother, and she not only acknowledges our branch of the family but is prepared to welcome us."

Mrs. Derange paused impressively. Alloa, feeling that something was expected of her, said:

"How lovely for you!"

"That's just what I say. It's a great opportunity for Lou. You'll have to impress on her what a lucky girl

21

she is. Don't forget, will you? She'll perhaps listen to you because you're young, and young people aren't as a rule interested in their ancestors. But I think those things are real important."

Alloa was to learn that it was only one of the many things which Mrs. Derange wished her to impress on Lou, but Lou remained singularly unimpressed by them all.

"Oh, shucks," she said when Alloa obediently began to speak to her about the Derange family. "You didn't fall for all that stuff of Momma's, did you? She only dug it all up because she wants me to marry the Duke."

Lou pronounced it "Dook".

"Marry the Duke!"

Alloa said in amazement.

The idea had not entered her head that there was anything behind Mrs. Derange's interest in the family tree.

"Yes, of course. She wants to get me away from Steve Weston because she fancies that he's after my money, and the best way she can think of is to bring out of the bag this French *Duc*."

Alloa gaped at her, uncertain what to say.

"Not that I'm particularly allergic to Dukes," Lou went on, painting her nails with a particularly virulent crimson nail varnish. "I'd like to be a Duchess, although I think an English one counts more than a French one. What do you think?"

"I suppose I think so because I'm British," Alloa said. "But a Frenchman would think that his own *Duc* came first. I suppose it's the same with a Spanish title or a German one."

"Say, you've got something there," Lou said almost in admiration. "But as we haven't got any Dukes they count for a good deal in America, I can tell you."

She glanced at herself in the mirror and smiled.

"*La Duchesse de Rangé-Pougy*. Sounds all right, doesn't it? Momma got hold of the pictures of the castle where they live. It's called the *Château Pougy*. It's pretty breath-taking I can tell you."

"Are you really considering marrying a man you have never seen?" Alloa enquired.

"Why not?" Lou answered. "If I can't marry the man I want to marry, it might as well be a French *Duc* as anyone else. Besides, I can always be a *Duchesse* first and Mrs. Weston afterwards."

"Lou, you can't really be talking like that," Alloa said in a horrified voice.

Lou put down her nail varnish.

"Have I shocked you?" she asked. "Gee, you're soft, aren't you? Well, perhaps I'm making it out worse than it need be. I wouldn't marry the *Duc* unless he's attractive and I like him. But, of course, Momma makes out that he's Apollo, Clark Gable and Errol Flynn all rolled into one."

"And does he want to marry you, not even having seen you?" Alloa asked.

Lou shrugged her shoulders.

"That's Momma's problem," she said. "According to her the French always arrange their marriages, and the *de Rangé* family would look quite favourably on a few millions of good American dollars. That's why I gather the Dowager *Duchesse,* or whatever she calls herself, and Momma have been getting together.

"The Federal Mail has been working overtime. Anyway, that's why we're here and I'm quite prepared to sit back and see what happens."

"And what about Steve Weston?" Alloa enquired.

Lou's rather hard expression softened for a moment.

"I guess I'm real crazy about him," she said. "But still, maybe Momma's right and he has got an eye on my dollars as well. It's very hard if you're an heiress not

23

to think everyone's trying to get their hands on your bank balance, so if you're at all practical you feel that you might as well sell to the highest bidder."

"I don't think you really feel like that at all," Alloa said. "I think you are just like every other girl, Lou. You want to love somebody who loves you. You want to be loved for yourself. And if you wait long enough you'll find the right person."

"Maybe Steve is in love with me for myself," Lou said a little wistfully. "How can one tell?"

"I feel somehow one ought to know instinctively," Alloa said. "It's awfully difficult for you, I can see that. Can't you tell if he is really sincere?"

"Oh, he's sincere right enough," Lou answered. "But I can't help wondering if he would be quite as keen on wedding bells if we had to live on just what he earns."

"And what does he earn?"

"That depends. He's in real estate. Sometimes things are good and sometimes they're bad. Oh, hell! Half the time I think Momma's right. She says he wants a rich wife and a lazy life, and you can't depend on love. On the other hand a title and a fine *château* are better company at breakfast than a cross husband."

Alloa had to laugh. But she could not help feeling sorry for Lou. She was certainly very attractive—slim, long-limbed, with large violet eyes and dark hair curling over her small head.

At the same time there was determination in her characteristically square chin, and though she sounded indecisive, Alloa, after a very short acquaintance, was quite certain that Lou would always go her own way.

Also nothing she or Mrs. Derange could say would alter Lou's mind once she had made it up.

Alloa had moved to Claridge's Hotel three days after her interview with Mrs. Derange and found herself fascinated and enthralled with this new life, which was quite unlike anything she had known before.

She had never imagined anyone could be as rich as the Deranges.

They surrounded themselves with an exotic luxury which left Alloa open mouthed. And the money which ensured their comfort was literally poured out like water.

Behind it all, however, Mrs. Derange had not lost her shrewd streak of common sense. She had not been well endowered when she married her husband who came from an ordinary small-town family and had made his great fortune when he was past middle-age.

There were moments when Susie Derange remembered the pence, or rather the dimes, and counted the cost of what she was doing.

"Although we appreciate that you're a very distant cousin," she said to Alloa, "you're coming to us as secretary and, of course, a kind of companion to Lou, and therefore it will not be necessary for you to eat with us downstairs. Your food will be sent up to your room. I'm sure you would prefer that."

"Yes, of course," Alloa said. "I would much prefer it."

"That'll be fine then," Mrs. Derange approved. "And I have managed to get you a room on our floor but at the back. It's not very big, but I feel sure you'll manage."

"Yes, of course," Alloa said, feeling a little embarrassed by the explanations.

She had not expected anything different; but at the same time, when she saw the tiny staff room which had been allotted to her, she could not help being amused at the way money was expended on other things.

Great corsages of orchids were bought for Mrs. Derange and Lou to wear every evening. They were only worn once and would then have been thrown away if Alloa had not rescued them and put them in water.

Bottles of champagne were opened every evening when friends came in to drink; and though perhaps only a glass or two had been poured out, the waiters removed the bottles when the party was over.

Mrs. Derange's maid was a French woman, Jeanne, who was longing to get back to France. At first, Alloa thought she was going to be hostile and a little difficult, but she had her own way of making friends.

Very soon Jeanne became obviously devoted to her and was grateful to her for taking many arduous little jobs off her hands.

"I don't mind ironing," Alloa said. "Let me do Miss Lou's things and that will give you time to concentrate on Mrs. Derange's."

"It's not right that you should do so much, *Mademoiselle*. You have all the letters to type," Jeanne protested.

"There are not very many of them and I'm very quick," Alloa smiled. "I will iron the things for you. Don't worry about it."

Jeanne had been profuse in her thanks, but Alloa found that Lou took it more or less as a matter of course. Within two or three days of her engagement she had become part of the *entourage*.

"Alloa, run down to the desk and tell them . . ."

"Alloa, go out and see if you can find out about . . ."

"Alloa, for goodness sake get this mess sorted."

She found herself enjoying every moment of it. It was all so different, so unlike anything she had ever done before. She had been entranced when she had first come to London and got a job as secretary to a doctor.

It was her mother who had insisted that she leave Scotland.

26

"It is so dull for you here, darling," she had said.

She looked out of the Manse windows on to the small fishing village of Tordale.

"I am perfectly happy, Mummy," Alloa protested; but her mother had smiled unbelievingly.

And so she had found herself in London, living in a hostel, bewildered at first by the noise and speed of the metropolis and yet, at the same time, fascinated.

She had not been lonely. She had worked too hard for that, and though she had been sorry to leave the doctor, when he retired, she had found a new interest and a new enthusiasm in the business world.

This job was again very different and was, Alloa decided, like something out of a fairy tale.

She moved across Lou's bedroom floor, tidying, putting things away in the drawers, and yet all the time it seemed to her she was conscious of a shadow standing by the dressing table.

She found herself remembering the sudden shock it had been when she had come into the room and seen the man standing there.

It was not surprising that the suite door had been left open. Lou never remembered to take the key. Mrs. Derange had spoken to her more than once about her carelessness.

"Oh, shucks," she said. "What have we got to burgle?"

"Our jewellery for one thing," her mother had answered. "And our mink coats for another."

"They are all insured," Lou said carelessly.

"It's not the right attitude at all," Mrs. Derange protested, and Alloa agreed with her.

How often her father had said: "It is wrong to put temptation in people's way."

Alloa wondered why the stranger happened to be passing along this particular floor.

Resolutely she put the thought away from her that he had intended to get in whether the door was shut or not. He had been very insistent that it was only curiosity.

She wanted to believe him, she wanted to be convinced that he had only been passing and had seen the door open. But what was he doing in the hotel? Had he a job here? Would she be seeing him again?

She had a sudden longing to know more about him, to find out if he really would find himself decent employment. Perhaps he would let her know? Yet she felt somehow that he would not write to her.

She would never know what happened. It was like an unfinished story, a book which came to an end after the first chapter.

She felt curiously despondent at the thought, and then had no further time for it because there was the sound of voices in the *entresol* and she realised that Mrs. Derange and Lou had returned.

They went into the sitting-room, their high voices both speaking at once; then Alloa heard a call:

"Alloa! Alloa! Are you there?"

She ran from the bedroom into the big sitting-room. Lou was standing in front of the fireplace lighting a cigarette.

"News, Alloa," she said, as Alloa came into the room. "Momma's fit to burst herself with glee."

"Now, Lou, there's no need to talk in that vulgar manner," Mrs. Derange rebuked her. "Yes, there is news, Alloa, and I know you will be as pleased as we are."

Mrs. Derange was holding a letter in her hand. Alloa saw that it was written on the thin, almost transparent paper which denoted a letter from abroad and that the long envelope which Mrs. Derange had thrown on the floor had two French stamps on it.

28

"A letter from the *Duchesse de Rangé-Pougy*," Mrs. Derange said impressively. "She says that she's delighted, yes delighted that we have come to Europe. She's looking forward to seeing us and she is going to speak to her son and suggest that he invites us to stay at their *Château*. What do you think of that, Alloa? It shows she's keen, doesn't it?"

"Keen?" Alloa questioned.

"On meeting us, of course," Mrs. Derange answered.

She spoke too quickly and Alloa knew well that that was not what she had meant.

"To tell the truth I've been getting a little anxious because the *Duchesse* hadn't answered my last letter telling her that we were sailing, but she says now that she has been away to Monte Carlo and that her letters weren't forwarded."

"Well, we just have to sit back and wait for the invitation from the *Duc*," Lou said. "In the meantime, Momma, you had better polish up your French. Do you know it took you nearly three-quarters of an hour to translate that letter?"

Mrs. Derange looked at her crestfallen.

"I used to speak French well when I was a girl," she said, "but I'm rusty, that's what I am. I expect it will all come back when I get to France."

She looked down at the letter again.

"The *Duchesse* says she hopes to be able to write again in a week."

"They're not hurrying themselves," Lou said. "They don't want to look as if they are snatching at the bait. They have their pride!"

She spoke semi-humorously. Mrs. Derange gave her a look which said more than words. Then suddenly she gave a little cry.

"I've got it!" she said. "I've got an idea! What are we sitting here for? Why should we wait a week or so for the *Duc's* invitation? As you said, my French is rusty. We'll go to France and polish it up."

"We can't arrive before we're invited," Lou said.

"I'm not talking of going to stay at the *Château*," Mrs. Derange said. "We are going to Biarritz. It's only about twenty miles away. The *Duc* can't avoid inviting us if we are sitting there on the very doorstep. And besides, I've always wanted to see Biarritz."

"Like hell you have," Lou said, laughing as she threw herself down in the armchair. "All right, Momma, it's your show. I'm game for anything, even to stalk the reluctant *Duc*."

"I have told you before, Lou, not to be so vulgar," Mrs. Derange said stiffly. "Alloa, will you go downstairs and ask them to telephone the best hotel at Biarritz for reservations? And we will fly there, of course."

"I will find out about the aeroplanes," Alloa said Then, she hesitated, with her hand on the door.

"Will you be taking me?" she asked in a small voice. Mrs. Derange did not look up.

"Of course," she answered absently. "And Jeanne. We might as well be comfortable."

"And, of course, the *Duchesse* wouldn't be impressed if she didn't think we moved *en prince*," Lou said incorrigibly. She winked at Alloa. "Go on, Alloa. Hurry up and get it over. Momma knows what she wants and she won't be happy until she gets it."

Chapter Two

Alloa snapped the suitcase shut and gave a little sigh of satisfaction.

Everything was packed. Her own things had not taken very long, there were so few of them, but she and Jeanne had laboured all yesterday with Mrs. Derange's and Lou's.

They had had to send out for new suitcases, new hatboxes, to try and get in the many purchases which the two Americans had made since they came to London. When it was done, Alloa had begun to think that if she ever heard the rustle of tissue paper again she would scream.

Her own packing was finished, too,

She thought now, with a wry little smile, that what she owned was not likely to take long. Two pounds, sometimes three, or—since she had come to work for Mrs. Derange—five pounds a week of her salary had gone speeding back to the little Manse overlooking the heather-covered hills.

She knew what it meant to her father and mother, but it left nothing for her to spend on herself.

Her appearance didn't matter, she thought, as long as she looked clean and tidy; and yet when she had moved into Claridge's she was lamentably conscious of how inadequate she appeared beside the expensively dressed Lou Derange.

White collars and cuffs, a belt of coloured ribbon, a flower on her shoulder—Alloa copied all the hints that were advocated in the women's journals for furbishing up an old dress, for making a cheap frock look like a Paris model. She washed and cut her hair herself.

She managed, with care and constant washing, to make her stockings last doubly as long as everyone else.

And yet somehow even then she found it hard not to spend money. There were so many things she wanted, so many things to tempt her in the shops.

She wondered, now, what else she would require in Biarritz. She had bought herself a couple of cotton dresses, a bathing dress and some sandals. She had been delighted with her purchases until she had seen the many garments which Lou had added to her wardrobe.

They were breathtaking in their variety and colours and their beautiful materials.

Alloa tried not to feel envious.

'Nobody is going to look at me, anyway,' she told herself with a little grimace at the wet roofs.

Then she remembered what lay ahead of her and felt her heart leap with excitement.

Mrs. Derange's plans had been changed at the last moment. She had originally decided that they should all fly to Biarritz, but when Alloa had told her how little luggage they would be allowed to take in the aeroplane, she had thought of another way of making the trip.

Mrs. Derange was not really a very clever or quick-witted woman, but she was a very decided one. She was the perfect type of what is called an "American committee woman"; and although Alloa was not to know this, she did recognise in her employer a streak of determination and obstinacy which made her an almost irresistible force once she had set her mind on something.

Mrs. Derange had apparently thought over what was the best and quickest way of getting her *entourage,* with all its baggage, to Biarritz. The upshot was that she found an American friend in London who lent her a large blue Cadillac.

"Lou, I and Jeanne will go by aeroplane," she said, "with just enough luggage to last us two or three days. Alloa will come with the car and the rest of the luggage. The only problem is that I have got to get a chauffeur from somewhere. My friends have lent me the car, but they want their chauffeur in London to drive the Bentley they have just purchased. Do you know where we can apply for one, Alloa?"

Alloa had hesitated for a moment and then she had said:

"I suppose you wouldn't like me to drive the car?"

"But, of course! That's a perfect solution!" Mrs. Derange exclaimed. "I can't imagine why I didn't think of it."

An English employer might have been hesitant about allowing a young girl of whom she knew so little to drive an expensive car across Europe. But American girls took such things in their stride and Mrs. Derange did not give the matter another thought.

It was Alloa who discovered that it would shorten the journey and make it easier for her to get to Biarritz in three days' time if the car was flown across the Channel.

Mrs. Derange agreed to everything, and Alloa, having made all the necessary arrangements with the Automobile Association and having got herself a licence to drive on the Continent, came back to the hotel, tired but triumphant, to start packing for Lou.

She saw very little of either Lou or Mrs. Derange.

Having only quite recently arrived in London and had a round of parties and festivities to welcome them, they were now doing a second round of parties and festivities in order to say goodbye.

In between their engagements they sandwiched fittings for their clothes; and page boys kept arriving with more and more dressmakers' and milliners' boxes, until Alloa and Jeanne gave up the unequal struggle and as each new batch was deposited in the suite telephoned for yet another suitcase.

'The car will look as if I am moving house,' Alloa thought to herself, and then laughed.

It was all so exciting, so thrilling to think of the journey ahead of her—alone, unhampered by either Lou or her mother, at the wheel of the long, pale blue Cadillac which had delighted her from the first moment she had set eyes on it.

How grateful she was now for the long hours in which she had driven her father's old and dilapidated Austin about the countryside.

Alloa had often said that if one could drive her father's car, which in irony they called *Pegasus,* it would be easy and a joy to drive any other car. Now she thought of herself speeding along the roads of France in a car that responded to her slightest touch, and she gave a little sigh of sheer delight.

She turned from the window and as she did so her eyes fell on the bunch of flowers standing by her bed— a bunch of lilies-of-the-valley which still, after three days, seemed to scent the room with their sweet, exotic fragrance.

They had been brought to her early in the morning as soon as she was called. There was a card attached to them, and even before she opened the little, narrow envelope Alloa had known from whom they came.

"Thank you, Dix."

She had read it several times and found herself wishing that he had said more.

Was he trying to get a job? Did he really intend to go straight?

It was so irritating not to know, and yet at the same time she felt that he would not have sent the flowers if he had not intended to do what she had asked of him.

She felt a little proud, and at the same time happy, that she had been able to help someone. She had kept her promise and prayed for him every night, praying long and fervently that he might have the courage to start again.

Now she looked at the lilies-of-the-valley and put out her hand to touch them. They were still at their best, and almost as if she felt she was deserting them, she said with a smile:

"I shall take you with me."

She wished she could leave a message in case Dix called or telephoned her.

She had half believed that he would do so; she had half hoped to hear his voice again. Yet she told herself there was nothing more she could say to him and it was impossible for her to leave a message as she did not even know his name.

She looked round the room and then picked up her handbag and a list which lay beside it on the dressing-table.

Mrs. Derange and Lou had gone out to lunch, leaving Alloa with a list of things they required to be done before they all left tomorrow morning.

There were flowers to be sent to the American Ambassadress and to a number of other friends; sunproof cream to be collected from a shop in Bond Street; a hat to be delivered for a final alteration; and innumerable small purchases ranging from lipstick to sunshades—all to be done in the last few hours before the shops closed.

Alloa hurried along the passage and went down in the lift. She reached the hall of the hotel which, late in the afternoon, was comparatively quiet.

Automatically Alloa stopped at the desk to say that

she would be out for the next hour or so, but hoped to be back by six o'clock. The Head Porter had the telephone receiver to his ear. When he saw her he put it down, saying:

"I was just telephoning the suite, Miss. You don't know what time Miss Derange will be in? This gentleman wishes to see her."

For the first time Alloa glanced at the man who was leaning on the corner of the desk. He was tall, square shouldered and square chinned.

One glance was enough to tell her that he was an American. She rather liked the seriousness of his face as he said:

"I'm very anxious to see Miss Lou Derange, if it's possible."

"She will be back for a few minutes this evening," Alloa answered. "But she will be going out almost immediately to a cocktail party and after that to dinner."

"I won't keep her long," the young man said. "I hear she is going away tomorrow."

Alloa nodded.

"Miss Derange is leaving with her mother for Biarritz."

"That's tough," the young man exclaimed. "But I've got to see her somehow. See here, Miss . . . Miss . . ."

He hesitated at her name and Alloa smiled.

"Derange. I'm Alloa Derange."

"Is that so?" he enquired. "Well, look here, Miss Derange. I should like to speak to you for a moment if I could."

Alloa thought, with a sense of despair at the list of urgent things to be done, that she could not very well refuse.

She walked across the hall to where under the wide,

overhanging staircase there was an empty sofa where they could talk undisturbed.

"How come you've got the same name?" he asked as they sat down.

"I am the British branch of the same family," Alloa said. "But don't let me deceive you. I have been engaged as Mrs. Derange's secretary and sort of companion to Lou."

"Then you're just the person I'm looking for," he said firmly. "Has she—I mean Lou—spoken about me? My name is Steve Weston."

"Oh!"

Alloa was surprised, and then she smiled.

"Yes, she has spoken about you," she said. "She told me that you . . . you are fond of her."

"I'm just crazy about her, if that's what you mean," Steve Weston said. "I thought we were going to be married, and then she ran out on me on this harebrained scheme of going to Europe."

"But why are you here?" Alloa asked.

He looked a bit shamefaced.

"To tell the truth, I don't quite know myself," he answered. "I've got a week's holiday and didn't know what to do with myself, so I just stepped on an aeroplane and here I am. I didn't like to cable Lou, or even to telephone her when I had arrived, in case her mother got to hear of it. She's a dragon, that woman; haven't you found her so?"

Alloa laughed. She couldn't help it.

"You mustn't ask me questions like that about my employer."

"There's a great deal more I could say about her," Steve said darkly. "Lou loves me, I know she does, but her mother's set on her making a fancy marriage. They're all the same, these American mothers. If their daughters get what they consider a smart husband, they

37

take all the credit for themselves. I haven't got a chance. I'm not smart and I'm not rich."

"I don't think that would matter if Lou really loved you," Alloa said.

The young man hit his knee with a clenched fist.

"She does love me," he said. "She loves me, only she won't admit it. She's bitten with the Society bug, too. Oh, I know that her mother's set on her having a handle to her name, making her a Duchess or a Princess or some such nonsense, but Lou's not going to be happy with anyone but me. I tell you, I know Lou. I've known her for years—since she was a kid in fact—and we've always been keen on each other."

"Have you told Lou this?" Alloa asked.

"She knows it all right," Steve Weston said miserably. "Though I haven't had much of a chance lately to get near her. That old she-devil started to write me off the moment the old man died. I was in love with Lou years ago, before I realised she was going to have so much money.

"I was in love with her when we were kids going to the same High School. I didn't know she was an heiress then, and it wouldn't have meant anything to me if I did.

"But when old Derange dies, then madam starts on me. Oh, I know what she said, because Lou told me. I'm a fortune hunter; the boy from next door who isn't classy enough to marry Lou now she's come into millions. I've no future ahead of me!

"I admit I can't compare with all the lah-de-dah titles out of which Lou can take her pick in Europe, but the rest is just hooey.

"Mother Derange was clever all right. She wrote me off almost before I realised what was happening. But I love Lou and if I could only get to see her I could make her see sense."

"Couldn't you have seen her when you were in America?" Alloa asked.

Steve shook his head.

"Not a chance. The old woman had me barred at the door. 'Miss Lou ain't at home,' the butler would say when I called. I knew he was lying and he knew he was lying, but there was nothing I could do about it.

"I tried telephoning, but that stuck-up secretary was always on the switchboard. 'I'm sorry, Steve, Lou isn't home,' she would say—and I knew she enjoyed saying it.

"I wanted to write, but I thought, 'Hell, what's the use? Lou won't get the letters.'"

"I thought American girls were so independent," Alloa said. "It sounds like something out of a Victorian novel to me."

Steve shuffled his feet and looked more unhappy than ever.

"Oh, I'm only telling you my side of it," he said. "Lou acquiesced all right. If she had wanted to see me she could have done so, but her mother got at her and then they whisked away without telling me they were going.

"I've taken to reading the social columns in the papers just for news of her, and that's where I learned that Mrs. Cornelius Derange had sailed for Europe with her daughter. It was a shock, I can tell you that."

"I am sure it was," Alloa said sympathetically.

"So here I am."

Alloa sighed.

"I suppose you want me to tell Lou that you are here."

"Would you?"

He smiled at her.

"I suppose so," Alloa capitulated a little ruefully.

39

"Although, if Mrs. Derange finds out, I shall very likely get the sack."

"I just want to see Lou for five minutes," Steve said, "You understand? Just five minutes alone. Just to tell her that I still love her and to have a chance to convince her that she still loves me."

There was something nice and straightforward and honest about him that Alloa could not help liking.

"I'll tell her," she said. "She should be back here at six o'clock, changing her dress before she goes on to a cocktail party. If you will let me go now, I shall be back about the same time waiting for her. Where will you be?"

"Down here," he answered. "Keeping out of sight of the old woman, but in the building. You just bring me the word and I'll go anywhere, into the cellars or up to the roof-tops, so long as Lou and I can be alone for a few minutes."

"I will do what I can," Alloa promised. "But, now, please I must go. There is so much to do. As you know, we are leaving tomorrow."

They rose to their feet and Steve held out his hand.

"Thank you," he said. "I think you're a real pal."

Alloa smiled at him, at the same time she felt a little apprehensive as she hurried out into the street.

She could understand, in a way, that Mrs. Derange did not want Lou to throw herself away on an unknown young American boy with no prospects and perhaps not even a very lucrative job.

Lou was a very rich young woman; she was, too, extremely pretty. At the same time, Alloa could not help being shocked at Mrs. Derange's notion of marrying Lou off to an unknown French *Duc*.

Marriages by arrangement might be quite all right for the French—they were used to them—but for an American or British girl who had known freedom, who had been brought up to believe that love is the only thing that matters in marriage, it was bound to be an almost revolting idea.

'I shall never marry anyone unless I love him with my whole heart,' Alloa promised herself.

She finished her errands and completed the purchases on the list that Mrs. Derange had given her; then, as she turned her steps towards Claridge's she saw it was a quarter-to-six.

It was then, for the first time, she began to wonder if she were right in acting as an intermediary between Lou and Steve. Shouldn't her allegiance be to her employer?

Wouldn't it be the right thing for her to go at once to Mrs. Derange and tell her Steve was there? But she could not help feeling that such an action would be a betrayal of the trust he had put in her; perhaps, in some way, a betrayal of her friendship with Lou.

How often her father had reproved her for acting on an impulse, yet every instinct of her body told her that it was right that Steve and Lou should be together, whether in friendship or in love, rather than that Lou should be chasing across Europe to meet some obscure *Duc* who was interested in her only because she was rich.

She went up in the lift and hurried to the door of the suite. Lou had not yet come in. Jeanne had laid out her cocktail dress and a little hat embroidered with jewels that went with it.

There were a bag, shoes and gloves all to match the deep blue of the dress, and there were, too, as Alloa knew, waiting in a locked drawer a necklace and bracelet of sapphires which would show up the magnolia quality of Lou's skin and make the blue of her eyes seem bluer than ever.

Alloa had only just put her purchases down on the

dressing-table when the door burst open and Lou came hurrying in.

"Oh, there you are, Alloa," she said. "I have enjoyed myself, I cannot think why Momma must take me away just when I'm having fun."

Alloa hurried across the room and shut the door which Lou had left open behind her.

"Listen!" she said. "There's someone downstairs who wants to see you."

"I can't see anyone now, you know that," Lou replied. "We are due at the party at half-past six."

"You haven't asked me who it is," Alloa said.

Lou turned her head at the strange note in Alloa's voice.

"Well, who is it?" she enquired.

"Someone who wants to see you very much," Alloa answered. "Someone who has come all the way across the Atlantic just on the chance of having a word with you."

"Not . . . not Steve?" Lou stammered in astonishment.

Alloa nodded her head.

"Yes, Steve. He is downstairs waiting in the lounge. He begged me to tell you that he is here. He wants to see you for just five minutes."

Lou stared at Alloa for a long moment. Then she turned her eyes away and looked into the mirror. Her face was rather pale and the smile had gone from her lips.

She sat and looked at her own reflection while Alloa waited, and when at last she spoke her voice was harsh.

"No!" she said. "No! I don't want to see him."

"But, Lou!" Alloa ejaculated. "He has come from America. He didn't wire or telephone because he was afraid of your mother."

"What's the point of my seeing him?" Lou asked.

"He will only argue and want me to marry him. I don't want to marry him—not yet at any rate. Not at all, if it comes to that. I'm having fun. Steve is too serious. I had forgotten him, or half-forgotten him anyway. If I see him, it will start all over again. What's the point?"

Alloa was astonished and for the moment could find nothing to say. Lou pulled off her diamond bracelet and threw it down on the dressing-table.

"Go downstairs and tell him he is to go back to New York. I didn't ask him to come here and I don't want to see him. I've got nothing else to say."

"But that is cruel," Alloa said slowly, remembering the look on Steve's face.

Lou shrugged her shoulders.

"We've all got to face facts sooner or later in life," she said.

Determinedly she started to undress. Alloa realised there was nothing more she could say. She went from the room and, feeling curiously unhappy about what she had to do, went down in the lift.

Steve was waiting in a corner of the further lounge which was kept for residents. His face lit up at Alloa's approach and he jumped to his feet eagerly.

"I'm sorry," Alloa said.

There was no need for her to say any more.

"She won't see me?" he asked.

Alloa shook her head.

"I was rather afraid of it," he said. "The lies that old dame has been telling her have stuck."

He squared his shoulders, but his face seemed suddenly very young and very vulnerable.

"What will you do?" Alloa asked.

"Go home," he said. "And hope that one day she'll come to her senses."

"And if she doesn't?" Alloa enquired.

"Then perhaps I'll come to mine," he said with a

fleeting smile. He held out his hand. "You've been swell. Thank you."

"I did my best," Alloa said unhappily.

"I can believe that," he said. "If ever you come to New York I'll try and repay you."

He squeezed her hand and then he was gone, almost as if he couldn't bear to stay any longer for fear of betraying his feelings.

Alloa watched him go with a little pain in her heart.

He was nice, she thought. Life with a young man like that would be uncomplicated and easy. There would be no heartaches, no problems and no worries.

She wondered if a man like Steve Weston would give someone like Dix a job, a chance in life. Would he understand what it meant to have a helping hand offered when in the past every man's hand had been against him?

Alloa gave herself a little shake. How ridiculous she was to think of such things! Steve was going back to New York and Dix was lost somewhere in London where she could never find him.

Solemnly she went upstairs and going back to the suite, stayed in the sitting-room, tidying and emptying the ash-trays, until Lou came out of her bedroom dressed ready for the party. She avoided Alloa's eyes.

"Is Momma ready?" she enquired.

"I'll go and see," Alloa answered.

She knocked on Mrs. Derange's door and went in to find her standing ready in the centre of the room, dressed in black lace which concealed the rather fulsome curves of her mature figure.

"Is Lou ready?" she enquired.

"I came to ask you the same question," Alloa smiled.

"We mustn't be late," Mrs. Derange said fussily. "I believe there are to be some of the younger Royalty present."

She bustled from the room into the sitting-room. Lou was standing staring out of the window, her face entirely expressionless.

"Let me look at you," Mrs. Derange said. "Well, you look nice, but you haven't got the brooch on that matches the necklace. I should put it on the waist-band. I've noticed one or two of the young things over here wear their jewellery in that way."

"All right," Lou said indifferently.

"And hurry," Mrs. Derange called after her as she went from the room.

"I am hurrying," Lou said nonchalantly, but a moment later she called Alloa. "Here, Alloa! See if you can find this brooch for me."

Alloa went into Lou's bedroom.

"I put it in this drawer last time I wore it," Lou said. "I'm certain of it. I remember sending the necklace and the bracelet downstairs to the safe by Jeanne, and when she had gone I found that I had forgotten the brooch. It was still on my dress, so I put it in the back of the drawer. It isn't there now."

"Oh, surely you must be mistaken," Alloa said. "Let me look."

She searched among the pots of face-cream, boxes of powder, combs and face tissues. There was no sign of a brooch.

"When did you last wear it?" Mrs. Derange asked from the doorway.

"Don't you remember, it was the day we had our own party downstairs. I had worn these sapphires for luncheon and I said to you, 'Shall I wear them tonight?' and you said, 'No, I didn't like them with that brown dress,' and so I put on my diamond brooch and bracelet."

"Yes, I remember," Mrs. Derange said. "Now, let me see. That must have been last Monday."

Alloa was suddenly very still.

It was on Monday night that she had gone into the room to find someone there! She could see him now, turning from the dressing-table, the miniature in his hand.

Had he already been to the drawer? Had he found the brooch and was it in his pocket?

She felt her whole being revolt at the thought. She had believed in him; she had trusted him. It was impossible to believe that all the time he had been so plausible the brooch had been in his pocket!

"Oh, we can't wait now," Mrs. Derange said sharply. "Alloa had better have a good look while we are gone. And in case we don't see you again tonight, Alloa, you've got everything ready for the morning, haven't you?"

"Yes, everything, thank you, Mrs. Derange," Alloa replied. "My tickets, passport . . ."

"Well then, we will see you in Biarritz. Telephone, of course, if anything holds you up, but try to get there as quickly as possible. Lou and I don't want to be short of clothes."

"No, of course not," Alloa agreed.

"Well, good night, and have a real search for that brooch."

"I'll look everywhere," Alloa promised.

"Good night, Alloa."

Lou was avoiding her eyes as she went from the room, Alloa knew that.

Somehow she felt less concerned with Lou and Steve than she had been a short time ago. She was thinking of how Dix had looked her straight in the eyes, how she had believed him and how hard she had prayed for him these past days.

And all the time he had been a thief! An ordinary, common, crooked thief!

46

Mechanically Alloa went through the pretence of searching the drawers, of looking under the white paper, of opening the various little cases and fittings which Lou had cluttered around her.

There was nothing there. Somehow Alloa had no hope that there would be.

She only felt a sense of despair that she herself could have been so easily deceived; that she should have thought she had been clever enough to convert him and change him by just a few words, by just the impact of her personality.

'It was vain and ridiculous of me,' she told herself. 'It was childish to think that anything I could say would alter a man already versed in crime. He must have been laughing at me.'

The thought hurt her until she remembered the lilies-of-the-valley, and somehow it was a little comforting to recall that he had the decency to send them and to say thank you.

She looked at herself in the mirror.

She looked so ridiculously young, her fair hair falling on either side of her pale cheeks, her eyes wide and dark—grey eyes which echoed the English skies and yet had a touch of green in them.

Now she looked sad and her little mouth was drooping at the corners.

She did not know why it should distress her so much, except that even as a child when anyone failed her it had always seemed to strike at her very soul.

She wanted to believe in people. She wanted them all to be as straight-forward and honest and good as she herself tried to be.

"If you go on trusting people like that, Alloa, one day you will have a rude awakening," a girl at school had said to her.

Alloa had never forgotten it; and yet so often when

she had trusted people her instinct had been right and other people who had disparaged them had been proved wrong.

Now she was wrong, and it hurt both her pride and something else, something which had made her believe this man was worth saving.

She shut up the drawers and went to her own room. Her two small suitcases stood ready for the morning, the wardrobe was empty except for her coat.

She tried not to think of the lilies-of-the-valley standing in a vase by her bed. She had meant to take them with her.

Now she knew she would leave them behind.

They had seemed a symbol of spring, a symbol of something beautiful and simple. Instead, they were symbolic only of betrayal—the Kiss of Judas.

Chapter Three

The drive from London to Lydd Aerodrome very early in the morning was exciting but uneventful.

At first Alloa could hardly believe that she was really driving a magnificent, smooth-running car which leapt forward at the slightest touch of her foot and was so easily manœuvrable that it could not be compared with the old, battered Austin which she had driven in the past.

She was not due to cross the Channel until eleven-thirty. But she allowed herself plenty of time, knowing that she must drive slowly to get herself used to the car, and also that it might be difficult for her to find the way. She had never been south of London.

She had gone to bed in tears the night before; but

she had awoken to find the sunshine pouring through the window and to discover that it was impossible to be depressed when so much lay ahead of her.

Last night she had told herself that she hated men and had lost her faith in human nature.

But in the morning she found herself smiling at the chambermaid who called her, at the waiter who brought her her breakfast, at the porters who saw her off with fatherly admonitions to take care of herself; and her heart was warm once again towards humanity.

Only deep down inside her, thrust out of sight for the moment, was a bitterness she had never known before, because she had been betrayed.

It was ridiculous, she told herself, to mind that a stranger had let her down.

And yet, because she had trusted him and because she had prayed for him, the wound rankled and it was an effort not to think about it.

She arrived at Lydd much too early, had a cup of coffee and watched the aeroplanes arriving.

It was fascinating to see the cars coming out of the insides of the big Silver Cities and watch them being loaded up again to fly off easily and gracefully into the pale blue sky.

The time passed so quickly that Alloa was quite surprised when she saw the Cadillac being driven into the aeroplane and heard her own name being called to go to the passport office.

Then it seemed to her only a few minutes later that she was up in the air, flying for the first time in her life, with England lying beneath her like a child's toy, the fields and gardens glimpsed for but a few minutes before the plane was over the sea.

Mrs. Derange and Lou were such experienced travellers that Alloa had not dared to confess to them that not only had she never flown before, but she had never been out of England.

She had not deliberately deceived them, because they had not questioned her as to what her experiences were.

But now, for the first time, she felt afraid, a little apprehensive in case she should fall short of the efficiency that they expected of her.

Already the coast of France was in sight, the sea lapping a long line of sand and the dunes stretching inwards for some distance.

Then the aeroplane was circling downwards. Alloa had a glimpse of red roofs, of a river spanned by a wide bridge.

There was a little bump and the aeroplane was taxiing towards some long, white buildings.

She was in France!

It took only a few minutes to pass through the French Customs and the formalities of the aerodrome, and then she was back at the wheel of her car, driving it through the aerodrome gates and on to the wide, wooded road which led towards Le Touquet.

"I must remember to drive on the right! I must remember to drive on the right!" Alloa said to herself.

She was terrified lest she should forget, lest she should smash up this beautiful car.

The left-hand drive was now a great help, while she had found it rather irksome in England. Soon forgetting her fears, she was eating up the miles on the long, straight roads on which the only other travellers seemed to be in farm carts or an occasional small Citröen.

She stopped about two o'clock and ate the sandwiches she had brought with her from London.

She was anxious not to waste time stopping for meals, but she could not help thinking how attractive the little *auberges* and *estaminets* looked as she passed them, and she rather regretted her haste.

On her way again nothing seemed fast enough to pass her except once, just as she was nearing Rouen, when there was a sudden shriek of a loud horn and a big red Mercedes swept by as she pulled over to the right.

She had a momentary glimpse of the driver at the wheel. He reminded her irresistibly of Dix. Such an idea was ridiculous she told herself.

Was every dark foreigner going to remind her of the man who had cheated her, a thief whom, if she had done her duty, she should have denounced immediately to the police?

Once again she began to blame herself for the theft of Lou's sapphire brooch.

It was not that the loss itself was very disastrous. Lou's jewellery was insured and, as she said herself, she had never liked the brooch particularly.

It was just that Alloa could not get out of her mind that she was an accessory to the crime.

If she had called for help the moment she had found the man standing at the dressing-table, then he would have been made to empty his pockets.

Perhaps other people in the hotel had suffered in the same way; perhaps he had made a really good haul by playing on her feelings, by inviting her sympathy. She scourged herself for her own softness.

'I am young, inexperienced and extremely foolish,' she told herself.

The first two were true enough, but never, until this moment, had she realised quite how inexperienced she was in dealing with this sort of world.

She had thought, because she had seen poverty, because she had worked with her father in the mining villages, that she had a good knowledge of human nature. She knew what it was like when people were up against fundamental things—lack of money, drunkenness, ill-health and even a certain amount of vice.

But none of these had prepared her for the heartlessness and the hardness of the social world, the indifference of people who had unlimited money, who were pandered to and protected from coming up against the fundamental difficulties of life.

No, of that type of superficial existence she was absurdly ignorant.

She did not understand how Lou could seriously contemplate marrying a man just because he could give her a title; she could not understand how a man could look at her with sincerity and frankness in his eyes and steal even while he persuaded her into believing in him.

It was getting towards the evening before Alloa realised that she was hungry. Now what was almost an ache within her told her that it was time to stop and feed herself.

She had been driving for nearly eight hours and she saw from the map that she was approaching the little town of Alençon.

The Guide Michelin told her that there was a restaurant there called *Le Petit Vatel*.

Alloa hoped it wasn't expensive, because she was well aware that food was very dear in France, and even though Mrs. Derange had given her the money for the journey she would doubtless want an explanation of how every penny was spent.

She drove into Alençon and without much difficulty found the restaurant. It was in a small, narrow street with an open space in front where it was possible to leave the car.

There were several cars parked there already, and when Alloa opened the door and walked in to the small lower room of the restaurant she saw that it was crowded.

It was a gay, typically French place, with red check tablecloths to match the curtains, and at the far end of the room a chef, with a tall white hat, bustled in and out, his carving knife in his hand. An attractive waitress greeted Alloa with a smile.

"*Une place, M'mselle?*" she enquired.

"*Oui, s'il vous plait,*" Alloa replied.

The waitress looked round helplessly and spoke to another girl who had just come down from upstairs. The latter shook her head and made a little gesture of hopelessness.

The room upstairs was obviously *complet*. The waitress looked round. At a table by the window there was one man sitting by himself. She beckoned Alloa and went across.

"*Avec votre permission, Monsieur?*" she enquired, pulling out the chair for Alloa.

"Yes . . . yes, of course," he assured. "I mean, *oui, je suis enchanté.*"

"Oh, you are English," Alloa exclaimed. "Do you mind if I sit at your table? Apparently everywhere else is full up."

"No, of course not," he answered.

She sat down. The man opposite was rather difficult to place.

He was almost flashily dressed and she had the impression that he was not as young as he appeared. He had brown hair, brushed until it shone, a neat little moustache and an almost ingratiating smile over very white teeth. .

"Are you staying here?" he asked.

Alloa shook her head."

"No, I'm on my way to Biarritz," she replied.

"By car?" he asked.

"Yes."

"But surely you are going to stay here the night?"

"I hadn't decided yet," Alloa answered. "I wanted to get as far as I could, but I don't particularly want to drive in the dark as I don't know the road."

"Then, if you take my advice you'll stay in this town. There's quite a good little pub here, the *Grand Cerf*. I'm staying there myself so I can show you where it is."

"That is very kind of you," Alloa said doubtfully. "I thought perhaps I might go on for another hour or so."

The man opposite looked at his watch.

"It's eight o'clock now," he said. "You're not likely to finish your dinner until after nine. The food is good but, as you know, in France one always has to wait for everything one has."

"Perhaps I should be wise to stay," Alloa said.

"I am sure you would be," the other diner answered.

He drew his chair a little nearer to the table and said:

"Let me introduce myself. My name is Basil Calvert."

"And mine is Alloa Derange."

"Well, Miss Derange—I suppose it's Miss," he said, glancing down at her ringless finger. "I think it's a bit of luck that we've met each other. I was just thinking how I'd like to have someone to talk to and here you are, like a present from Heaven, so to speak."

"Don't you speak French, then?" Alloa enquired.

"Oh, I speak French all right," he answered. "As a matter of fact I'm a representative of a wine firm— you may have heard of them, Hardacre and Watford in St. James's Street."

"No, I'm afraid not," Alloa said.

"Oh, well, they are very well known, and I come over two or three times a year, so I can promise you I know

54

my way about. But you don't get a chance of meeting many people on these trips. It's mostly business, business all the time. One can be jolly lonely in the evenings, I can tell you that."

"I can quite believe it," Alloa said. "It must be a very interesting job though."

"It's a job, that's all that matters," he said.

Mr. Calvert struck Alloa as being a rather dull, unimaginative person, and she wished that she could have her dinner alone and watch the rest of the people in the room. But there was no doubt at all that her companion liked to talk.

"I'm a friendly sort of chap," he was saying. "You may wonder why I haven't got married. I suppose it's because I've never met the right girl—not that I haven't met a lot of girls if it comes to that.

"They call me Don Juan at our local tennis club and tease me about my lady friends, but I always say to them, 'I can take it.' What I mean is that if you've got a sense of humour yourself you shouldn't mind being teased. Don't you agree with me?"

"Yes, yes, of course," Alloa said.

She found that Basil Calvert did not expect her to say very much.

So long as she agreed with what he was talking about and smiled occasionally at his rather ponderous jokes he was completely happy to keep up what amounted to a monologue.

He was quite right about the time it took to have dinner. In fact it was nearly a quarter-to-ten before Alloa had paid her bill and he had paid his.

"The service is included," he said authoritatively. "You don't need to leave a tip. Don't forget when you are in France always to look and see if they have done that; and, if you'll take my advice, you'll add up the

55

bill, too. It's always a good thing to be on the safe side when you're dealing with foreigners."

"Yes, yes, I suppose it is," Alloa said, thinking what a bore the man was.

The dinner had been delicious, and if Alloa could have done so without evoking a storm of criticism from her new-found tutor she would have left a few extra francs for the waitress.

But she felt it was impossible to do so with Mr. Calvert's eyes upon her and they went out together into the cool of the evening. It was almost twilight and Alloa saw at once that it would be unwise for her to go further that night.

"Could you tell me the name of the hotel you mentioned?" she said.

"I'll take you there," Mr. Calvert replied. "You don't mind giving me a lift, I suppose?"

"No, of course not," Alloa answered.

They got into the car and drove down a narrow street to a beautiful old square. The *Grand Cerf* was a small, extremely clean hotel with a great deal of solid comfort without being the least pretentious.

"I've brought you another customer," Mr. Calvert said jovially to the man behind the reception desk. "A countrywoman of mine who's on her way to Biarritz. She's got a very fine American car with her which we've just parked in the garage. I hope nobody steals it before the morning."

"The car will be quite safe, *Monsieur*," was the somewhat repressive answer.

Alloa felt uncomfortable in case the people should think that she was casting aspersions on their honesty. A pageboy came forward to take her suitcase, and she held out her hand to Mr. Calvert.

"Thank you very much indeed for bringing me here," she said. "Goodbye! I hope you have a good trip."

56

He took her hand, then held on to it.

"I was just going to speak to you about that," he said. "You've got to go through Tours tomorrow, and that's exactly where I'm going myself. I was going to take the bus, but I should be very much obliged if you would give me a lift. You'll doubtless be leaving earlier and drive much more quickly. You'd be doing me a real kindness."

Alloa hesitated. She had no desire to saddle herself with this bore, and yet what else could she do?

"Yes, of course," she said. "But I want to get off early tomorrow morning. Shall we say about nine o'clock?"

"Suits me," Mr. Calvert said heartily. "Well, good night, and pleasant dreams."

He shook her hand effusively and Alloa escaped upstairs to her room.

What a nuisance it was, she thought when she was alone. It would spoil the whole of her drive tomorrow, having to listen to Mr. Calvert droning on beside her. He was so conceited and had obviously nothing to talk about except himself.

He was not even particularly interested in the wine trade or the vineyards that he visited. She was quite certain that there were entrancing things that he might learn about them if he wished.

She wondered if she could have had the courage to say that her employer did not wish her to take anyone else in the car.

Then, somehow, she knew it would have been unkind. After all, poor man, he was a traveller like herself, and her father would not be pleased if she refused to do anyone a good turn just because she thought him a bore.

At the same time she knew that tomorrow would be a tiresome experience, if nothing else; and as she fell asleep Alloa wondered if she would ever make the trip with someone she was fond of, someone it was a joy to be beside.

She awoke in the morning to learn, where yesterday had all gone smoothly, today was to be one of difficulties.

She was up and downstairs by a quarter-past-nine, only to find, as she tried to get the car out of the garage, that something had gone wrong with the starter.

It was, of course, Mr. Calvert who fetched someone from the local garage.

A mechanic in blue overalls and a beret pulled jauntily over one eye burrowed into the bonnet of the car and then announced that it would have to be towed to the garage for the necessary repairs to be done.

"Please don't wait for me," Alloa said to Mr. Calvert. "You catch the bus."

"Now, you can't expect me to behave like that to a lady in distress," he said. "I'll see you through this, and don't you worry. It's not difficult to mend; the trouble with these chaps is that they talk so much you can't get them to do any work."

"But I know you want to be in Tours as soon as possible," Alloa said. "I promise you I shall be quite all right."

"I wouldn't think of it," he said.

Alloa's heart sank at the thought that she would have to listen to him for even longer than she had anticipated.

Having got the car to the garage, it appeared that the mechanics knew exactly what to do, and Alloa's hopes rose as they diagnosed the trouble and then said that they actually had the part that was necessary. But they did not hurry themselves unduly.

People kept dropping into the garage to say good morning, to have a chat about the car they were taking

58

out or bringing in, and invariably they stopped to admire the Cadillac and to talk to the mechanics who were working on it.

That is, they were working until spoken to, then they stopped and exchanged compliments, talked about the weather and compared the speed of the American cars with their French counterparts.

It all seemed to Alloa to take an immeasurable amount of time, and Mr. Calvert appeared to enjoy every minute of it.

At last it exasperated her so much that she slipped away from the crowd of men standing around the Cadillac and walked across the road to where she had noted a beautiful old mediaeval church.

She pushed open the door and went in. Instantly her irritation fell away from her.

There was peace in the cool, incense-filled darkness of the high nave. The glass in the windows was beautiful, casting sapphire and ruby lights on the stone floor.

There were many flickering candles lit before the statues in the chapels, and Alloa stood for a long moment feeling as if she had stepped straight into another world.

There was something in the atmosphere of a Catholic church which always moved her. She told her father so once, and he had answered:

"God is everywhere. Only we notice it particularly where two or three have gathered together in His name for centuries."

It must be faith that made the atmosphere so poignant, Alloa thought; the faith of those who had prayed for what they wanted with an intensity of soul and heart.

She moved up the nave and then went into a beautiful little Lady chapel which was decorated with flowers and alight with candles.

She knelt down, praying for her father and mother, for herself, and then, because she could not help it, for the man who had proved himself a thief.

"Help him, God."

There was so little she could say. She had failed, but she felt that somehow Dix would still have another chance.

She rose to her feet, feeling newly invigorated, as if she could face anything—even Mr. Calvert. She dropped some francs of her own into the poor box at the end of the church and then went out into the sunshine.

She was greeted with the news that the car was nearly ready.

"Ten minutes, *M'mselle*," the garage proprietor assured her.

But, of course, it was almost an hour before the work was finished, the car filled up with petrol, oil and water, the bill paid and the *pourboires* distributed.

"It is nearly twelve o'clock," Alloa said with a little sigh. "It has taken us all morning. It is almost time for lunch."

"I thought of that," Mr. Calvert said, settling himself by her side. "And so I nipped back to the hotel and got them to put us up some sandwiches and a bottle of wine. I thought we might picnic on the way. What do you say?"

"I think it is an excellent idea," Alloa answered. "Very kind of you to think of it."

"It will save time, won't it? We shan't get to Tours now until about six o'clock."

"How annoying," Alloa said.

"Well, if you stay the night there you can get to Biarritz tomorrow, that is if you put your foot down on the accelerator. It will be a long day, but you'll be there in time for dinner. With a car like this, distance is nothing."

"Perhaps I could stay beyond Tours," Alloa suggested.

"I don't quite know where," Mr. Calvert said. "As a matter of fact I was going to ask you to dine with me tonight."

"It's very kind of you," Alloa said. "But I think I shall have to push on."

She made up her mind at that moment that nothing would make her stop in Tours if it meant dining with Mr. Calvert.

"Now don't be hasty," he said. "You've got the whole day to think about it. But I thought you and I could tootle off together, have a really good dinner—you can trust Basil to know the right places—and then we might go to a night club. What do you say to that? I know a place that would really make you open your eyes; the cabaret's a bit hot stuff, but, as I always say, 'When in Rome, do as the Romans do'."

"It is very kind of you," Alloa said firmly, "but I feel sure I can get further than Tours—that is, if we hurry."

Mr. Calvert seemed to take no notice of her refusal. She had the uncomfortable feeling that he was quite convinced she would dine with him.

"You know, the trouble with you," he said, "is that you're too serious. At your age you ought to be out for a bit of a laugh. After all, you're only young once."

"You forget that I am doing a job of work," Alloa said, feeling that some comment was expected of her.

"Well, it's the sort of job I wouldn't mind having," he said. "A car like this, all on my own, with a chance of picking up a pretty girl like you. Now, go on, say the right thing, say it was a bit of luck meeting me."

61

Alloa began to feel very embarrassed.

It was quite obvious that Mr. Calvert was trying to flirt with her and she wished now that she had had the courage to tell him that she couldn't take him to Tours.

Why, she wondered, hadn't she got up early and slipped away long before nine o'clock? But even if she had tried to do so, he would have caught up with her owing to the trouble with the self-starter.

Without realising in the slightest that she was disliking his conversation, Mr. Calvert started looking about him.

"Now we want a nice, cosy, secluded place for lunch," he said.

"I don't want to go off the main road," Alloa said. "The car might break down again."

"Well, we can walk into one of these woods," Mr. Calvert suggested.

"It will all take time," Alloa said firmly. "Besides, I should like to keep my eye on the car. One never knows that someone might come along and steal it or the luggage."

"It is locked up," Mr. Calvert suggested.

"I feel I have got to keep my eye on it," Alloa said firmly.

"Well, there's a place just ahead of us," he said. "You can draw off the road a little and the trees will be nice and shady."

Alloa slowed down. There was, she could see, a natural clearing in the trees. There was no possible objection to stopping there and she swung the car over and on to the clearing and stopped only a few yards from the road.

Mr. Calvert got out and stretched his arms.

"The smell of the pines is like nectar to me," he

said, sniffing. "It makes me feel strong and virile. What do you feel about it?"

"I want to eat my lunch quickly," Alloa said, ignoring his question. "I feel so apologetic at having delayed you so long that I want to get you to Tours as soon as possible."

She took the large paper bag with the luncheon in it from the back of the car and sat down on the grass beside the car in full view of the road. Mr. Calvert looked as if he might protest, and then slumped down beside her.

"Now don't you worry about me," he said. "Shall I make a little confession to you?"

"I can guess it," Alloa said sharply. "You weren't in a hurry to get to Tours at all."

"Bull's-eye first time," Mr. Calvert said gleefully. "I haven't got any appointment until tomorrow morning. I can just take my time. As it happens, I was going to take the afternoon bus."

"Then you shouldn't tell lies," Alloa said severely.

"All's fair in love and war," Mr. Calvert said complacently.

Alloa stiffened. She busied herself with taking the food out of the paper bag and putting the bottle of wine in front of Mr. Calvert so that he could open it.

The luncheon consisted of rolls, crisp, fresh and thickly buttered, with slices of ham between them. There was an apple and a banana each and two glasses for the wine.

It was a picnic which Alloa knew she would have enjoyed enormously had she been alone or with someone she liked.

But now, despite the resolution to remain calm and to ignore the familiarities of Mr. Calvert, she felt her heart thumping a little and her mouth becoming dry because she was afraid of what he would say next.

"I am going to enjoy this," he said, looking at the food and taking the cork out of the bottle. "Wait till you taste this wine. It's the right stuff, I can tell you. It'll trickle down your throat like velvet. You can trust Basil when it comes to choosing a good wine, you see if I'm not right."

He held out a glass to her and she sipped it. It was rather sweet and heavy but, at the same time, extremely delicious.

"You'll like that," he said. "It'll warm the cockles of your heart and perhaps make you a little kinder to yours truly. You wait and see."

He put out his hand as he spoke and laid it on hers. Alloa jerked it away as if she had been stung by a wasp.

"Let us eat our lunch quickly," she said sharply. "If you are not in a hurry to get to Tours, I am."

She picked up a roll resolutely as she spoke and took a mouthful of it. She had an uncomfortable feeling that Mr. Calvert was watching her all the time. She did not look at him.

She only wished there was more traffic on the road. She supposed that, as it was Sunday, all commercial vehicles were at rest and at this particular hour the Frenchman was enjoying his lunch, not snatching it quickly as was an English habit, but settling down to two hours' solid contemplation of his food.

Mr. Calvert filled up her glass to the brim.

"Drink up."

He raised his own glass to her.

"Cheers!" he said. "And here's to the prettiest pair of eyes I've seen for a long time."

Alloa did not answer him.

She went on eating with what she hoped was bovine stolidness, even though the food seemed to stick in her throat, and she took a sip of the wine simply because she was thirsty.

"Go on, have a good drink," Mr. Calvert admonished. "There's plenty more in the bottle."

"You forget I am driving the car," Alloa replied. "And, as I have already told you, I'm in a hurry."

Mr. Calvert emptied his glass and then turned towards her.

"Listen," he said. "You're young, and it strikes me that you're a bit frightened. There's no need to be. I promise you Basil Calvert wouldn't hurt a fly, you ask anyone who knows me.

"I'm not saying I haven't got an eye for a pretty girl and I like a bit of fun when it comes my way. But I'm not going to hurt you—you can be sure of that.

"What harm is there in enjoying ourselves? I'm a man and you're a jolly attractive girl. Neither of us is going to miss a kiss or two."

"I think we ought to get on," Alloa said quickly.

She tried to get up, but Mr. Calvert reached out his hand and caught her wrist.

"Now, now," he said. "What's the hurry?"

"Please let me go," Alloa said stiffly.

She tried to drag her arm away, but his hand encircled it and she might as well have tried to shake off a boa constrictor.

"I like girls with spirit," he said. "I don't mind them even when they're hard to get. It's the ones who are hard to shake off who are the trouble."

He pulled her suddenly towards him and Alloa, who was kneeling on one knee, was taken by surprise.

She lost her balance and his arms went round her, pulling her down beside him on the grass.

She fought him wildly. It seemed to her as if her strength was utterly ineffective. His arms enclosed her and she knew that his mouth was seeking hers.

She struggled against him desperately, conscious all the while that while she was fighting, activated by her

65

own terror, he was laughing at her efforts, confident of his eventual success, quite sure in the smug conceit of his own mind that eventually she would surrender to him.

"Let me go! Let me go!"

She writhed and struggled and his mouth was drawing ever nearer.

"I'm crazy about you," he said.

Now there was a note of excitement in his voice which frightened her more than anything else.

"Crazy, do you hear me? Here, give over, you little hell cat."

She had got one hand free and thrust it in his face, scratching his cheek with one of her nails. He released his grip for a moment and she sprang to her feet, running away from him in a frenzy to escape.

He was quicker than she had anticipated, jumping up and catching her before she had gone a few yards.

Now they were struggling together on the verge by the roadside, and as she struggled Alloa knew that he was winning.

Her heart was thumping, she could feel her breath being squeezed from her as he drew her ever closer, while, with her hands, she strove desperately to push him away.

And then, as despairingly she tried to scream, tried to avoid the smiling lips fastening themselves upon her mouth, she heard a sudden voice ask:

"What is going on here?"

The sharpness of the tone, the sudden surprise at the interruption, made Basil Calvert slacken his grip, and with an effort Alloa staggered away from him and then looked up, wide-eyed and incredulous, at the man who was standing there.

A few yards down the road—it must have passed them and they had not noticed it in their struggle—

was a big red Mercedes, and bare-headed in the sun-shine, his mouth grim, was the last man Alloa could have imagined might come to her rescue.

She gave a little gasp and in a strangled whisper, because her voice seemed to have left her, she called his name.

"Dix! Dix!"

She did not quite know how she reached him.

Her legs felt as if they must give way under her, but somehow she was beside him, holding on to his arm.

"Who is this man?"

She had never thought it possible to be so pleased to see anyone.

"It is . . . someone to whom I gave . . . a lift," she stammered breathlessly. "Help me to . . . get away. I have got to . . . get to . . . Tours."

He looked down at her as she held on to him. Almost instinctively she straightened herself.

"Are you able to drive?"

"Yes . . . of course."

She had control of herself now, the terror had gone.

She put her hand to smooth her hair; she tidied her blouse, thrusting it into the band of her skirt where it had come apart.

"Then get into your car. Go straight down the road for about three or four miles and then stop. I will catch you up."

She obeyed him without question, thankful that he had taken command of the whole proceedings, wanting only to get away. She did not look to where Mr. Calvert stood gaping at them.

She ran towards the Cadillac, got in and started it up.

As she went she heard Mr. Calvert's voice raised shrilly as if in explanation.

She saw Dix going towards him, she saw his fist

clenched, and then the Cadillac was on the road and she was moving at seventy miles an hour, wanting, if she could, to put hundreds of miles between herself and that terrifying moment when she had realised her own weakness.

'Why are women always at a disadvantage?' she asked herself savagely. 'Why, when it comes to anything physical, are they completely helpless beside the strength of a man?'

She had gone for over five miles before she realised that she must stop and let Dix catch up with her.

It was only then that she remembered that, though he had saved her from a moment of horror and misery, he was still a thief. He had tricked and betrayed her.

Should she go on? Should she drive away from him and refuse to speak to him?

It was what she ought to do, she felt; and yet, because he had saved her, because he had come at just the very right moment, she knew she could not do it.

She was not a coward and yet she was afraid to see him, afraid of what she might say.

What was the point of accusing him, of berating him? It was as hopeless and ineffective as fighting against the strength of a man like Basil Calvert.

She felt her utter inadequacy to cope with such things, and yet she drew the Cadillac to a standstill at the top of a hill looking down into a sunlit valley below.

The world was so beautiful. She felt her heart almost turn over at the beauty and the wonder of it. And yet people despoiled it. Why could not man be as lovely as the world in which he lived?

As she asked herself the question she heard a car stop behind her.

It was only then that she remembered her appearance, and taking a vanity case out of her bag, powdered her nose. She was combing her hair in the mirror over the windscreen as Dix opened the door and got into the car.

Alloa did not look at him. She put her comb away and said in a stiff, formal little voice:

"Thank you for coming when you did."

"It was fortunate, wasn't it?" he said. "I thought I passed you yesterday, but then I was sure I must have been mistaken. When I stopped in Alençon for petrol, I got out to stretch my legs while they were filling the tank and the garage hands were arguing about the performances of Cadillacs.

"I heard them speak of one that had been there that morning and I asked them to whom it belonged.

"They described you and I had a feeling I had not been mistaken. They told me that you had gone to Tours and so I thought that I might pass you. A Mercedes is a quicker car!"

She knew that his eyes were twinkling. Still she did not look at him.

"It was kind of you to stop," she said.

"How could you be such a little fool as to pick up a man like that?" he asked.

She was so surprised at the words that she turned now and looked straight at him.

His eyes were severe, but there was a smile at the corners of his mouth. She was just about to make some explanation when she remembered.

"I am not a very good judge of people, it appears," she said, and he did not miss the bitterness in her voice.

"What is the matter?" he asked. "Are you sorry that you gave me another chance?"

"Another chance!" She turned at that, stung out of her pretence of indifference.

"You were laughing at me," she said accusingly. "I gave you a chance, I believed in you, and all the time you were tricking me. Oh, it must have been very amusing to you, quite part of your usual stock in trade, to persuade a gullible fool like me that you meant to go straight, and all the time you must have had it in your pocket."

"What are you talking about?"

Dix bent forward and to Alloa's surprise put his hands on both her shoulders and turned her round to face him.

"What are you accusing me of?" he asked.

"I am accusing you of being a thief," she said hotly. "Oh, you didn't take the miniature which I found in your hand, but you had taken the brooch already and you didn't put that back."

Dix gripped her shoulders until she could feel his fingers digging into them.

"What are you talking about?" he said. "What brooch?"

"Lou Derange's sapphire brooch which was in the drawer," Alloa said. "It was there that evening, before she went out to the party. She remembers putting it there. When we came to look for it some days later, it had gone."

"So I took it, did I?"

"Of course you did. Why lie?"

She tried to twist herself away from him, but he would not let her go.

"Why lie to me?" she repeated. "I believed in you. I prayed for you as I said I would."

He released her shoulders and picked up both her hands. There was a sudden gentleness in the movement which surprised her.

"Listen, Alloa," he said, and his voice was different, no longer harsh and demanding but soft and tender. "Listen to me very carefully. If the brooch is missing, it is not my fault. I stole nothing—do you hear me?—that evening that you found me."

Her eyes were raised to his.

"Are you sure?"

"Quite sure. I swear it."

She searched his face; his eyes seemed utterly sincere. There was no twist at the corner of his mouth, his expression was serious.

"But it had gone," she said.

"As I have already said, if it has been stolen it was not I who took it. I swear to you, on anything which you hold holy—on your own head if you like—that when I went from that room that night, when you let me go, I took nothing with me but the memory of someone who had been kind and generous and merciful."

Her eyes fell before his and her fingers quivered in his hands.

"I believed in you," she said in a low voice, "until . . . until the brooch was missing, and then I hated you."

"And now?" he asked.

Her eyes looked up at him again.

"I want to believe you," she said. "I want to, but it is difficult."

"I can offer you nothing but my word," he said.

She searched his face again, her own eyes troubled, her lips quivering a little.

"You couldn't look like that and lie," she said. "Or could you?"

"Will you believe me when I say I couldn't lie to you?" he said. "To anyone else, perhaps, but not to you."

"Is that the truth?" Alloa asked.

"It is the absolute truth," he answered. "Say that

71

you believe me, say that you will trust me as you did before."

His eyes seemed to be looking down into her very heart.

She tried to withstand him, tried to think logically and clearly and knew it was impossible. She was conscious only of the warm strength of his hands, of his nearness and of his eyes looking into hers.

The rest of the world had vanished.

"I believe . . . you," she said at last in a whisper.

Chapter Four

Alloa was suddenly conscious that Dix was still holding her hands. With a quick, rising sense of embarrassment she made a little nervous movement and instantly she was free.

He sat back and drew a cigarette case from his pocket.

"May I smoke?" he asked.

"Of course."

She nodded her head automatically, noting that his cigarette case looked as if it was made of gold and that his lighter was obviously expensive.

"Why are you here?" she asked.

She was conscious, even as she spoke, that she could not keep her voice as light or as casual as she wished.

He glanced up at her quickly. At the same time, she felt that he considered before he answered her question.

"I am, as you see, driving a car down south," he said. "To Bayonne, to be exact."

She turned round to look at the big, red Mercedes, its chromium plate glinting in the sunshine.

"It is a beautiful car," she said. "Have they . . . have they . . . employed you to drive it?"

There was a strange look on his face and in his eyes as he said, half mockingly, half seriously:

"Are you suggesting politely that I have stolen it?"

"No, no, of course not," Alloa protested.

But she could not help the colour creeping into her cheeks or the lack of sincerity in the tone of her voice.

"I would rather you told me what you are thinking," he said.

"You haven't stolen it, have you?" Alloa said. "Tell me the truth, please tell me the truth."

He looked at her for several minutes and she thought there was something hard in his face and in his eyes that had not been there before.

"I want to trust you," Alloa said miserably, feeling as if it were she, and not he, who was on the defensive.

There was almost a sob in her voice and he softened perceptibly.

"Why should you worry about me?" he asked. "I am not worth it. But to set your mind at rest I will reassure you that I have not stolen that car."

"And you have got a job?" Alloa persisted.

Again it seemed to her that he hesitated before he replied.

"A sort of one," he admitted at last.

"I am not being impertinent in asking you these questions," Alloa said. "I suppose, if . . . I am honest, that . . . I feel sort of responsible for you."

"Because you let me go?" he enquired with a sudden smile. "But you don't know what you are taking on. Anyone who accepts any responsibility for me runs a chance of disillusionment, regret and—dare I be presumptuous enough to add?—unhappiness."

"But why?" Alloa enquired.

"Because, as you already know, I am what you call

73

in England a bad hat, the black sheep of the family, the one who prefers going to the devil in his own way."

"And yet you can't really like that sort of life," Alloa said. "It doesn't make you happy."

"How do you know that?" he enquired.

"Because you don't look happy, not all the time," Alloa answered.

"And you, who are so virtuous," he said. "Are you happy?"

"Yes, terribly happy," she answered.

Her thoughts shied away from the nights when she had worried over him, when she had felt both angry and let down because of Lou's brooch.

"And yet your virtue appears to get you into somewhat uncomfortable, if not unhappy situations," he said.

She flushed at that and then said impulsively:

"I haven't thanked you for rescuing me. I was frightened, terribly frightened."

"If I hadn't found you . . ." he began, and then stopped. "Forget it. It never does to think of that sort of thing. Be more careful another time. You can't trust everyone as you did me."

"But that was different," Alloa smiled. "What happened this morning was so unexpected. I . . . I never imagined that . . . anything like that could happen to me."

"How do you do your hair?" he asked.

She turned large, astonished eyes towards him.

"My hair?" she enquired.

"Don't you ever look in the glass?" he explained.

"You . . . you mean that . . . my face attracts people like Mr. Calvert?" Alloa said. "Oh, no! Not as a rule. I have never had any trouble like that before—except . . . except the other evening."

She suddenly remembered the man who had followed her in the park; but feeling that she could not explain what had happened, she was silent, looking away down the long, empty, sunlit road.

Dix glanced down at his wrist-watch.

"If we start now and go fairly steadily, we should be at Tours by half-past six or seven o'clock," he said. "I am going to find you rooms in a decent hotel and then I am going to take you out to dinner."

"But . . . but I think I ought to press on," Alloa said.

"Nonsense," he replied. "You will have done quite enough today by the time you reach Tours. Besides, I want the pleasure of giving you dinner."

Alloa looked away from him.

"I suppose really I ought to say no," she said. "After all, I don't know you and . . ."

"Your mother has warned you about accepting invitations from strange men," he said with a smile. "But am I so strange?"

Alloa had to admit to herself that she felt as if she had known him a long time.

It was almost as if he had become a part of her life. She had thought of him continually since that evening in Lou Derange's bedroom.

She had prayed for him. She had been hurt and miserable because he had failed her. And now he had come to her rescue, at a moment when she had been terrorised and helpless.

"I am being silly," she said, capitulating. "And I should love to have dinner with you—so long as you will let me pay my share."

"Are you trying to insult me?" he asked.

Alloa shook her head.

"You know I am not trying to do that," she said. "But I am poor, too. I know what it is to have to count every penny, to give up something that you want

75

very much so that you can do something else. Mrs. Derange has given me the money for my journey. I must pay for my own dinner, although it is very sweet of you to suggest that I should be your guest."

He was silent for a moment as if he was thinking over what she had said, and then he laughed.

"Your honesty is unbelievable," he said. "Don't you think that if you are hard up it would be much better to dine with me, let me pay, and put the money that you would have spent on your dinner in your pocket?"

"No, of course I wouldn't do a thing like that," Alloa answered. "It wouldn't be straight. Besides, I should have to lie, and you know as well as I do that isn't right."

"Yes, I know it," he said. "But I am wondering if anyone these days lives up to such standards."

"My father does," Alloa said. "And there must be millions of people like him, men and women who try to do the right thing, whatever the cost to themselves, however difficult it may be."

"Do you really think I could be one of them?" Dix asked.

She turned swiftly to look into his eyes.

"I know you could be," she said. "I knew it the very first moment I saw you. You are not an ordinary type of . . ."

She hesitated for a word.

"Crook?" he suggested with that little twist of the lips she knew so well.

"It is a horrid word," Alloa said passionately, "but you know what I mean by it. Forget your past, all the things you have done of which you are ashamed, all the things you want to forget. Start again, doing all the things that are worth while, all the things that are right, which will give you self-respect, make you proud to be yourself."

"You make it sound easy," he said.

"If I do that, I am deceiving you," Alloa said. "It is hard, terribly hard at times, and yet you would never regret it, I am certain of that."

"You are very persuasive," he said. "Shall we go now and talk about it at dinner?"

"Yes, of course," Alloa agreed.

She felt a little guiltily that she might have bored him by being too intense. She mustn't preach, mustn't sermonise.

She had heard her father say often enough how impatient the boys and girls in his youth clubs were when people came down and lectured them on how to behave.

At the same time she felt as if every moment was precious; she mustn't waste one in not doing what she could to help Dix.

He had come into her life for a moment and then he had vanished. And now that he had reappeared again, there was nothing to make her believe that he would be with her for more than a very short time.

Then their paths would separate once again and unless she had really changed him he would go back to the senseless, wasted life that he had been leading in the past.

"I am going to follow behind you," Dix said as he opened the door of the car. "That is just in case you get involved in any more adventures. The road is well sign-posted so you cannot miss the way. Go as fast as you like, I shall be able to keep up."

"I am well aware of that," she smiled.

"But don't take any risks," he commanded as he shut the door and came round to stand beside her window. "You know, that car is really too big for anything as small as you."

"It is the most wonderful car I have ever driven,"

Alloa said. "I keep wondering if it is really true, that I have really got the chance to be here, in France, for the first time in my life."

"You have never been to France before?" he asked almost incredulously.

She shook her head.

"Then there are a lot of things I want to show you," he said. "Don't let us waste any more time on this dull road. Forward to Tours. Stop just before you get to the town and I will lead you in. I know where the hotel is where you are to stay."

Alloa started the car, and turned on the wireless. As she drove along she found herself humming the gay tunes which came throbbingly over the air.

The road was very straight and there was very little traffic, save in the small towns they passed through.

In the fields on either side of the road farmers were working, and overhead there was an occasional aeroplane, glinting silver against the blue sky.

Otherwise the world seemed clean and empty. There was only the fresh wind blowing through her hair and that indescribable, pungent smell of spring which seemed to pervade everything.

Alloa put her foot down—the car leapt forward to sixty, seventy, eighty miles an hour.

It gave her a sense as if she was carried on wings. In the little driving mirror she could see the Mercedes keeping just behind her, always at about the same distance, giving her a sense of safety and security.

They reached Tours almost exactly at half-past six, and when they came to the outskirts of the town Dix took the lead and led her through the wide boulevards and along the river Loire until they came near the centre of the town.

He slowed down outside an hotel which looked on to a gay municipal flower-bed and a fountain sparkling with the colours of the setting sun. Alloa stopped her car before the front door. Porters came hurrying to take her suitcase and direct her to the hotel garage.

She drove the car in through the narrow entrance and was ushered into a lock-up garage. As the attendant closed the door and handed her the key she found Dix beside her.

"This is too grand," she said to him. "I don't suppose for a moment I can afford to stay here."

"It is respectable," he said, "and they will look after you. I have spoken to the reception clerk and he will give you a bedroom at the back which will be quiet. You have got a long run in front of you tomorrow."

"I am sure it is terribly expensive," Alloa said apprehensively.

"Mrs. Derange can well afford it," he said firmly. "Now, stop worrying and go and get ready for dinner. I shall call for you in half an hour."

"Aren't you staying here too?" Alloa asked.

She did not know why, but she hated the thought of his going away even for a short time.

"I have already booked somewhere else," he said. "Don't worry, you will be properly looked after."

There was nothing else she could say and she felt almost forlorn as she followed the page-boy along the passages to her bedroom. It looked out on a square courtyard.

The hotel had originally been an old coaching inn which had been cleverly modernised and there was a bathroom attached to the bedroom. There were only the small-paned windows with their pretty chintz curtains to remind one of less luxurious days.

Alloa lay in her bath and felt the tiredness of driving such a long time soak away from her into the warm water.

She wished she had something beautiful and gay

79

to wear, but there was only her black silk dress with its white collar and cuffs and neat black leather belt.

It was very demure and very suitable for an unobtrusive little secretary.

Alloa had a sudden vision of herself in one of the tulle and sequin cocktail dresses which Lou wore for informal dinner parties, or a dress of soft chiffon worn with a cape of velvet and fox.

She sighed, then laughed at her own fancies.

The only thing she could do to improve herself was to brush her hair until it shone like gleaming gold, to touch her mouth with lipstick and to let the powder lie so softly on her cheeks that it was like a bloom on a newly plucked peach.

She was ready exactly at the time Dix had said he would call for her.

Yet she hesitated before going downstairs. She was suddenly shy at the thought of dining alone with him.

He would never believe her, she thought, if she told him it was, in fact, the very first time she had ever dined alone with a man.

It was not surprising that she was excited, she told her reflection in the glass; and then, half ashamed at the light in her eyes, she picked up her handbag and ran from the room.

Dix was waiting in the hotel lounge, being eyed furtively by two old ladies sitting in the corner and two young French girls who were seated on either side of their somewhat corpulent father.

He had changed into a dark-grey suit, and yet however sombre his clothes, Alloa could see that there was something rakish and rather dashing about him. He looked like a buccaneer from an eighteenth-century print, or perhaps there was the touch of a brigand about him.

He might have been one of those adventurers who

would sail all over the world not only in search of loot, but because the dull and prosaic existence at home was intolerable to them.

Alloa smiled at Dix, who, without giving her any greeting, put his hand under her elbow and led her out of the hotel. The red Mercedes was waiting at the door. They got into it and still without a word drove off.

It was even more luxurious than Alloa had imagined.

She sank down into the comfort of the well-padded seats and noted the beautiful pale-blue enamel Saint Christopher which had been attached to the dashboard.

"Wouldn't you like to own a car like this?" she said, more to herself than to Dix.

"I would prefer a Bentley," he replied. "I tried one the other day in London and thought they were superb."

"I've never been in one," Alloa said.

"I must . . ." he began, and then suddenly stopped.

Alloa wondered what he was going to say and then felt uncomfortable.

It was impossible to face the questions which kept arising in her mind. How had he had the chance to try out a Bentley? What was he doing with this magnificent car?

Had he really been commissioned to drive it to Bayonne? She wished that her mind was not besieged by such ideas. Try as she would, she could not shut them out entirely, could not trust him as she wished to do.

She was thankful that their journey did not take long. They drew up outside a restaurant and a few minutes later they were inside.

The room was small, the tables were arranged in small alcoves so that each diner was ensured of the maximum amount of privacy. There was a grill at the far end of the room and at it two white-capped chefs were busily turning chickens on a spit.

Alloa looked around her with wide eyes.

Nearly every one of the alcoves seemed to be filled and there were several tables in the centre of the room which were, perforce, being taken by late arrivals.

"I have already ordered dinner," Dix said. "I want you to try all the specialties in this place and, as you know, they take time to prepare."

'This is going to be very expensive,' Alloa thought with dismay.

She had planned that she would say she was not hungry and would choose something on the menu that was not priced at all high; and now she was not going to be given the choice, and she hoped, uncomfortably, that she would not run out of money before she reached Biarritz.

The dinner, when it came, was superb.

There were *langoustines,* done with a special sauce, wild duck, and to follow them *crêpes suzettes* which were cooked in front of the table and then set on fire before finally they were placed, rich with liqueurs, on Alloa's plate.

Dix had ordered a wine which had a bouquet so subtle and yet so fragrant that Alloa felt she could almost taste the grapes and the sunshine which had gone into the making of it.

They talked of trivial things: of the restaurant, the journey, the history of Tours; and yet all the time Alloa felt this was one of the most exciting evenings she had ever spent in her life.

"I have always read about places like this," she said. "Somehow I never thought I would come to one. For that matter, I never thought I would get to France."

"One day you must go to Paris," he said. "It is the most beautiful city in the world and there is something in the air which makes people gay and happy and care-free, so it is not by chance it is called 'The Gay City'."

"Is your home in Paris?" Alloa asked.

"I have lived there quite a bit of my life," he answered evasively.

"And yet you left it to come to London. Why?"

"As a matter of fact I was only staying in London this last time. I had a reason for being there."

"I somehow thought you lived there," Alloa said. "To tell the truth I was not certain what nationality you were. I just knew you weren't English."

"I come from the south," he said. "Sometimes I call myself a Basque, but actually my family are French. My home is not far from the Pyrenees."

"And you are going home now?" Alloa asked.

"Eventually," he answered.

She told herself it was no concern of hers; she should not catechize him.

Yet she knew she was curious, not only because he was naturally reserved, but also because she suspected, try as she would to disbelieve the idea, that he was concerned in something which would not bear investigation. The car, the money, his cigarette case, his clothes.

How could she reconcile these with a man who was prepared to risk his liberty for the sake of picking up a few jewels or trinkets in an hotel bedroom?

There was something behind all this which she knew, sooner or later, she must discover, even though she was afraid of what she might learn.

She gave a little sigh. He looked up at her apprehensively.

"Are you bored already?" he enquired.

"No, no, of course not." She smiled at him. "I was just thinking how different this was from anything I have done before."

"I don't suppose you make a habit of dining with crooks," he said, speaking provocatively.

"I didn't mean that," she answered quickly. "I don't make a habit of dining with anyone, if it comes to that."

"Are you seriously asking me to believe that you have not got a boy-friend?" Dix enquired.

Alloa shook her head.

"No, of course not. I haven't had the opportunity of meeting men in London, and when I was at home we lived a very quiet life and saw very few people except in the shooting seasons.

"Then the lodges are full, but although the people who own them are nice to us and often ask us to luncheon on Sundays when they are not fishing or shooting, one never sees them again until the next year."

"And so you came to London. Was it to find a husband?"

Alloa drew herself up a little stiffly. Instantly Dix bent forward apologetically.

"Forgive me," he said, touching her hand. "I shouldn't have said that. I was just finding it hard to believe that, looking as you do, you should not have men asking you out to luncheon, dinner, dances, to any and every sort of amusement."

"They couldn't ask me if they didn't know me," Alloa replied. "And living in a hostel one really doesn't meet people after office hours. Sometimes I have been out to a cinema with one of the other girls; once or twice I went to a theatre by myself; but usually I just sat at home and read."

"Didn't you feel you were missing something?"

"I suppose sometimes I did," Alloa said. "There was nothing I could do about it."

"Nothing ventured, nothing gained!" he quoted.

She laughed.

"I didn't know where to venture to."

"And so you have never been in love?"

"No."

"Supposing you fall in love with someone, what then?"

"Then I hope I shall be able to marry him," Alloa said. "What else?"

"What else, indeed!" he repeated. "It is, of course, the journey's end, so to speak."

She looked at him with a little puzzled frown between her eyes.

"What are you trying to say to me?"

"I am trying to find out about you," he replied disarmingly. "I find it hard to believe that anyone so attractive and so pretty could have escaped reality for so long."

"It depends on what you call reality," Alloa answered. "If by 'reality' you mean love, then it is true. If you mean life, then I don't agree. I didn't find the people I met in London any different from those I had known in Scotland.

"They were all filled with their own problems and difficulties. They were all struggling and striving for something—whether it was money, position, or somebody else's affection."

"And you want none of these things."

"You are trying to make me sound a prig," Alloa said. "Of course I want them all. I want to earn lots of money; I want to be in the position where my father and mother would be proud of me; and I want to fall in love, madly and crazily, with somebody who is in love with me."

"Do you think this will happen without any effort on your part, without your doing anything but just sitting at home and reading a book?"

"If it is meant to be, it will be," Alloa said. "As an old woman in the village used to say when I was a child: 'Mister Right will come along one day. There's not a wind blowing off the sea that can prevent it.' "

"Superb fatalism!" Dix said. "I wonder if we do things better in France?"

"You mean . . . have . . . *marriage de convenance*?" Alloa asked.

"So you know about such things?" Dix enquired.

"Yes, of course," Alloa answered. "Why, Mrs. Derange . . ."

She stopped suddenly, remembering that it was not her secret and she should not, in loyalty to her employer, reveal her private affairs to a perfect stranger.

". . . Mrs. Derange has spoken of it to me," she finished. "I understand that in France, even today, in the very best families marriages are still arranged."

"Amongst the peasants and the middle classes I believe it is a general rule," Dix replied. "Some of the aristocracy, those who are in the more cosmopolitan set, have kicked over the traces, but the majority stick to the customs of the past."

"And what do you think about them?" Alloa enquired.

"I have seen instances where they are extremely successful," Dix replied. "But, of course, in those cases it is usual for both parties to marry knowing that the husband and wife will, where their hearts are concerned, go their separate ways."

"You mean that they will love other people without breaking up their marriage?" Alloa enquired.

"Yes. The man will take a mistress, the wife a lover, and neither party will object."

"I think that is wrong and horrid," Alloa said. "And supposing . . . supposing the girl should love with all her heart the man she marries, while he has just allowed it to be a legal contract arranged by his parents? What happens then?"

86

"It will be a legal contract for her also," Dix replied. "If she falls in love with him, perhaps she will be fortunate enough to make him in love with her too."

"I am sure it is wrong!" Alloa cried. "Quite, quite wrong. Love must be the only reason for marriage."

He smiled at the intensity in her voice.

"Supposing," he said, "that you had the chance of marrying someone in a very advantageous position in life who could give you everything you wanted, could look after your father and mother, who would be kind and who would love you, but you knew that you could never have for him more than perhaps a respect and affection? What would your answer be?"

"It would be, no," Alloa said. "I would never marry anyone unless I loved him."

"On the other hand," Dix said, "supposing you fell in love with someone who could give you nothing, someone of whom your parents would not approve, someone whom you could not really respect or admire, but with whom, despite yourself, you were in love. What then?"

It seemed to Alloa as if the restaurant was suddenly very still, as if everyone was silent, waiting for her answer, waiting for her reply.

The question seemed to be repeating and repeating itself in her brain, as if it were written there in letters of fire. And in a whisper she gave her answer:

"I don't know! I don't know!"

Chapter Five

Driving along the road in the morning sunshine, Alloa felt as if she was seeing France for the first time.

She had been nervous about the car the day before and so distracted by her passenger and his subsequent behaviour that she had had no eyes for the wide open countryside with its exquisitely tinted colours of soil and forest and the little whitewashed villages with their ancient churches.

Now she began to notice the beauty in everything she saw—in the grey *châteaux* standing back from the road behind wrought-iron gates and in the glimpses she sometimes got of grander, more imposing buildings encircled with trees through which shone the shimmer of a lake.

She noticed the magnificent pairs of white Percheron horses working in the fields; the goats tethered by the roadside; the priests with their wide-brimmed hats.

There was so much that was new to see that Alloa resented the fact that if she was to reach Biarritz that night she must not waste time on the journey.

Yet Dix had been insistent that they should have luncheon together in Bordeaux.

"I will give you a meal that you will enjoy and a wine that you will never forget, in the heart of the grape country," he promised.

Alloa felt uncomfortable at accepting his hospitality even though she knew she was looking forward to their meal together.

Last night when the bill was presented after dinner he had not let her see it.

"Your share is *un mille*," he said.

"But that cannot be right!" Alloa protested. "Think what we have had to eat. Please, you must be fair over this. I know you can't afford it."

He had smiled at her in that disarming manner which she found exceedingly difficult to combat.

"Your share is exactly *un mille*," he said, holding out his hand.

He had refused to argue, refused to discuss it further, and eventually she had meekly given him the *mille* note and pretended not to notice how many others he pressed under the folded-over *addition*.

Dix had taken her home early. She had gone to bed, but had not been able to sleep.

Instead she had laid awake, going over what had been said at dinner, worried because she knew that his attitude had altered from the moment when she had refused to give him a straight answer to his question about marriage.

She saw now how stupid she had been. He had not been asking her what she would have done in a particular case, even though the question was framed like that.

What he had really been trying to find out was whether he had a chance of marrying some decent girl who would love him for himself. Fool that she had been not to realise that!

She was furious at her stupidity in being so obtuse, in letting her fastidiousness and her almost ridiculous sense of honesty prevent her from helping him as he should have been helped.

Of course she should have said that love was more important than respect, that love would overrule any other considerations.

'I failed him.'

She told herself that miserably when she was alone in

the quiet bedroom which looked out over the courtyard. And yet she asked her conscience:

'What else could I have said?'

She could see Dix's face, stern and unsmiling, after he had heard her reply to his question. She could see that the warmth he had exuded towards her had gone and in its stead was an almost repellent coldness.

'I must try to make it better,' she told herself miserably, yet wondered what she could possibly do.

He had seemed quite normal this morning when they met in the garage yard of the hotel.

But their greetings, in front of the attendant, had only been formal. He had checked the Cadillac to see if there was plenty of oil and petrol in the engine, and then told her the way out of Tours.

"We should be at Bordeaux by one o'clock," he said. "Wait for me to guide you to the restaurant where we are to lunch. It is near the market but rather hard to find."

It was only when she was at the wheel of the Cadillac moving out of Tours that Alloa knew that in her heart of hearts she was relieved.

She had hardly dared to formulate, even to herself, the fear that because of last night Dix might not have repeated his invitation asking her to have luncheon with him today.

He might have just slipped away and not even have turned up at the garage as he had promised to do.

She wondered then what she would have done. Would she have hung about waiting, hoping against hope that he would appear? Or would she have accepted the inevitable and started off on her own?

"I mustn't rely on him too much," Alloa whispered, and knew that the corrective was only a movement of the lips and quite without foundation in her thoughts.

The road was straight and it was easy without any

effort to cruise along at quite a high speed. It was a warm day but not too hot. There was a gentle wind blowing across the fields and rustling through the bright spring green of the trees.

It was only just after half-past twelve when Alloa arrived at the outskirts of Bordeaux and waited to let the big red Mercedes drive past her. She had a quick glimpse of Dix sitting back comfortably at the wheel.

She thought that he looked as if he was the sort of person who was born to have a big, expensive car of his own.

"Perhaps some people are made that way," she sighed.

She thought how impossible it was to imagine Lou washing up at the kitchen sink or digging in a potato patch.

She found it just as impossible to imagine Dix being a mechanic in a garage, working at a machine in a factory, or going down a coal mine.

He was essentially masculine, essentially a strong man; and yet she could only visualise him at the wheel of a luxurious car, riding a spirited horse or at the helm of a yacht, sailing over the rippling water.

'And yet he has got to work,' Alloa told herself. 'This sort of job, driving another man's car, is only giving him expensive tastes which he will never be able to indulge."

Her thoughts shied away from the gold cigarette case, the watch on his wrist, the well-cut clothes. Those were all things that belonged to the past.

The future might be hard, but at least it would be honest.

She puzzled over how she could encourage him to do what was right and not discourage him by telling him how irksome it would be at times.

She had a sudden feeling of fear that these moments

were going too quickly. They would be at Biarritz to-night, and she dare not ask the question whether, after that, she would ever see him again.

He stopped outside an unpretentious, rather ordinary-looking restaurant standing in a side street off the big, covered market-place.

For a moment Alloa felt disappointed. She had expected something more original; but when she got inside she gave a little exclamation of delight.

The dining-room of the *Chapon Fin* was built as if it were a grotto. There were big rocks on one side, out of which flowers and ferns were growing quite naturally.

There was a fountain playing into a basin filled with water lilies, and in the whole restaurant there was the dim, mysterious atmosphere of a vast cave.

"What an enchanting place!" Alloa exclaimed as they seated themselves at a table in the corner.

"The most important thing here," Dix told her, "are the cellars."

For a moment Alloa did not understand him, and then, as he picked up the wine list, she smiled.

"You mean it is famous for its wine?" she said.

"Very famous," Dix smiled.

The *maître d'hôtel* came hurrying to his side and they spent a long time discussing various wines and vintages and ordering the right food to go with them.

Alloa was too interested in her surroundings to listen. She felt here as if she had walked into a fairy tale.

There was only the soft music of the fountain, the lowered voices of the waiters to persuade her that it was not just a dream or that she was not watching a film at the cinema.

"I have ordered what I hope you will like," Dix said at last and turned to smile at her.

"I am afraid it will be very expensive," she said.

"Forget money for once," he said. "Do you know, when I was coming along I was thinking that you have no idea how to enjoy life. You are like all the people who are too good. They are brought up to suspect everything which is enjoyable or naturally gay.

" 'It must be wrong,' they say. 'I'm liking it too much.' "

"Oh, but I am not like that," Alloa protested hotly. "I was just thinking how happy I was and how lucky to be here, to experience all this—to have you to help me."

"I am glad I come into it somewhere," Dix said.

"But of course you do," Alloa replied. "I want you to know how grateful I am for all you have done for me. If it hadn't been for you I should not have seen all these interesting places, or known what to eat or drink, or learned about the countryside. I am grateful, I am, really."

"So, even a thief can have his uses," Dix said.

Alloa glanced at him quickly as he spoke and knew that he had not forgiven her for last night. The hurt was still there, the barrier still stood between them.

Impulsively she put out her hand and laid it on his arm.

"There is something I must say," she said in a low voice. "Something I must tell you. I . . . I thought about what you said last night . . . the question you asked me. And . . . I know the answer."

"Yes?"

He made no pretence of not understanding to what she was referring.

"When you . . . asked it," Alloa went on, "I had not . . . had time to . . . think, to consider. It was not a question that had ever . . . occurred to me before. But now I know that the answer is—yes. A girl, or a

93

woman, if she loved enough, would marry a man she loved regardless of anything he had done in the past."

"You are sure of this?" Dix asked.

"Quite sure," Alloa said positively. "You see, if she loved him and he loved her, then there would be no question of his ever doing again things which were wrong or which had caused her not to respect him."

"Supposing," Dix said slowly, "supposing even after they were married or had admitted their love to each other, the man continued to be what he was and what he had always been—a blackguard, in one way or another, even if he didn't go to the extremes of being a criminal. What then?"

Alloa took a deep breath.

"I do not know very much about love," she said. "Though I think that once it is given it is not something that can be taken away. A woman might still go on loving a man whatever he did."

Dix looked full into her eyes.

"You are talking about some mythical woman or some mythical man," he said. "Last night, if I remember rightly, I was asking you if you could love someone whom you did not respect."

Alloa looked down at her own hand as it lay on his arm.

He had seen through her efforts, she thought. He had guessed that she was trying to help him, speaking not so much from her heart but because she thought it was the right thing to say.

He had called her bluff, and now she must tell him the truth.

She felt herself tremble and wondered for a moment, wildly, how she could give him an answer. And then almost magically her answer was there.

"It is a question I cannot answer," she said, "because I have never been in love."

"I suppose that is the nearest to the truth I shall get," he said.

She wondered for a moment if he was angry, and then he smiled at her.

"I almost suspected a white lie because you thought it would help me."

She flushed as she looked up at him.

"I try always to speak the truth," she said.

"That is obvious," he replied.

He put his hand suddenly over her fingers which in her agitation had tightened on his arm.

"Don't think about it any more," he said. "Perhaps one day I will ask you the question again and you will give me a different answer. For the moment let us talk about you. Tell me about your home, your childhood."

Alloa answered his questions, feeling as she did so a warm happiness of relief and thankfulness, because he was no longer angry with her.

She thought, as she watched him, that there was something very sensitive about the fineness of his features, the lines beginning to show at the corners of his eyes. She remembered her father saying once:

"The more highly strung a man is, the harder it is for him to face up to the roughness and brutality of life."

Was it, she wondered, just escapism which had made Dix choose the life he led?

They talked on for some time, and then, when the food came and with it two wines—red and white—of almost unbelievable delicacy, they ate for a short time in silence. *Filets de Sole Chapon Fin* were followed by *Tournedos diplomate*. When Alloa had finished a dish of wild strawberries and was waiting to drink a cup of fragrant black coffee, she said:

"And now I have got something more to thank you

for—the second most delicious meal I have had in my life."

"It was good," Dix admitted carelessly.

"Good!" Alloa exclaimed. "Don't you dare be so unappreciative. I have enjoyed every mouthful, and I didn't believe that wine really existed which tasted like bottled sunshine."

"We will tell the proprietor what you say," Dix said. "The shortest way to any Frenchman's heart is to praise his cuisine and his cellar."

"It is not difficult to praise anything that is so good," Alloa said.

"Except that the British always keep their thoughts and their feelings a secret. Whether they are pleased or displeased, they still manage an aloof silence. I find it very disconcerting."

"Oh, we are not all like that," Alloa said. "In Scotland we are very friendly. The Scottish are supposed to be dour, but I think they are much more hospitable than the English, and I find them always ready to pay a compliment and say something nice."

"I quite see I shall have to come to Scotland," Dix said. "Will you invite me to your home?"

It was a challenge and Alloa knew it.

"But, of course," she said quickly. "I would love you to meet my father."

"So that he could complete my reformation?"

"No! Because he would like you and you would like him," Alloa answered. "And when I tell my mother how kind you have been to me, she will love you."

"I wonder if I can believe you," Dix said.

"But, please, you must believe that to be the truth," Alloa said quickly. "Surely you don't think that I am such a snob as to be ashamed of you, after all you have done for me?"

"You would really take me to your home?" Dix asked.

"Of course," she said.

There was no doubting the sincerity in her voice.

"I am only afraid that you would find it a very poor place after all the luxury that you are used to. Not that I think it is right for you to be used to it; it is merely that you have let it become a part of your life, and now it is something from which you have got to cut away."

"I see no reason why I should give up anything so long as I can make enough money honestly to keep it," Dix said.

"Of course, that is the ideal," Alloa said. "But can you? What can you do that would bring in enough for this sort of thing?"

She made a little gesture with her hand.

"There are ways and means," Dix said evasively.

"Yes, but are they the right ways and means?" Alloa asked. "Oh, please listen to me. It is awfully hard to put into words, but I have got to make you understand. Go straight and do the right thing. It is going to mean a lot of self-sacrifice; it is going to be hard, desperately hard, for you at first.

"But if you can win through those first moments of despondency, those first uncomfortable moments when you have to do without money and the things that have come to be necessities in your life, then gradually the peace and self-respect which you will have instead will be worth so much more than anything you can buy."

"How much do you want me to give up?" he asked.

"Everything that you haven't come by absolutely honestly," she said. "Everything that hasn't been earned, everything that isn't entirely your own."

She spoke in a low voice, not looking at him.

It was the first time he had really come into the open,

97

she thought, and she was terrified lest by some unconscious word she should antagonise him again.

"And supposing I told you that many of the things
that you are suspicious of do belong to me, genuinely
and without any other tag upon them?" he asked.

"Then, of course, I should be very glad," Alloa said.
"It will make it so much easier for you; it will not mean
such a big renunciation as it might do otherwise."

"Supposing," he asked after a moment, "supposing
they weren't mine? What would you suggest I should
do?"

Alloa took a deep breath.

"Then you must send them back," she said. "It will
be a wrench; you will feel empty and perhaps unhappy
about them. But whether they are money or goods,
whatever they may be, if they are not yours genuinely
and completely honestly, then they must go back to
their original owners."

She was thinking of his cigarette case, of his wrist-
watch, as she spoke. Perhaps, too, he had a flat somewhere, filled with his ill-gotten gains. Perhaps even his
clothes had been stolen or obtained from a tailor under false pretences.

It seemed to her a long time before he spoke again,
then he said quietly:

"You are very drastic, aren't you, in your convic-
tions?"

"It is the only thing to be," she said. "You must see
that."

"Yes, I see what you are trying to tell me," he said.
"I wonder if you would say the same to a stockbroker
who has got his money through being one jump ahead
of the other man; or an industrialist who has managed
to scramble his way to success by bankrupting his com-
petitors; or a politician who makes promises that he
knows he can never keep?

"Aren't these people cheats and crooks just as much as the man who takes some small object that does not belong to him?"

"Morally, of course, they are," said Alloa. "And even if there are a number of people who behave in such a way, there are equally a large, or larger, number who behave decently and do only the things which they believe and know to be right, who go out of their way to help their fellow beings and who would not tell a lie or do something wrong under any circumstances."

"It is a pity I never meet such people," Dix said.

"Perhaps you never give yourself the chance," Alloa replied. "Come to Scotland and I will introduce you to many who are as straight as a die and proud of it."

"Perhaps one day I will accept your invitation," he said. "In the meantime I think we ought to be pressing on if you are to get to Biarritz in time for dinner."

Alloa felt as if her heart dropped a beat.

This then was the end of their luncheon together; perhaps the last time they would talk together seriously about things that mattered.

"We will fill the cars up with petrol before we leave Bordeaux," Dix was saying as he signalled for the bill. "We might stop for a drink or a cup of coffee at about five o'clock. I shall be behind you all the way and when I think there is a good place I will pass you and show you where to stop."

"I would like that," Alloa said.

She knew it was a reprieve. She had not yet got to say goodbye and her heart was the lighter because of it.

Once again she was back on the road—a wide, very fast road, which she had seen on the map ran straight from Bordeaux to Bayonne. It kept a little inland so that she could not see the sea, but all the time Alloa was conscious of it.

There was something in the air, some tang, something invigorating and yet nostalgic which made her think of the great, grey rollers coming in from across the Atlantic, of the winds blowing from the golden west.

She wondered as she drove whether it would be possible to find Dix a good job in America.

She wondered if Lou could help him, and then she knew that it was impossible for her to speak of him either to Lou or to Mrs. Derange.

How could she explain how she had met him? How could she tell of his capabilities or even ask them to assist him, knowing what she knew?

She began to see how difficult it was for a man who had once been branded as a black sheep ever to make good. There was always that question of references, of being able to furnish details of one's past.

She felt as if such questions tortured her. She felt as if her whole being was tense and strained in her anxiety to help. And yet she felt utterly helpless.

She was so distraught by her thoughts that when finally five o'clock came she did not even realise the time was imminent until the red Mercedes suddenly hooted and drew ahead of her just outside a small village.

To her surprise Dix did not stop at the *estaminet* but drove a little way off the road, down a narrow lane until they came to a small *château*.

There were umbrellas in the garden and Alloa could see that what originally had been a private house had been turned into a restaurant.

A wireless was playing gay Viennese waltzes; but there were only two or three other couples there. Dix chose a secluded table where they were out of sight of everyone and had an uninterrupted view of the flower-filled garden.

"What a sweet little place," Alloa exclaimed. "How did you know of it?"

"I sometimes stop here on my way south," he said.

"Do you do this journey often?" Alloa enquired.

"Quite frequently," he said.

"And always by car?"

There was an impish smile on his face as he replied: "If I can beg, borrow or—steal one."

Alloa knew he was laughing at her, and felt herself blushing. She did not have to reply because the waiter came at that moment and Dix ordered tea for her, coffee for himself and a selection of rich cream cakes.

"We have made good time," he said, looking at his watch. "You should get to Biarritz by half-past seven. That will give you time to unpack, have a bath and dress for dinner."

"I shall not have to dress up a lot just to eat it from a tray in my bedroom," Alloa smiled.

"Is that how they treat you?" he enquired. "What damned cheek!"

Alloa laughed.

"It is nothing of the sort," she said. "I'm doing a job and there is no reason at all why Mrs. Derange or Lou should ask me to dine with them in the restaurant."

"But you are a relation."

"A very, very distant connection," Alloa said. "I am not even sure that I believe Mrs. Derange's stories of us all being descended from the family of the *Duc de Rangé-Pougy*."

As she spoke she realised that it was the first time she had mentioned it to Dix.

"I expect it is true if she says so," Dix remarked. "These Americans are pretty thorough in their investigations when they want to find something out."

"Well, it won't affect me at any rate," Alloa said, "I don't expect I shall meet the *Duc*, and I am quite certain he won't be interested in me."

"Why shouldn't he be? You are as much a connection as Lou Derange."

"Yes, but I haven't got the dollars," Alloa said. "A few Scottish bawbees don't compare, now do they?"

Dix laughed.

"It's the first time I have ever known you cynical," he said.

"I am not being cynical," Alloa corrected. "I am just being severely practical. They say the French are a very practical nation—and they certainly seem to be when it comes to marriage!"

"While the Scots, of course, never give a thought to money," Dix retorted.

Alloa laughed.

"Touché," she said. "Though we are not so mean as all the stories about us make out."

Dix finished his coffee and looked at his watch.

"We ought to be moving on."

"Please let me pay my share," Alloa said quickly.

He shook his head.

"I reserve the right to be your host for our last meal together," he said.

"Yes, of course; this . . . this is our last!"

Alloa felt as if the sun had suddenly gone in.

"I hope you will still think of me sometimes," Dix said. "Still go on praying for me. That is, if you remember."

"I will remember," Alloa said through lips that felt suddenly a little stiff.

"I shall think of you," he said. "All the time that I am struggling to give up the things which matter so much."

Alloa felt a sense of hopelessness sweep over her. What more could she say? What more could she do to help him?

She watched him pay the bill, then turned and

walked through the flower-filled garden to where the cars were waiting in the drive.

She stood for a moment at the door of the Cadillac, the sun shining on her fair hair, her eyes blinking a little from the glory of it. And then, as Dix reached her side, she held out her hand to him.

"Thank you," she said in a low voice. "I wish I could say it a little more adequately."

He took her hand in both of his.

"Does it mean anything to you?" he asked.

She did not understand his question and looked at him a little bewildered.

"Mean anything?" she repeated.

"Saying goodbye like this."

"But of course," she answered. "I have told you how grateful I am that you came to my rescue, that you have been so kind to me these past few days. I . . . I shall pray for you always."

"And that is all?" Dix asked.

"What else?" she replied.

"What else?" he echoed, and she thought mockingly.

She did not understand him, could not gather what he was trying to say. Because she was embarrassed she turned away a little abruptly.

"Goodbye!" she said.

"*Au revoir!*" he answered, and went towards his own car.

Alloa felt the tears pricking her eyes as she drove back on to the narrow lane and turned on to the main road. What had he meant by his question? Why had he said goodbye in such a strange manner?

Once again she felt that she had failed him, and yet she did not know how. She only knew that all the joy and happiness seemed to have gone from the day.

'What did he mean? What did he want me to say?' she asked herself as she drove down the road.

Angrily she blinked away the tears. If she wasn't careful, she wouldn't be able to see where she was going. It would be a pity to have an accident at this last moment, after she had come safely for so far.

She drove on, glancing every so often in the driving mirror. The red Mercedes was just behind. She wondered what he was thinking. Was he, also, a little sad, a little despondent because their journey had come to an end and their ways had got to separate?

She had the sudden feeling that she had tried to enclose in a very small cage a brilliant, exotic bird which would only die in captivity. Better let Dix live his life in glory and beauty for a short time than be imprisoned by convention.

'Why am I thinking like this?' Alloa asked herself a little wildly. 'I know what is right and I know what is wrong. What Dix is doing is wrong and he must give it up.'

She looked in the driving mirror. There was the red Mercedes purring along the road a little way behind her.

She had an impulse to stop the car, to go and speak to him, to tell him that there was so much more they must talk about, so much more they must decide.

And then she knew that she dare not stop, because when she came face to face with him she could not say what she wanted.

She thought of his dark eyes looking down into hers, of his smile and of the touch of his hand; and she knew, in that moment, that she had nothing to offer him except words, and—words were no use.

She felt then how utterly ineffective she was; how helpless and of how little consequence. The tears were running down her cheeks. She brushed them angrily away.

They were coming into Bayonne, crossing the bridge

over the river, and then on the right she saw a signpost marked 'Biarritz'. She glanced back.

The red Mercedes was still following her and she turned down a road which was bordered on either side by pine woods.

The sea was on her right—deep green with a pattern of gold and crimson in the glory of the setting sun. It seemed to sparkle and glitter so that it was hard for Alloa to keep her eyes on the road. The pine woods stretched right down to the sands.

She had a glimpse of brightly coloured villas nestling amongst the trees, and then the road opened out and she saw ahead of her the lighthouse, the hotels and houses of Biarritz.

It was just as she had imagined it would be—standing in a small semi-circle beside the sea, colourful and beautiful; while behind in the distance the Pyrenees with their snow-covered peaks were silhouetted against the blue sky.

Instinctively she slowed down and then looked back.

For a moment she could not believe what she saw. She drew the car to a standstill and turned her head, looking searchingly back along the dusty white road.

The red Mercedes was no longer following her. There was nothing in sight!

Chapter Six

Lou was in her bedroom changing for dinner when Alloa was shown up to the suite by one of the reception clerks. She turned round from the dressing-table and held out her hands with a genuine exclamation of delight.

"Alloa! I'm so pleased to see you. I thought you would never get here."

"I have come as quickly as I could," Alloa said. "I had a little trouble with the car at Alençon or I should have been here sooner."

She wondered, as she said it, if it was indeed the truth or whether, even if everything had been perfect, having once met Dix she would not have lingered on the way. But Lou was not interested in the details of her journey.

"You have brought the luggage safely?" she said.

"It is coming upstairs now," Alloa reassured her.

"I have been praying you would arrive quickly," Lou said. "I think we are going to have fun here. Momma has found a whole heap of friends and we're getting booked up with dinner parties and invitations to lunch."

"I'm so glad," Alloa smiled, and then added because her curiosity prompted her: "What about the *Duc*?"

"Not a word from him yet," Lou replied. "Momma's hopping mad with rage, but she won't say so. Of course, most of the people we know here are Americans, so they can't give us any information."

Alloa was just going to ask further questions when the door opened and Mrs. Derange came in.

"Jeanne told me you were here," she said. "How are you, Alloa? You have brought the luggage safely?"

"Quite safely," Alloa answered.

"I hope you remembered the typewriter," Mrs. Derange said. "My secretary has sent me a huge pile of correspondence from New York, but I haven't attempted to open any of it until you arrived."

"We will get it all sorted out tomorrow," Alloa said with a smile.

Mrs. Derange hesitated and then she said:

"Well, perhaps you will have time to look some of it over tonight after you have had some supper."

Alloa said nothing. She was suddenly aware how tired she was.

It was not only the strain of driving, but all the emotions she had experienced in the last forty-eight hours and that sudden empty feeling in her chest because Dix had left her without saying good-bye. She realised that Mrs. Derange was waiting for an answer.

"Yes, yes, of course," she said. "I will do what I can."

"You will find them all in the sitting-room," Mrs. Derange said. "But I have asked them at the office to have a desk put in your bedroom. It will be more convenient for you to work there."

"Thank you," Alloa said. She gave a little sigh and turned towards the door. "Now if you will excuse me I will go and find my own room. I've been travelling all day and I am very dusty."

"There are one or two things I wanted to tell you before we went down to dinner . . ." Mrs. Derange began.

But for once Lou was perceptive enough to realise how tired Alloa was.

"Oh, leave her alone, Momma," she said. "Can't you see she's all in? It's quite a journey when one comes to think of it."

Mrs. Derange had the grace to look ashamed.

"Perhaps you had better rest tonight, Alloa," she said. "Your dinner will be brought up to you. It's *table d'hôte*, don't forget, because that's in the *en pension* terms. This is a very expensive hotel."

"Which we can well afford," Lou drawled from the dressing-table.

Mrs. Derange looked at her warningly.

"There is no need to be extravagant, Lou. As I have told you often enough, you may be rich, but your father worked hard for every dime of it."

"Nonsense!" Lou retorted. "He struck lucky and you

know it. And if you talk in that cheese-paring way, Momma, the *Duc* won't think we've got any money to spend at all."

"That reminds me," Mrs. Derange said. "We will ask if there's a letter downstairs. I don't trust that hall-porter. He is so stupid he may have got our names muddled with someone else. I feel quite certain the *Duchesse* would have replied by this time."

"Perhaps she's not so anxious to see us as we are to see her—or, rather, her son," Lou suggested.

Mrs. Derange snorted with annoyance, and then, realising that Alloa was still in the room, said sharply:

"Run along, Alloa, and rest. If you are too tired to do any work, you might as well go to bed. I'll see you in the morning immediately after breakfast and we'll get down to those letters."

"Thank you," Alloa said. "Good night, Mrs. Derange. Good night, Lou."

She slipped from the room and as she went she heard Lou say:

"You are disagreeable, Momma. You might have thanked Alloa for bringing the car half across Europe."

"Thank her! Why should I?" Mrs. Derange enquired. "She's paid for it, isn't she?"

Alloa heard no more, but she was laughing as she went down the passage.

Her room was on the same floor, but on the other side of the hotel, looking out not over the sea but over the front door and a large, open courtyard where the cars were parked.

This meant, as she well knew, that she was likely to be kept awake very late at night as guests arrived or departed, slammed their car doors and talked at the top of their voices regardless of those who might be wishing to sleep.

But she was not prepared to find fault with the way

she was housed. It was a thrill to be in this large, luxurious hotel, and in Biarritz. The only thing was that at the moment she felt too tired to appreciate it.

Dinner was brought up to her by a white-coated waiter.

It was delicious, and after she had eaten it she felt revived and not so sleepy, although that little aching depression in the region of her heart was still there when she thought of Dix.

She wished she understood him. She wished that she was certain she would ever see him again.

She crept into bed thinking that she would lie awake, but she slept peacefully and dreamlessly and awoke to find that the depression and queries of the night before had vanished entirely.

Instead she felt excited and expectant of what the day would bring.

She had dressed and had her breakfast long before Mrs. Derange was called, and so she slipped out of the hotel and down on to the sea-shore which lay directly beneath it.

The sea was as blue as the sky above it, the rollers coming in from the Atlantic were white-crested as they broke on the golden sands.

There were very few people about and Alloa found herself running, the wind blowing back her fair hair from her cheeks, the sun sparkling in her eyes so that everything seemed enveloped by a rainbow of golden glory.

She ran back breathlessly to the hotel and arrived to find Jeanne looking for her along the passage to say that Mrs. Derange was ready.

The blinds were half-lowered over the big bow window in Mrs. Derange's bedroom and she was sitting up in bed, looking every minute of her age.

"Oh, here you are," she said as Alloa came in the door. "There is no need to ask you if you are rested."

"I slept wonderfully, thank you," Alloa answered. "I hope you did."

"I had a terrible night," Mrs. Derange replied. "We stayed at the Casino until four o'clock and I lost a lot of money too."

"I am sorry to hear that," Alloa said.

"I was a fool to let them persuade me into gambling," Mrs. Derange said. "What my late husband would have said at such stupidity I can't imagine. He always believed that money should be spent wisely and on things that really are necessary. You remember that, child. It is a good rule. Never waste money in case you may need it some day."

"I have never had any to waste," Alloa said gently.

"No, I suppose not," Mrs. Derange said.

When she added quickly as if she was slightly embarrassed at the turn the conversation had taken,

"Well, let us get down to work."

It was obvious that Mrs. Derange was not in her best form this morning.

In dictating her letters she contradicted herself every other word, hesitated over what she should say, and then, having said it, changed her mind again.

Alloa's notebook was full of crossings out and corrections, and she was beginning to think that they were not going to get very far when Jeanne brought in a letter.

"This has just come by hand, *Madame*," she said.

Mrs. Derange's eyes lit up and, though she said nothing, Alloa knew perfectly well that she thought it was from the *Duchesse*. But when she opened the envelope her face dropped.

"It's from the Cartwrights," she said. "They are in

110

San Sebastian and want us to go over there for dinner on Thursday."

"The chauffeur is waiting for a reply, *Madame*," Jeanne said.

"Well now, let me see," Mrs. Derange said. "San Sebastian is in Spain. We have our visas all right, but what about the car? You had better telephone down, Alloa, and find out."

"I don't think there will be any difficulties," Alloa said. "The Triptique is made out for Spain as well as France. But I will just check to be quite sure."

She picked up the telephone and got through to the hall porter.

"Will it be all right for Mrs. Derange to take her Cadillac to San Sebastian?" she asked.

She asked the question in French and then had a little difficulty in understanding the reply. Then she put down the receiver.

"I think I had better go downstairs with our papers," she said. "I can't quite understand what the porter is saying."

"Oh, I am sure it will be all right," Mrs. Derange answered. "I will write an acceptance, then Jeanne can wait with it until you return."

"I won't be more than a few minutes," Alloa promised.

She collected the Triptique from her bedroom and hurried downstairs in the lift. The hall porter looked at it very carefully and then said:

"That is quite in order, *M'mselle*. But only you can take the car into Spain and bring it out again. The Triptique is in your name and therefore no one else can drive it."

"But I don't think I was asked to dinner," Alloa exclaimed. "I think Mrs. Derange will want her daughter to drive the car."

"That is impossible, *M'mselle*," the hall porter said. "You see, there are very strict rules about taking cars into Spain. The driver who takes a car in must bring it out."

"But, why?" Alloa enquired.

The porter smiled.

"There has been a lot of trouble," he said. "General Franco has made it almost impossible for Spaniards to afford foreign cars, and yet somehow they get into the country."

"You mean they are smuggled in?" Alloa asked.

"I wouldn't know, *M'mselle*," the porter said with a twinkle. "But the Spaniards undoubtedly have very smart cars, even sometimes a Cadillac."

Alloa laughed.

"Well, they mustn't have ours," she said.

She went upstairs again and told Mrs. Derange what the porter had said.

"How ridiculous!" Mrs. Derange protested. "Of course, I meant Lou to drive us over—or I could drive myself for that matter. Naturally the Cartwrights haven't asked you. They don't even know you are here."

"Let me take you over," Alloa suggested, "and then I will go and get myself something to eat in San Sebastian. I don't mind waiting."

"We might be late," Mrs. Derange said.

"I still don't mind. I can sit in the car and wait for you. Please don't give it another thought."

"Well, that's real nice of you," Mrs. Derange conceded. "You can take the note downstairs, Jeanne."

Jeanne hurried away with it and Alloa picked up her shorthand book again. But Mrs. Derange's heart was obviously not in her correspondence.

After a moment she put down the letter she was holding in her hand and said:

"Has Lou said anything to you about the reason why we have come here?"

"You mean to meet the *Duc de Rangé-Pougy?*" Alloa enquired.

"So she has told you," Mrs. Derange said. "I hope, Alloa, that you will do your best to make her see how sensible such a marriage would be. It would give her position, it would make her into somebody of real importance."

"Supposing she was not happy?" Alloa asked.

Mrs. Derange hesitated for a moment, then she said:

"On the other hand, suppose she married somebody quite ordinary, an American boy, and then she isn't happy? What has she got left but the heartache?"

"But if she loved him and he loved her she would at least have a chance of being happy," Alloa said in a low voice.

"And suppose he married her for her money?" Mrs. Derange asked. "Alloa, money makes life very difficult for a girl—especially a girl with the amount Lou has inherited. How is she to be sure that anyone loves her merely for herself? The answer is, one can't be sure.

"People with money are, in many ways, different inside themselves because they are rich. It is no use speculating what Lou would do if she wasn't rich. She is rich and therefore, as her mother, I have got to decide what is best for her, what will give her the greatest happiness in the long run."

Alloa looked worried.

"Supposing," she said, "supposing she doesn't like the *Duc?*"

"She will like him," Mrs. Derange said confidently. "Think what he can offer. The *Duc* is head of one of the most distinguished families in France. They have great properties, they have a house in Paris. Alloa,

113

you have got to help me. I know what is best for my child, but you can make her see it from her own point of view."

Alloa suddenly felt there was no point in arguing.

"I will do what I can," she said. "But I am glad it isn't me."

"You are different altogether," Mrs. Derange said crushingly. "No one would marry you except for yourself, and so the problem doesn't arise."

"No, of course not," Alloa agreed. "And that is why I am sorry for Lou."

"Lou is a very lucky girl," Mrs. Derange said sharply.

Alloa tried to convince herself this was the truth. But when she went along to her own room she found several letters on her dressing-table. Jeanne gave her an explanation of their presence there.

"I am sorry, *M'mselle*, I forgot to give them to you last night. They arrived at Claridge's just before we were leaving. The hall porter asked me if I would bring them along for you. I forgot about them until this morning."

"That's all right," Alloa said, seeing that the one on top was from her father.

She looked at the others. One was from a girl with whom she had been at school. The one underneath was in an unknown handwriting.

She opened it first because she was curious, turned to the signature and saw it was signed 'Steve Weston'.

It was a surprise to hear from him. She read it quickly.

Dear Miss Derange,

After I had left, I thought that I had not thanked you enough for trying to help me. I realise you did all you could and I am grateful.

I don't want to be a nuisance or bother you, but if

at any time you think Lou would like to see me, will you let me know? You know I love her, and I believe in her heart she loves me, too. Anyway, if you ever write or cable me at the above address, I will jump a plane and will be with you just as quickly as it can get me there.

Thank you again.

Yours,

Steve Weston.

Alloa looked at the address on the top of the writing-paper, then folded the letter and put it carefully away in her despatch-case.

She felt sorry for Steve Weston and she was certain that, whatever Mrs. Derange might say, he loved Lou for herself and not for her money.

'I know whom I would rather marry if it was a choice between Steve and the *Duc*,' Alloa told herself.

Then she laughed, because there was no likelihood of her ever having such a choice.

She typed for the rest of the morning, had lunch and went on typing most of the afternoon. When she had finished, it was nearly four o'clock. Lou had gone off to play tennis. Mrs. Derange had not yet returned from a luncheon party.

Alloa, with a little sigh of relief, realised that her time was her own, and after glancing at herself in the looking-glass she ran downstairs to the beach. She was wearing only the simple cotton frock she had bought in London.

Even so, she seemed overdressed beside the women lying on the beach in Bikinis, abbreviated shorts and bathing dresses that were little more than a wisp of ribbon.

Alloa turned aside from the more crowded part of the sands beneath the hotel and walked away to the right to where there were only bare rocks and a few scattered villas reached by long, twisting steps cut in the cliff side.

Soon she found a deserted stretch of sand and sitting down in the sunshine, her hands clasped round her knees, she stared out to sea.

She thought of Dix, somehow thinking of him made her feel he was there beside her. His dark eyes boring at her quizzically, his lip twisted in a half humorous, half cynical smile. . . .

She came back to reality to find it was much later than she had meant to be out. She hurried back to the hotel, up the little twisting streets, to find that Mrs. Derange was waiting for her.

"Where have you been, Alloa?" she said. "There are some letters which have come this afternoon that I particularly want to answer."

"I'm sorry," Alloa said. "I looked in about half an hour ago. There was no one here."

"Well, we have got time to do them before dinner," Mrs. Derange said.

Alloa fetched her notebook and was just about to sit down when Lou came into the sitting-room.

"Look what I found downstairs," she said, holding up a letter.

There was no mistaking the high, pointed writing on the long, thin envelope.

"It is from the *Duchesse*," Mrs. Derange cried.

She got up hastily from her chair and took it from Lou's hand.

"I wonder how long this has been here?" she added crossly. "They really are hopeless in this hotel. My letters were in the wrong pigeonhole just now."

"This was lying on the desk," Lou said. "That's how I saw it."

116

"Well, thank goodness it has come," Mrs. Derange said, pulling the thin sheets out of the envelope.

The letter was written in French. It took her some time to translate it, but at last she gave a cry of excitement.

"She wants us to go over and have luncheon tomorrow," she said. "Yes, tomorrow. We are asked for twelve-thirty. Oh, Lou! Think of it. I have been waiting for this moment."

"What else does she say?" Lou asked in a tone curiously devoid of excitement.

"She says that her son has not yet returned home. Now that's real disappointing. I hoped we were going to see him. But he may be back any day—yes, that's right, any day."

Mrs. Derange put down the letter.

"If you ask me, the *Duchesse* wants to have a look at us first. After all, I can understand it. I should feel the same myself if it were my son. Oh, Lou! I hope you will make a good impression."

"I don't know why I shouldn't," Lou answered.

"Well, you know what these French people are," Mrs. Derange said. "The Ambassadress was telling me what airs they give themselves and how conventional and staid they are in their own homes. You'll have to watch everything, Lou."

"O.K., Momma," Lou remarked.

"There you go," Mrs. Derange said with a gesture of hopelessness. "What an expression. And don't call me Momma. I have told you often enough. It started as a joke when you were a little girl and you have just gone on with it. People don't understand, they think you don't know any better."

"What do you expect me to call you?" Lou asked. "Susie?"

"No! I think that's worse," Mrs. Derange said in

117

all seriousness. "I don't like girls calling their mothers by their Christian names. Oh, I know a lot of your friends do it, but I never have thought it was right."

"Well, the *Duchesse* will just have to put up with Momma," Lou said. "I can't change myself overnight and I shall never remember anything else. Besides, just remind her how good the exchange is at the moment! What an enormous amount of francs go to one nice green dollar bill! You'll see, she'll think anything I say is just charming!"

"Lou, you are not to be cynical," Mrs. Derange said. "And don't start being difficult either. I am thrilled about this, really thrilled. I want to meet the *Duchesse*, I want to see the *Château*."

She looked down at the letter again.

"Twelve-thirty! We mustn't be late. Will you find out how long it takes us to get there, Alloa?"

"Yes, of course," Alloa answered.

Mrs. Derange looked at her and smiled. There was an air of almost effusive geniality about her as she said:

"But, of course! You are interested, too. We mustn't forget that they are your relations as well as ours. Well, I will tell you what we will do, Alloa. You shall drive us over. Lou won't want to crease her frock anyway. You can take your lunch and eat it in the car. It will give you a chance of seeing the house and grounds. You'd like that, wouldn't you?"

"Yes, of course," Alloa said quickly. "It is very kind of you to think of it."

"We shall all be very interested in seeing the *Château*," Mrs. Derange went on. "I wonder what you had better wear, Lou? You want to be smart and at the same time look quiet and respectable—the sort of girl whom anyone would want for a daughter-in-law. I want you to make a really good impression. First

118

impressions are always important. Now, which dress of yours do you think would be best?"

"I really don't know," Lou said. "I shall leave it to you, Momma, to choose."

"I shall go and look in your wardrobe right away," Mrs. Derange said.

She marched out of the room and Lou looked across at Alloa and winked.

"Momma's in her element," she said.

"And what do you feel about it?" Alloa asked in a low voice.

Lou shrugged her shoulders.

"I haven't seen the *Duc* yet. It seems to me he's being pretty elusive."

"Do you really intend to go through with it?" Alloa asked.

"Why not?" Lou said in a hard voice.

Alloa had no answer to this, and as if she sensed her thoughts Lou said suddenly.

"I suppose you are thinking of Steve. Well, forget him. He played on your feelings as he would have played on mine if I had seen him. There are other men in the world besides Steve Weston, and, as I have told you before, I should like to be a Duchess."

Lou was speaking defiantly and Alloa knew that she was not so much arguing with her as with her own thoughts.

The door opened suddenly and Mrs. Derange stood there with a dress in her hand.

"Really, Lou," she said. "You are careless. I have spoken about it before; and Jeanne is about as bad. She unpacked for you."

"What are you talking about?" Lou asked.

"Look at this dress," Mrs. Derange said. "Look at it."

Both Lou and Alloa stared at the dress that she

held up by the hanger so that it swung high above the ground.

It was a pretty dress of flowered silk with rather a complicated pattern, so that Alloa, looking for spots or tears, could see nothing wrong with it.

And then suddenly, with a little leap of her heart, she realised what Mrs. Derange was talking about.

Pinned at the V of the neck, so that Lou must have taken it off without noticing it, was the sapphire brooch which they had all believed had been stolen.

Alloa felt a sudden flood of relief sweep over her. Dix had been telling the truth then.

She had believed him—and yet, deep in her heart, a tiny doubt had remained.

Chapter Seven

Alloa sat outside *Château Pougy* and watched the sunlight sparkling on the moat.

The flowers in the exquisitely laid-out gardens were blowing a little in the warm wind and marble statues stood sentinel on the green lawns. The chestnut trees in blossom and the massed banks of flowering shrubs looked like something out of a fairy story.

It was more like a palace than a house, Alloa thought, and wondered if anyone would mind if she slipped from the car and explored the gardens.

She longed, too, to look at the stables, which she could see a little way in the distance beyond a sixteenth-century Orangery.

The *Château* was one of the most beautiful houses she had ever seen. A long flight of steps led up to the front door over which a huge coat of arms carved in stone proclaimed the *de Rangé-Pougy* to be of Royal descent.

When they had arrived, footmen wearing heavily gold-laced velvet uniforms hurried down the steps, and even Mrs. Derange seemed a little awed as she and Lou walked slowly through the front door, leaving Alloa behind them.

For the moment Alloa could understand Mrs. Derange's ambition to see Lou as chatelaine of this wonderful place. With all her money there could be nothing in America to compare with this.

And yet, Alloa wondered, even though the *de Rangé* blood ran in Lou's veins, would she ever feel at home? Even as she asked the question she knew the answer. It all depended on the *Duc.*

It was not really possessions that mattered one way or another. Happiness came from people, and exquisite and wonderful though her surroundings might be, only if Lou liked her future husband would she be happy here.

And from here, Alloa's thoughts inevitably went to Dix. She wondered if he was still at Bayonne? Where he was staying? What he was doing?

Would he think of her at all? she asked herself. Perhaps, she thought, she would never see him again.

In which case he would merely become a name in her prayers, and gradually, she supposed, she would cease to think of him, to wonder about him, or really to trouble herself whether he was going straight or had gone back to his usual mode of life.

She wondered in what sort of place he had been born. Perhaps in one of the poor farms which they had passed on their way to the *Château.*

Perhaps in one of the tumbledown buildings in the villages which were picturesque enough with their washing hanging over the balconies, but doubtless were insanitary and squalid if one had to live in them.

She had a sudden longing to see Dix's family. She was certain that that was the clue to his behaving as he did.

How often she had heard her father say that behind every juvenile delinquent there stood a guilty and neglectful parent. Were Dix's parents directly responsible for the life he was leading?

She was somehow convinced in her own mind that that was the answer.

"Alloa!"

She heard her own name called and turned her head quickly. Lou was standing at the top of the stone steps just outside the front door. Alloa opened the door of the car and got out.

"What is it?" she asked, running up the steps.

"The *Duchesse* says you are to come in," Lou said. "She asked us how we got here, and when Momma explained about you she said she wanted to meet you."

"Oh!" Alloa drew a deep breath. "I will get my handbag."

She ran back to the car and only as she opened the door did she realise that Lou had followed her.

"Alloa, it's wonderful!" Lou was saying in a soft voice. "You've never seen such a magnificent house. And the *Duchesse* is sweet. I'm thrilled, I am really. Momma was right! There is no question of anyone else now I have seen this place."

Alloa did not say anything to damp her enthusiasm. Instead, she smiled at her and slipping her handbag over her arm said:

"Are you quite sure the *Duchesse* wants to see me?"

"Yes, of course. She had the most exquisite manners. She's just like someone in a film. One can hardly believe that she's real. And when she heard your name was

Derange, she said, of course, she couldn't allow one of the family to wait outside. The way she said 'the family' made me quite tingle. I believe there is something in all this family tree business after all."

Alloa wanted to laugh but felt that Lou would be offended. By now they had entered the house and her attention was distracted by the beauty and grandeur of the hall.

She had never believed that so much ornate decoration could yet be in such perfect taste. The painted ceilings, door and wainscoating were vividly colourful in soft blues, greens, yellows and reds.

There were tapestries on the walls of the wide staircase which with gold banisters and a crystal handrail swept upwards under a domed ceiling.

"The *Duchesse* is in the *Grand Salon*," Lou said in an awed voice.

Alloa was not surprised that she was awed when she saw the room.

A symphony of gold and rose pink, the walls were hung with what she was to learn later were Aubusson tapestries except where pictures by Titian, Raphael and Watteau decorated painted panels. The furniture was all sixteenth century and covered in needlework.

Seated on the sofa was one of the most beautiful women Alloa had ever seen. Her skin appeared to be made of alabaster, her white hair was piled high on her head.

She was dressed in black. Round her neck were string upon string of exquisite pearls, and her hand sparkled with diamonds as she held it out towards Alloa.

"So this is another relation," she said in French.

"Alloa belongs to the British branch," Mrs. Derange replied. "My husband did try to trace what happened to them, but he died before we could get to England to finish his research."

"I am very pleased to meet you, dear," the *Duchesse* said to Alloa.

"It is very kind of you to ask me in, *Madame*," Alloa said.

"Your French is good," the *Duchesse* smiled. "Have you been to France before?"

"No, unfortunately," Alloa confessed.

"Then it must be your ancestry which makes you speak so perfectly."

Alloa felt herself flush with pleasure. The *Duchesse* rose to her feet.

"Come, we will go into luncheon," she said.

The meal was served in a huge Dining-Hall as beautiful in its own way as the *Grand Salon*.

There was a footman behind every chair, and Alloa found it difficult not to stare at the wonderful gold ornaments which decorated the damask-covered table.

Mrs. Derange, however, seemed quite unabashed by her surroundings. She chattered away in excruciatingly bad French, continually and Alloa thought embarrassingly harping on Lou's wealth and the great possessions which were theirs in America.

"I am afraid I have never crossed the Atlantic," the *Duchesse* said. "I have been to England, of course, many times. But now I am older I am content to stay at home, to look after this estate for my son and to play hostess for him until he brings home a bride."

She spoke quite naturally and did not look at Lou as she spoke; but Alloa, glancing across the table felt there was no doubt at all that the *Duchesse* had already accepted Lou as her son's future wife.

When the luncheon was over, the *Duchesse* suggested that they might like to see round the house.

"It is one of the few great *châteaux* in France which still have their owners living in them," she said. "I hope I do not live to see the day when my son must retire to one of his smaller houses and this must become a national museum."

Her hand rested, as she spoke, on a Chinese lacquer cabinet; and as her fingers touched the wood, Alloa thought to herself,

'She loves the place. That is why she wants her son to marry, to have an heir, so that the line will be continued.'

The long, thin fingers trembled and Alloa thought: 'She is frightened. I wonder why?'

She looked up suddenly and saw the *Duchesse's* eyes were fixed on Lou.

'Why is she afraid?' Alloa asked herself again, but could find no answer to the question.

They went over the house, finding every room more magnificent and, if possible, more beautiful than the last.

The great State bedrooms with their huge, canopied beds and the armoury with its ancient weapons and suits of armour were breathtaking.

So was the Ballroom with its rows of glittering chandeliers, and the music room with a spinet which was supposedly the earliest ever made.

There were treasures everywhere. Pictures, tapestries, furniture, miniatures, ivories and china—each, in its own way, a collector's piece; some of them so unique as to be priceless beyond imagination.

Alloa could see that Lou and her mother were overwhelmed and impressed by everything they saw, but were without real appreciation of each particular object.

As she moved round the house, she found herself becoming increasingly grateful for the hours her father had spent making her study the catalogues of all the great museums and showing her the books on period furniture which were among his most prized possessions.

"I shall never own beautiful things myself," he said. "But in this way I can appreciate what others have."

She and her mother had often laughed a little tenderly at her father for his preoccupation with antiques.

Now Alloa could understand that his love for beautiful things had been born in him. He had never seen the *Château Pougy* but the treasures that were contained here were all part of his heritage.

The heritage he had inherited from the ancestors who had been forced by command of the King to leave France and go to the great, undeveloped acres of Canada.

"Oh, I wish my father could see this!" Alloa said suddenly.

She was standing in front of a beautiful picture by Watteau which hung in one of the small Ante-rooms.

"One day we must invite him to come here," the *Duchesse* said kindly.

"I am afraid it would be impossible, *Madame*," Alloa answered. "But it is very kind of you to think of it."

"Then you must tell him about the *Château*," the *Duchesse* said. "I can see that you love beautiful things."

"I have been brought up to love them," Alloa said. "But I never realised until now what a difference it makes to see a fine piece of furniture or a lovely picture in its proper setting."

The *Duchesse* smiled at her.

"Now you understand why I want the house to remain exactly as it is," she said. "Sometimes my son wants to move something to our place in Paris or to a villa that we have near Monte Carlo. But always I say: 'No! Buy new, if necessary; but the things that belong to the *Château* must remain here'."

"I am sure they would feel lost and lonely anywhere else," Alloa said softly.

126

The *Duchesse* smiled at her again, almost as if they had a secret between them that the others could not understand.

"I think I have shown you nearly everything," the *Duchesse* said at last. "You must forgive me if I do not take you outside. I have not been very well lately. I suffer a little with my heart and too much exercise is not good for me. I should like you to have seen the orangery, the herb gardens and the maze, but you will be able to see them when you come to stay."

There was a little glint in Mrs. Derange's eyes as she said quickly:

"When will you be expecting us, *Duchesse*?"

The *Duchesse* hesitated.

"I think my son is returning tomorrow or perhaps the day after," she said in her soft voice. "I am waiting to hear from him. The moment he is back I will tell him that you are here in Biarritz and I know he will want you to be his guests."

"We should enjoy that very much," Mrs. Derange said. "Wouldn't we, Lou?"

"Yes, I should love to stay here," Lou answered. "And to meet the *Duc*."

She looked straight at the *Duchesse* as she spoke and Alloa knew that she was telling her, without words, that she accepted the marriage even without seeing the bridegroom.

Mrs. Derange was about to say something more when the butler came into the room and bent to say something softly in the *Duchesse's* ear.

"My maid has sent to remind me that it is time for my rest," she said. "I hope you will not think me impolite or inhospitable, but the doctor has been very insistent that I must obey his regime. Please stay as long as you like, if there is anything further you would like to see; but I am afraid I must retire."

"No, we will go now," Mrs. Derange said. "And thank you very much, *Duchesse*, for having us. We shall look forward immensely to our visit to you."

"And I shall look forward to it, too," the *Duchesse* said.

She shook hands with Mrs. Derange and Lou, then she turned to Alloa.

"I hope you will come as well," she said. "There are many other treasures which I know you will appreciate and which you will also be able to describe to your father."

"Thank you, *Madame*. It is very kind of you," Alloa said.

The *Duchesse* touched her shoulder.

"There is a distinct likeness to some of the pictures in the gallery. I did not have time to take you there today, but when you see the family portraits you will know what I mean."

She smiled at Alloa again; and then they had made their final farewells and almost, Alloa thought, before they had time to get their breath, they were driving away down the drive.

"Well!" Mrs. Derange ejaculated at last. "I expected something big and important, but nothing as splendid as that."

"It's swell, Momma! Really swell!" Lou said enthusiastically. "At the same time, I shall always be scared to death that I might break something."

"You needn't be frightened of that," Mrs. Derange said soothingly. "If there's one thing you're not, it's clumsy. I always said when you were a little girl that you didn't romp about like other children or smash things. No, Lou! That's the perfect background for you, dear."

"I wish she had shown us a photograph of the *Duc*," Lou pouted.

"I am sure they wouldn't have had anything so ordinary as a photograph," Mrs. Derange replied. "A portrait, maybe, but I didn't see any modern portraits."

"Perhaps there is a picture gallery which we didn't see," Alloa suggested, and wondered if the *Duchesse* had deliberately avoided taking them there.

"Yes, of course, a picture gallery! That's where they would be," Mrs. Derange agreed. "Did you notice the jewels and the snuff boxes? Why, each one of those must be worth thousands of dollars. You'd think that they would be frightened of burglars."

"Not with all those retainers about," Lou said. "It's like stepping back into the Middle Ages. Oh, Momma! What parties I'll give there!"

Alloa said nothing.

She suddenly had a vision of Lou's gay young friends jiving and jitterbugging in the *Grand Salon*. She could not bear to think of it.

The house was so beautiful. It had such an atmosphere of peace and tranquility that it was sacrilege even to think of blaring modern music disturbing it or of loud, shrill voices echoing around those beautiful walls.

"I can't get over it all, I can't really!" Mrs. Derange kept saying. "The people back home would never believe that a place like that still existed. It's . . . it's mediæval, that's what it is."

Alloa could not help smiling to herself.

Mrs. Derange had been very scornful about some things in London. She had found much in the hotel and in her friends' houses which compared unfavourably with the comforts and amenities in New York.

For once she was awestruck, and Alloa could not help being pleased that *Château Pougy* had exceeded her expectations.

They got back to Biarritz just about tea-time, but there was no question of Alloa having a cup. To Mrs.

Derange and Lou the British habit of having tea at half-past four meant nothing.

In America they went from luncheon to cocktail time without anything to eat, and it never struck them that Alloa was longing, as tea-time came round, for a drink of real English tea such as was always waiting for her at home at that particular hour.

"We have got at least two hours' work ahead of us," Mrs. Derange said as they reached the hotel; and Alloa followed her upstairs to start taking down in shorthand the long-winded letters she wrote to her friends, her lawyer and the chairmen of her committees.

As Alloa started to type them out, she wondered for the hundredth time why Americans took so long to say something which other nations could manage in a few words.

The letters this afternoon were longer than usual. Mrs. Derange could not resist describing *Château Pougy* in every letter she wrote.

"My husband's family home," she phrased it.

When the letters were finished, Alloa was sent downstairs to see if there was any possibility of buying postcards of *Château Pougy*.

"I will see what I can do, *M'mselle*," the hall porter told her. "I think some pictures of the *Château* are obtainable."

"Then please get as many as you can. Mrs. Derange will, I think, want at least three dozen of each different view."

The hall porter became more attentive. It was obvious that his particular commission on such a large number of postcards would be well worth while.

Alloa went upstairs to write to her father, giving him a long description of *Château Pougy*. When she had finished, it was dinner time and her meal was brought up to her as usual.

After she had eaten it she looked out of the window to see that it was still light although the sun had just begun to set.

Mrs. Derange and Lou would already have left to dine with some friends at another hotel. Alloa picked up a short coat and slipped it over her dress. She would go for a walk, she decided, along the beach.

She looked into the sitting-room, put the letters that she had typed for Mrs. Derange on the desk ready for her to sign, and then went downstairs.

The beach was practically deserted. There were only a few men fishing and a dog or two gambolling along the sands.

Alloa moved towards the rocks and when she found she could go no further along the sea shore, she climbed up a twisting, narrow path which took her past the lighthouse on towards the pine woods which lay between Biarritz and Bayonne.

She must have walked for nearly half an hour before she realised that she was getting tired.

It was still not dark but the sun had sunk in a blaze of gold and crimson glory. She was in the middle of the pine woods and they stretched right down to the sea.

She sat down with her back against a gold and brown trunk fragrant of resin and stared at the waves coming in, emerald and sapphire, from the horizon.

How different the colours were from the sea she knew so well at Tordale.

And yet she had a sudden longing to be home, to open the heavy oak door of the Manse and run across the dark, cramped hall into the cosy warmth and light of the sitting-room.

Her father and mother would be seated reading on either side of the fireplace. She wished now she could tell them about *Château Pougy* and about the *Duchesse*.

It was so irritating to have to wait for her father's

reply to her letter and not to be able to see the expression on his face when he read how wonderful it was.

Lined and thin with over-work and ill-health, he was still a handsome man, and she wondered if she would recognize his features amongst the portraits in the picture gallery.

'We belong there,' she thought of herself as saying to him.

Then with a little laugh realised how ridiculous she was being.

There was no doubt where she belonged—to the small, poverty-stricken Manse with its rough wood floors and rooms that were sadly in need of paint.

How long she sat thinking of her home Alloa did not know. She was suddenly conscious that the sun had vanished and that it was growing dark. She glanced up at the sky.

The evening stars were coming out and the pale moon had appeared, which would soon bathe the world in a silver light.

She was not the least afraid of being out in the dark.

She was used to walking over the moors and of finding her way home by the stars when she no longer recognised her surroundings. It was not cold and the wind blowing in from the sea was soft.

'I won't go back yet,' Alloa thought.

It was then that she became aware of a flickering light some distance away. Somebody was moving through the trees with a torch. It looked rather pretty, she thought; almost like a firefly hovering in the still of the evening.

Then another torch flashed. There were faint sounds, but she was not certain what they were.

She watched for some time and then rose curiously to her feet. Perhaps some people were having a midnight bathing party, she thought, but there was not the shrieks of laughter that usually accompanied such escapades.

She walked slowly through the trees, the pine-needles covering the ground muted the sound of her light footsteps. The lights were further away than she thought and it took her some little time to reach them.

The ground was gradually sloping down towards the shore; so that, as she approached, the torches disappeared completely and there were only the faint sounds to guide her onwards.

She saw then that the sea came inwards at this point, forming a small natural bay. The cliffs were no longer high—in fact they vanished almost completely and the ground sloped down sharply towards the sea.

Suddenly she stood still, amazed at what she saw beneath her.

Almost completely hidden, except from someone standing above, men with torches in their hands were working on something large and dark which stood on the very edge of the water.

For a moment Alloa could not see what it was; and then, going a little nearer still, she recognized it as a car. Had there been an accident? she wondered. Had the car driven into the sea by mistake?

Now she saw that the men were not trying to rescue the car from the sea.

A fishing boat was standing only a few yards out in the bay. A ramp connected it with the shore and the car was to be driven up the ramp and onto the boat.

The men were moving silently about their task. Four of them were at work, two of them were standing watching. An order was given, but in little more than a hoarse whisper.

"*À la droite! À la droite!*" she heard one man say, while another cursed suddenly and shook his fingers as if he had hurt himself.

Alloa watched them with fascinated eyes.

She moved a little nearer still and at that moment her foot slipped, a pile of earth slipped away from beneath it.

It made only a slight sound, but the men below her heard it. A torch was flashed in her face. She heard an exclamation, a coarse oath was rasped out.

Two men came running up the incline towards her. She had no time to think, no time to escape even if she wished to do so. Her arms were seized roughly, she was dragged down on to the beach.

"Stop! What are you doing? Where are you taking me?"

Frightened, she spoke in English. Then suddenly her captors stopped, bringing her to a halt before the two men who had stood apart from the rest.

"Une femme," she heard one of her captors say, and when he said it he spat.

There was a sudden babble of voices. Alloa managed to distinguish a little of what they were saying.

"What is she doing here . . . ?"

"Ask her who sent her . . . ?"

"Who is she . . . ?"

"What are we going to do . . . ?"

"Silence!"

Someone spoke in a voice of command, and then once again a torch was flashed in her face. She could see nothing, was only blinded by the glare, but at the same time was suddenly terrified.

What had happened to her? Into what predicament had she got herself?

She was afraid. She knew there was danger, knew it without even being conscious of the hard hands on her arms and the rough way she had been dragged over the soft ground.

Someone had once told her that in the war he could smell danger.

She knew now that there was danger all round her, danger that she did not understand and yet which had the effect of making her knees feel as if they were turned to water.

And then out of the darkness a voice spoke.

"Let her go!"

For a moment the voice meant nothing to her, and then suddenly an arm went round her shoulders—an arm protective and comforting, an arm which drew her close.

"It is all right," someone said in French. "I know this girl. She is a friend of mine."

It was Dix!

She turned to him with what was almost a sob of relief; without her conscious volition her hands went out to cling onto him.

It was only now that she knew how frightened she had been, how frightened she still was. But he was there. Nothing could happen while he was there.

"What's she doing here?"

There was no doubt of the suspicion behind the question.

She felt Dix shrug his shoulders lightly.

"I presume she has come to see me."

"How can we be sure of that? She may have been sent. How can we know that that is the truth?"

The man who was asking most of the questions was the same man who had spat. Alloa could not see him, for her eyes were still blinded by the torch, but she could sense his hostility.

"We can ask her for one thing," Dix said.

She felt that he was smiling as his head turned towards her.

"You came to meet me, didn't you, Alloa?"

She felt his fingers press her shoulder lightly. Obedient to what was required of her she answered:

"Yes."

"I told you to wait for me at the lighthouse. Do you remember?"

Again his fingers pressed her shoulders.

"Yes," Alloa answered.

"How can we be sure she's telling the truth?"

"Does she look like a liar?" Dix enquired. "Besides, are you suggesting that there is no reason for a pretty girl to wait for me? I am not yet without attraction, *mes amis*."

There was a grunt of laughter at this and then the man who was most insistent said:

"We will tie her up. We are not going to risk letting her get away until we have gone."

"Oh, tie her up if you please," Dix said. "I am sure she'll not have the slightest objection."

"Are you sure she's your girl?" the man asked in an ugly voice. "If I thought you were doing the dirty on us, I'd slit her throat here and now."

"You'll have to slit mine first," Dix said lightly. "And as to her not being my girl, I can assure you that she is and that we love each other very much. Is that not true, *ma petite*?"

Obedient to the pressure of his fingers Alloa murmured:

"Yes, of course."

"But you can't prove it," the ugly voice said from the darkness.

"No, I can't prove it," Dix replied. "Except like this."

Before Alloa was aware of what he was about to do he put his hand under her chin and turned her face round to his.

Then he bent his head and before she could draw in her breath with surprise he had laid his lips on hers.

For a moment he held her prisoner. She was too surprised to resist him, too surprised even to move. She felt her mouth quiver beneath his and then suddenly she was free.

"Oh, come on," someone said. "We haven't time for this sort of . . ."

He used an ugly French word which made Dix stiffen almost instinctively, and then Alloa felt rough fingers dragging her hands behind her.

Her wrists were bound together by a cord which bit into her flesh.

"Now her feet," someone said.

"I will bind her myself," Dix said slowly.

He bent down and picked Alloa up in his arms.

He carried her a short distance away and set her down on the sand. Someone handed him a rope and she felt his hands put it gently round her ankles.

"It's all right," he managed to say very softly. "Don't be frightened."

It was impossible to answer him, for the man who had bound her hands was still beside them. The others had moved back to the car. A light was flashed on her feet as Dix rose.

"She'd better not get away or you'll pay for it," the man said.

"I can't think why you should worry," Dix said. "She doesn't want to run away. I suppose with an ugly face like yours you know nothing about women."

"I don't want to have anything to do with . . ."

The man used a filthy word and spat again, and before Dix could answer he walked away towards the car.

"You'd better come and help get her off," he said. "We haven't got much time before the tide turns."

Now that the light was no longer in her face Alloa could begin to see more clearly. The men were still working on the boat which was rocking now on the waves.

Her bound hands were hurting her and for the moment she felt almost faint as Dix moved away and she was left alone on the sand.

What did it all mean? It had all happened so quickly, it had all been so frightening, she felt as if she had been holding her breath from that first moment that her foot had slipped.

The men were dangerous. That was one thing that was quite certain. She had known it even before Dix had rescued her, and she had known that he, too, was fearful for her even while he held her securely against him.

Yes, he was afraid, too. She had known that; known it, she thought, in the touch of his lips when they had rested on her mouth.

She longed to raise her fingers to her mouth to feel if her lips were still the same. She could not move. He had kissed her, kissed her because, in some way she still did not understand, it had saved her.

The men were still moving round the car which now stood on the deck of the fishing boat. They were using their torches to see that the ropes were bound securely. The torch was raised again.

Alloa saw the glint of colour. The car was red!

She felt her heart give a sudden leap. She knew now what car was being loaded.

She remembered what the porter had said to her when Mrs. Derange had wished Lou to drive the Cadillac to San Sebastian. This was the clue to everything, the clue to what Dix had been doing with the red Mercedes.

They were taking the car round to the coast of Spain.

This was how the Spaniards got those expensive cars of which the porter had spoken.

This was how they evaded the payment of taxes which would have been imposed on them at the frontier. Alloa understood now exactly what was happening.

She saw the boat with its heavy cargo begin to move. The smugglers came splashing back to the shore.

Yes, they were car smugglers—and Dix was one of them!

Chapter Eight

It had grown very dark. Clouds had come up to cover the stars.

Even though her eyes were now accustomed to the darkness Alloa found it difficult to see what was going on.

She found it increasingly uncomfortable to sit with her hands bound behind her and her legs, tied at the ankles, stretched straight in front of her.

But there was nothing she could do about it and there was at the moment no one even to whom she could complain.

Dix and the other men had covered the car with a tarpaulin and were now having great difficulty in getting the boat off on the tide. Finally, however, they managed it.

The boat moved out and Alloa could see it silhouetted against the sky.

She realised then how clever they had been. The car, covered and camouflaged, appeared to be only some rather heavy superstructure on an ordinary fishing vessel.

No coastguard seeing it move along the coast would give it a second thought.

It was then, with one agonizing moment of fear, that Alloa thought that Dix had gone with the boat. She could see the heads of the men aboard and for a moment she could not see him in the darkness of the little bay.

Then she realised that Dix and another man were left behind.

They came walking over the sands towards her and when they were only just within earshot, stopped.

For a moment their French was so rapid that she found it difficult to understand what they were saying. She realised, however, that the other man, whoever he might be, was giving commands and Dix was listening to him.

There was no doubt at all who was in authority. She heard the words 'safety' and 'safe arrival' mentioned several times, and at last understood what the other man was saying.

It was imperative that she should not be released until the cargo that the boat carried had been unloaded safely on Spanish territory.

Dix was not arguing; he was merely saying that he would be responsible for her, that he could promise that she would not have the slightest chance of communicating with the police. Their voices rose a little.

The other man said severely, and in no uncertain terms, that when engaged in dangerous traffic of this sort it was lunacy to be cluttered with women.

Women always talked; in his opinion they were a menace which should be avoided.

Dix said in a voice which was outwardly humble but held a hint of laughter in it that he always did his best to avoid trouble, but trouble had an uncomfortable habit of following him wherever he went.

The other man was apparently not amused.

Again he reiterated that Alloa was to be kept captive for at least two hours and her silence was to be assured by every possible method.

"You are sure you can trust her?" he said at length.

"I am quite sure," Dix said quietly.

"If you are mistaken, it will be the worse not only for you but for her," the man said.

There was a menace in his tones which no one could mistake.

"I understand," Dix said.

The man turned and walked away, his footsteps making no sound in the soft sand. Dix stood and watched him go.

Alloa was certain that he would come to her side immediately, but he just stood looking out into the darkness although she was certain that he could no longer see anything or anybody.

She was just about to call his name, to cry out that her wrists were hurting her almost unbearably, when there came the sound of a car being started up. She could hear it running for a moment and then moving away down the road.

As if it was the signal for which Dix had been waiting, he turned instantly and came across to Alloa.

He dropped down on his knees beside her; then flashing his torch on her bound wrists he cut the cord with a sharp knife.

She felt her shackles fall away and the utter relief at being able to move made her forget everything else.

She began to rub the circulation back into her wrists. Dix cut the cord that bound her ankles before, without saying a word, he switched out the torch and put his arms round her.

"I'm sorry, my darling," he said in a voice she had never heard him use before.

141

Then his lips were on hers and he was kissing her.

It was quite different from the kiss he had given her before. It took her completely by surprise.

After a moment of astonishment she struggled against him, pressing her hands against his chest, striving to free her mouth from beneath his, to no avail.

Even as she struggled, she felt an ecstasy and a joy shoot through her such as she had never known before in the whole of her life.

Quite suddenly she was still—immobile with surprise and with the almost unbelievable rapture that his kiss was awakening in her.

She felt a flame flicker through her like a fire that had just been kindled and her body became limp against him, her mouth was soft beneath the possessive hardness of his lips.

"I'm sorry! Oh, darling, I'm sorry!"

She hardly heard his voice, she only knew that her whole being was alive, tingling with a wonder and a glory beyond anything she had ever dreamed of feeling.

She knew then that this was love. This was what she had sought and not understood.

This was love, which made a kiss seem something divine, something sacred; at the same time something so utterly and completely thrilling that she could hardly draw breath because of the glory of it.

At last he released her. She knew that he was looking down at her, his eyes searching for her face in the darkness.

It was only as her lips were free of his that she remembered—remembered the glimpse of red that she had seen on the boat, remembered what had happened and who had been involved in it.

She felt a sudden chill creep over her. She must have

been mad to have even for those few seconds forgotten what he was.

As if he sensed what she was feeling, he said:

"Why did you come here? You have no idea how dangerous it might have been for you."

"How could I know?" she asked. "I believed in you . . ."

"I know."

His voice was rather harsh.

She tried to struggle to her feet and he helped her.

"How could you?" she asked in a sudden agony. "How could you do this?"

In answer he put his arms round her once again.

"But you love me!" he said exultantly. "Whatever I am, however bad I may be, you love me!"

For a moment she fought against the triumph in his voice and against him; and then, because it was impossible to resist the urging of her whole body, she let his lips find hers and they clung together once again.

"You love me!" he said a moment later.

"Yes, I . . . love . . . you," she said unsteadily.

She shivered as she spoke, not only from the night air but from something that seemed to come from her very heart, that seemed to envelop her like a dark cloud.

He felt her shiver and put his arm round her shoulder.

"You are cold," he said. "I oughtn't to keep you here. You will catch a chill. We will go back to the car, it's not far."

"I must go back . . . to the hotel," Alloa said a little wildly.

"Not yet," he said.

Now she felt afraid—afraid of what she did not understand and most of all of herself.

143

He put his hand under her elbow and they walked in silence.

Their feet sank into the sand and it made their progress slow until the ground grew firmer and they moved under the pine trees to where, hidden from the road, Alloa saw vaguely the dark shape of a car.

Dix opened the door and she got in the front seat.

A moment later he sat beside her at the wheel. He bent forward and switched on the lights on the driving panel and started the engine.

"I will put on the heater," he said. "You will be warm in a few minutes."

She sat saying nothing, trying not to look at him, but vividly conscious of his nearness.

"Alloa!"

His voice was enticing and yet she did not turn her head.

"It is no use," she said. "I can never trust you again."

"I have not lied to you about anything which concerns us personally," he said. "I would not lie to you about that."

Despite her resolution she turned to look at him.

"What do you mean?" she asked.

"You know what I mean," he answered. "I love you. I think I loved you from the first moment that I saw you."

"But that is ridiculous! How could you?" Alloa asked.

Even as she said the words she knew that it had been true of herself.

She had not known it, but she had fallen in love with him at that first meeting. She remembered how she had thought about him afterwards; how she had prayed for him; how her heart had leapt when she had taken his lilies-of-the-valley from the box in which they had come.

144

She remembered what she had suffered when she had thought that he had taken Lou's sapphire brooch. Of course she had been in love with him, although she had not realised it or understood it.

He was watching her face with that faint smile on his lips that she knew so well.

"Well," he said softly. "It is so ridiculous?"

"No, no!"

She put her hands up to her face.

"You must go away, I cannot see you again—not after tonight."

"Do you really mean that?"

He asked the question, but he did not sound as if he was afraid of the answer.

Instead he slipped his arm along the back of the seat and then suddenly drew her close to him. Her head fell back against his shoulder and he looked down into her eyes.

"Do you really mean that?" he asked again. "Do you want me to go away? Do you want not to see me again? Do you wish to deny our love? Do you?"

He shook her gently and then, masterfully, as she quivered and could not answer, he put his hand under her chin and turned her mouth up to his.

A long time later, it seemed to Alloa, she rested her head against his shoulder and said in a weak, dazed voice:

"But how can I love . . . you? It's . . . wrong, I know that. I should hate you, and yet when you touch me I . . . love you so much that I can think of . . . nothing else."

"Isn't that enough?" he asked.

With an effort she gathered herself together to answer him.

"No, it is not enough," she answered. "I want to respect you, to admire you, to know that you are

145

honest and trustworthy and truthful. And . . . and . . ."
Her voice broke on a sob. "You are none of these
things."

"And yet you love me!" he said exultantly.

"Yes, I . . . love you," she answered. "But I
shouldn't . . . I know I shouldn't. . . ."

He drew her a little closer.

"My poor darling," he said. "You know so little
about life, don't you? And yet you think you know so
much. It has been so easy up to now. Black has been
black and white has been white, and you've never been
torn by having your brain think one thing and your
heart another."

He held her closer still against him and then he gave
a little laugh.

"It's not that you're too young," he said, "you're too
old. You've never learned to laugh, to enjoy life just
for the sheer joy of living. That is what I am going
to teach you."

"But I mustn't listen to you," Alloa said. "We can't
mean anything to each other. Can't you understand?
How could I tell my father about you? How would I
explain to him and my mother that I love you?"

There was a little silence and then Dix said:

"So you really want me to go away?"

"No! No!" Alloa spoke involuntarily. "I couldn't
bear it, I couldn't. You must change. . . . You must
promise me . . ."

He interrupted her.

"Would you really believe those promises?" he asked.
"Would you?"

"I would try," she replied.

He laughed gently.

"You know in your heart you would never be convinced," he said. "No! I shall make no promises. You
must love me as I am or I must go away. There must

146

be trust in love—there I agree with you—and there can be no trust where there is insincerity, where there is hypocrisy and pretence.

"You see me as I am, little Alloa. Love me because I am myself and not some fairy-tale figure that you have created in your mind."

Alloa shut her eyes. She could not be hearing this, she thought. It could not be true. The decision was too hard.

She could not believe that he was making her face something so incredible that her mind seemed, at the moment, incapable of understanding it.

"Oh, why are you like this? Why?" she said at length.

Her voice was so low that he had to bend his head to hear it.

"I am what I am," he replied.

"But you can change," Alloa persisted. "Surely you can see that?"

"Perhaps," he agreed. "Everyone alters as they grow older. Everyone changes for the better or the worse every day of their lives. I have not said that I shall not try to change, that I shall not attempt to be what you want of me.

"I am only saying that at the moment I will not lie to you or act as being any different from what I am. You see me for what I am and I believe, despite it, that you love me. That is all I ask. The future we can leave to itself.

"What I am asking you to accept now is the present, and to accept it with your eyes open."

"But surely I am accepting that?" Alloa questioned. He shook his head.

"Not really," he answered. "You're still playing a nice little game with yourself. You're still saying in your heart that I can't be as bad as I appear. You want me

147

to promise you that I shall never again do anything of which you disapprove.

"You want me to repent. In other words you want me to be anything but myself. As I have said already, I am as I am."

His arms had slackened round her and now Alloa moved a little away from him.

She had a sudden vision of her father's face as he stood in the pulpit exhorting his congregation to resist temptation, to follow the Commandments.

She knew quite well what he would have her say at this moment. She knew what was the right thing to do, the thing she should do.

And then even as she moved away from Dix she turned back towards him again.

"I . . . can't, I . . . can't!" she whispered.

The tears came into her eyes and overflowed down her cheeks.

He held her for a moment with a tenderness that had no passion in it; then he raised her face once more, looked down at her cheeks wet with tears and kissed them gently away.

"I shall never forget those tears," he said. "They are the most precious things that have ever happened to me."

He spoke very soberly and then he said gently:

"Stop crying, darling, and tell me when you will marry me."

Alloa opened her eyes and stared up at him.

"M . . . marry . . . you?"

"But, of course," he said. "The inevitable end to a happy love affair, isn't it? I will swear to you one thing, on the Bible if necessary, that with all my nefarious crimes I have never been married. Nor, I may add, have I ever before asked anyone to marry me."

There was a pause until he said softly:

"You will marry me, darling little Alloa, won't you?"

Alloa turned her head away from him, afraid of the look in his eyes.

"It is too . . . soon," she answered. "I can't . . . think of it yet. I can't give you . . . an answer. I have got to . . . . think."

She felt him stiffen and then he said in a very different voice:

"Of course, I had forgotten that you must decide whether you can face the shame of being married to a thief."

"No, no, it isn't that," Alloa cried. "It is my father and mother. I shall have to explain to them, I shall have to tell them. I couldn't lie about this. They will have to know the truth."

"I see."

He spoke slowly as if he was cogitating a problem and then he said:

"And supposing they refuse to give their consent? What then?"

"They won't refuse; they couldn't," Alloa exclaimed. "They will be hurt, they will find it hard to understand. But they won't refuse to let me marry anyone I want to marry."

"And suppose they do?" he insisted. "Suppose they absolutely forbid it?"

Alloa twisted her fingers together. She could see her father's face, white and strained, not with anger but with pain; the disappointment in her mother's eyes. They had hoped so much of her.

They had wanted to give her so much that they could not afford; and all the time they had made sacrifices, tremendous sacrifices, for everything that she had received at their hands.

She was their only child. All their hopes, all their ambitions, all their wishes were centred in her.

"Well, what is your verdict?"

Dix was waiting for an answer. She knew she had to give it to him.

She tried not to be conscious of his closeness; tried not to remember that he was there beside her, that her lips were still warm from his kisses. Yet somehow nothing else seemed to matter.

The world had disappeared; there was no other life, no other people, nothing—they were alone, alone in a kingdom of their own and everything else had vanished into the darkness outside.

It seemed to her then as if all her past life was gone too. Even her father's teachings, which had meant so much to her that she had come to believe there was nothing more important.

Then vaguely at the back of her mind she could remember a quotation which was the clue to everything, which was the answer she sought.

Slowly it seemed to her that she was spelling it out, remembering it, saying it:

"*Amor vincit omnia*—Love conquers all things."

That was her answer. That was the reply for which Dix was waiting.

Love, when it came, was greater than prejudice, rules and regulations, beliefs or even a standard of life. It was love that counted. Love which could forgive everything and which could eventually, in its greatness, understand everything.

She turned impulsively in his arms.

She looked up at him, her eyes shining in the light of the dashboard. Her lips trembled a little as she spoke, but her voice was steady:

"I will marry you," she said. "Because, oh, because . . . I love you so . . . much."

Hours later, or it may have been much less because time had ceased to exist. Dix kissed her eyes and said:

"I'm going to take you somewhere where we can have something to eat and drink. I've just remembered that I have eaten nothing since lunch time. Also I want to make quite certain that you won't catch a chill."

"I'm not cold," Alloa answered.

It was true enough. Her body was warm and tingling with the exhilaration of her love. Her cheeks were flushed and her mouth seemed to burn from the violence and passion of the kisses that had been rained upon it.

"If you look at me like that," he said, "I shan't be able to start the car."

She laughed softly and moved a little away from him, only to have his arms reach out swiftly for her and draw her back again.

"I can't let you go," he said. "Not even for a second. I think you have bewitched me. Never in my life have I felt like this about a woman. I never believed it possible that I should lie awake night after night thinking about one."

"Have you done that?" she enquired.

"Almost every night since we first met."

"And yet you didn't write to me, you didn't try to see me again in London," Alloa said.

"I wanted to," he answered. "But there were reasons why I couldn't come back to Claridge's."

Alloa's eyes flickered and she dared not look at him. She could guess what those reasons were, but she said nothing, thinking in a kind of agony that this was just one of many occasions in her life when she must accept the inevitable and not ask questions.

"Kiss me," Dix murmured against her ear. "You are so sweet, so utterly adorable, so lovely beyond words. One day I will buy you clothes that will make people realise how beautiful you are."

'And who will pay for them?' Alloa longed to ask, but she dared not do so.

He kissed her again lingeringly so that she felt her heart throbbing and the blood racing through her veins. Then he moved his arms away from her and started up the car.

Dix stopped outside the gates of the hotel and took her in his arms.

"I shan't be able to see you tomorrow," he said. "But I shall be thinking of you every moment and every second of the day. I will let you know what can be managed on Friday."

"Where will you be? Where are you staying?" Alloa asked.

"I'm sorry, darling, I cannot answer those questions," he replied.

"But why not? Why . . ." Alloa began.

He silenced her voice with a kiss.

"There are many things I cannot tell you yet," he said after a moment. "But one day you shall know them all, I promise you that."

"But why . . . why can't you tell me now?" Alloa questioned. "Can't you see how difficult it is for me? Can't you understand what I feel when you disappear?"

"I know only too well," Dix answered. "But there is nothing I can do about it."

He kissed her again almost as if his thoughts were elsewhere; and suddenly, as if some spark was ignited between them, they were clinging together.

Alloa's arms were round his neck, and he was raining wild, passionate, hungry kisses on her face and neck, eyes and mouth.

"I love you! Oh, God, how I love you!"

He said it again and again, his voice low, hoarse and deep with emotion.

Then, as if she could bear it no longer, Alloa turned away from him blindly and opened the door of the car.

"I'm all right. Don't get out," she said, her voice broken and breathless from the fire of his kisses.

Before he could answer, she ran through the gates, down the courtyard and in through the big, brilliantly lit doors of the hotel.

It was only when she reached her own bedroom, to stand, panting, with her back to the door, that the elation she was feeling ebbed slowly away from her and her eyes lost their brilliance.

"I love him! I love him!"

She said the words out loud, but now they were almost a protest against the questions and queries that came flooding in on her.

Why could he not tell her where he would be? Why couldn't he see her tomorrow? Would he be with those terrible men again? Was he engaged in something so dangerous that he dared not speak of it?

She felt herself tremble at the thought of danger, yet she was sure that that was why he could not speak of what he was doing.

She remembered the menace in the other man's voice when he had spoken of her; remembered the man who had spoken of slitting her throat.

These men were desperate criminals, she was sure of that. They would stick at nothing.

She sat down at the dressing-table and covered her face with her hands. How could Dix be so mad, so crazy as to become involved with men like that? Was any money worth the risk of death or mutilation at their hands?

She looked at her clock and saw that it was one o'clock in the morning. But she was not tired.

She went to the window and looked out. The court-

153

yard lay before her and she could just catch a glimpse of the road where she had left the car.

Now the road was empty. The diners and dancers in the hotel had all gone home. There was only the silence of the night and the glimmering street lights to keep her thoughts company.

After a little while she undressed; but even as she got into bed she knew she would not sleep. She could only think of Dix driving away into danger; of her parents, blissfully unconscious of what she had to tell them.

She thought then for the first time how little she knew about Dix. He had told her nothing of himself and what she knew it was almost impossible to put into writing. And yet she could never lie to her parents.

She must write the truth. She must tell them the worst and beg them to accept it for her sake.

"Dix! Dix!"

She heard herself whispering his name into her pillow, and then realised that she did not even know his name.

How impossible it all was, she thought despairingly. How could she write to her father and mother that she was about to marry a man and she did not even know his name?

She wondered why she had not thought to ask it of him, and then she knew it was because she was utterly bemused by his love-making. That at least was true and without pretence. He loved her.

She knew it by the look in his eyes and the sound of the words on his lips; knew it in the tenderness of his hands and in the wild passion which had made him hold her strained against him while his lips seemed like fire against her mouth and throat.

"I love you! Oh, Dix, I love you!"

She said it again and again as if it gave her reassurance.

Then at last, when torn between happiness and terror for him she thought she could not sleep, she fell into a dreamless slumber.

She awoke to hear a knocking on her door. For a moment she was so sleepy that she heard it and yet it meant nothing to her.

Then with a start she awoke. It was half-past eight. She saw that her breakfast had been brought up and placed by her side and she had not eaten it. The curtains had been drawn, too, and yet she had never woken when the chambermaid entered the room.

The knocking continued and at last she got out of bed hurriedly and opened the door. A small page-boy stood there with an enormous bouquet of flowers.

"These have just been left for you, *M'mselle.*"

"Who left them?" Alloa asked quickly. "Was it a gentleman? Is he still there?"

The page-boy shook his head.

"I do not know, *M'mselle.* The hall porter told me to bring them up to you."

How silly she was being, Alloa thought to herself. Even if Dix had left them he would have gone by now. She took the flowers and realised, with a little leap of her heart, that there was a letter attached to them.

"Thank you," she said to the page-boy and shut the door.

She stood in her bedroom looking down at the flowers in their wrapping of cellophane.

He had sent her a bouquet of red roses and she knew without it being said in so many words that red roses meant love.

She opened the bouquet and buried her head in the fragrance of the roses. Then, regardless of the time, she sat down on her bed and drew out the letter.

There were only three lines, each one containing the same number of words.

"I love you. I love you. I love you."

She kissed the note, then held it against her heart. The fears and terrors of the night did not seem so ominous now that morning was here and the sun was shining outside.

Alloa had her breakfast and then dressed slowly. The chambermaid brought a vase and arranged the red roses on the dressing-table.

"They are beautiful, *M'mselle*," she said. "You have a *beau*? That is good."

Alloa could not help smiling. It was so typical of the French to go at once to the heart of the matter, to be quite convinced that flowers could only mean one thing—an attentive lover.

She read Dix's note again, then slipped it into the front of her dress, feeling as she did so that she was being absurdly Victorian, but unable to prevent the impulse.

She wanted it to lie against her heart, she wanted to feel as she moved the crackle of the paper.

What was he doing? she wondered. Where had he gone? Had he brought these flowers and this letter on his way somewhere, or had he sent them by someone else?

She wondered if he had slept; if he had thought of her as he had lain in bed; if he had longed, as she had longed, for a security which meant there would be no secrets between them, no mysteries.

At length she was ready, and turning from her dressing-table she picked up her note-book and went along to Mrs. Derange's bedroom.

She knocked at the door and heard Mrs. Derange's nasal tones call out:

"Come in."

She turned the handle of the door.

"Oh, there you are, Alloa," Mrs. Derange said

briskly. "I was just going to ring for you. You're late this morning."

"I'm sorry," Alloa apologised. "I overslept."

"You're fortunate," Mrs. Derange snapped. "Personally I didn't sleep a wink all night. But, there, I've been a bad sleeper all my life."

She looked down at her letters and then touched one which lay on the top of the pile with what seemed to Alloa an almost caressing movement.

"I've heard from the *Duchesse* this morning," she said. "It came just a few minutes ago. She's asked us all to go and stay at the *Château* the day after tomorrow. Isn't that wonderful?"

"Does she mean me, too?" Alloa asked.

"You, too," Mrs. Derange said. "I think that particularly nice of her. But, then, what a charming person she is in every possible way!"

Alloa felt her heart sink. How would she be able to see Dix? What would happen if she were staying at *Château Pougy* and he wanted to see her?

"Of course, under the circumstances," Mrs. Derange was saying, "Lou and I will not bother to go over to San Sebastian tonight. Between ourselves, I'm not sorry for the excuse."

"I had better telephone Mrs. Cartwright at once," Alloa said.

"Oh, there's plenty of time," Mrs. Derange answered. "At the same time you can telephone this list of people and ask them in this evening for cocktails. We'll give a party instead of going to one. They're all local numbers so it won't take you long."

"Very well," Alloa said.

Mrs. Derange looked up at her.

"I'm very pleased indeed with you, Alloa," she said. "I should like to take this opportunity of telling you

157

that I think you've been very satisfactory, both as my secretary and as a companion to Lou."

Alloa made an inarticulate reply.

"I don't mind confessing to you now," Mrs. Derange went on, "that I was a little worried as to how Lou would feel about this marriage with the *Duc*. Of course, I didn't expect the *Château* to be as magnificent as it is, and I'm not saying that wasn't the deciding factor.

"But Lou and I had a little talk last night and she told me that she thought I had been very wise in not letting her marry Steve Weston. She told me then that he had tried to see her in London and that you had sent him away.

"That was quite right of you, Alloa, though I think you should actually have told me that he had called."

"I didn't quite know what to do," Alloa said. "He asked particularly to see Lou alone."

"Well, I think it must have been in some way your tact and good sense that prevented her from doing anything of which I should have disapproved," Mrs. Derange said generously.

Alloa felt she was taking praise that was not really her due; but before she could say anything more Mrs. Derange continued:

"I'm a very happy woman this morning, Alloa, I don't mind saying it. This is something I've worked for for a very long time. It's a dream that occasionally I felt would never be fulfilled. I've always wanted Lou to have a title. I've wanted her to be important, to take her place in European society.

"But that *Château*! Well, it really took my breath away. The *Duchesse* told me privately, too, that the family jewels are some of the finest in all France. She has promised to show them to Lou when we go to stay there."

"I hope Lou will be very happy," Alloa murmured.

Even as she said the words she felt a deep compassion and a pity for the American girl who would never feel as she was feeling now; would never know what it was to love somebody to the exclusion of all else, or be prepared to throw everything aside for one man who could give in return nothing, nothing except himself.

"Oh, well," Mrs. Derange said. "There's still a lot to be done; there are still a lot of plans to be made. Now, just run and ask Lou if there's anyone else she wants invited to the cocktail party, and then I'll give you the rest of my letters."

Alloa got obediently to her feet. She walked from Mrs. Derange's room and knocked on Lou's door.

"Come in."

Lou was sitting up in bed with her breakfast beside her. She was wearing a little dressing-jacket trimmed with pale pink marabou and her dark curls were tumbling riotously over her head.

She looked very attractive and she smiled as Alloa came into the room.

"Good morning, Alloa! What excitements are there today?" she said with her mouth filled with fresh *croissant* covered with butter and honey.

"Your mother wants to cancel the dinner party at San Sebastian tonight," Alloa began.

"Good," Lou interrupted. "The Cartwrights are crashing bores. I'd pay not to spend an evening with them."

"And instead," Alloa went on, "she suggests having a cocktail party here. She has given me a list of the people to invite and wants to know if there is anyone else you would like me to ask."

"Can't think of a soul," Lou answered indifferently.

She finished her breakfast, pushed the tray aside and picked up the pile of newspapers.

"How I hate not having today's newspapers," she

159

exclaimed. "Look, the *New York Times* is three days old."

"The London papers are yesterday's," Alloa told her.

"I know. But I'm only interested in the American news. At the same time, there's something dead about it when it's happened so long ago."

She picked up a French paper.

"Here's the local rag," she said. "Momma sent in a list of our dinner party the night before last. She felt it would impress somebody, but Heaven knows who."

She turned over the pages.

"Shall I read you the list for the cocktail party?" Alloa asked.

Lou didn't seem to hear her. She was looking at the pictures in the French paper, staring at one intently.

"Look!" she cried.

There was something arresting in her voice, something in her pointing finger which made Alloa hurry quickly to her side. She bent over her shoulder.

The picture, which was badly printed, was of an aeroplane and a man being taken from it. He was a small man and he was seated in a wheel-chair which was being lifted by several attendants from the door of the aeroplane to the ground.

Alloa looked at the picture and then read the caption beneath it, at which Lou's brilliantly varnished fingernail pointed.

"*The Duc de Rangé-Pougy,*" she read, "*arrives at Biarritz Aerodrome on his return from Baden-Baden where he has been taking a cure.*"

"He's a cripple!" Lou said in a strange tone. "A cripple!"

Her voice rose to a sudden scream.

"A cripple!" she repeated.

Then, horribly, so that Alloa longed to put her fingers to her ears, she started to laugh.

160

Chapter Nine

Lou abruptly stopped laughing and her eyes were hard as she repeated grimly:

"A cripple!"

She threw back the bedclothes and got out of bed.

Without saying any more she slipped her arms into the beautifully cut rose satin dressing-gown which lay over a chair; then, with her feet in high-heeled velvet mules she walked across the bedroom carrying the newspaper in her hand.

Alloa knew where she was going and had a feeling of compassion for Mrs. Derange. She knew how the older woman's hopes and ambitions had been centred on Lou's becoming a *Duchesse*.

She felt she could not bear to see her aspirations crumble away just because of a photograph in the newspaper. Impulsively she put out her hand.

"Wait, Lou!" she said. "Think a moment."

But Lou did not seem to hear. Instead, she stalked on towards her mother's bedroom. Only as she reached the door did she stop for a moment and turn back.

"Come with me, Alloa," she said. "I want you to hear what I'm going to say."

Alloa wanted to refuse, to leave mother and daughter alone to have this out together; but somehow she felt this was not the moment to argue with Lou or to bother about her own feelings.

So obediently, without saying anything, she followed Lou into Mrs. Derange's bedroom, trying, because she was embarrassed, to make herself as inconspicuous as possible as she stood just inside the door.

Lou walked across to her mother's bed and put the open newspaper in front of her.

"Look at that," she said.

"What is the matter?" Mrs. Derange asked.

She put out her hand to fumble for her horn-rimmed spectacles which she habitually used when reading.

"Look at it," Lou repeated.

Mrs. Derange found her spectacles and set them on her nose. Lou watched her mother's face.

"A picture of the *Duc*," Mrs. Derange said after a moment. "It must have been taken yesterday afternoon on his return from Baden-Baden."

"Do you see him?" Lou said. "Do you see what he is like? You told me he was attractive, handsome. You've stuffed me with a lot of lies about him. Now do you see the truth?"

"He has been ill," Mrs. Derange said, but her voice somehow lacked conviction.

Lou snatched the paper from her.

"You knew," she said accusingly. "You've known all the time."

"Now, Lou, don't work yourself up . . ." Mrs. Derange began.

"Tell me the truth," Lou interrupted. "You knew he was a cripple, didn't you?"

Mrs. Derange looked uncomfortable.

"Mother, how could you do this to me?" Lou asked, her voice rising a little. "I thought you were fond of me; I thought you loved me; and yet you could deceive me like this. Do you think I want half a man as a husband? Do you think I want to spend the rest of my life pushing a little squirt like that about in a bath-chair?"

Mrs. Derange's face was pale, but Alloa could not help feeling she was behaving with dignity.

"There is no sense in talking like that, Lou," she

said. "And there is no reason to marry the *Duc* if you don't want to."

"Want to!" Lou cried. "Do you think I want a husband who looks like that?"

"You haven't seen him yet," Mrs. Derange replied reasonably. "Newspaper photographs are notoriously caricatures of anyone they wish to depict. I've seen some of you which were certainly nothing to be proud of."

"You knew he was a cripple," Lou reiterated.

"I do not know that he is a cripple or that there is any reason to suspect that the fact that he is in a wheel-chair is anything but temporary," Mrs. Derange said.

"Are you trying to tell me he's had an accident?" Lou asked.

"I don't know," Mrs. Derange answered. "I only knew he had been ill because the *Duchesse* told me so. She did mention in one of her letters that he could not lead a very active life, having been delicate ever since he was a child. The fact that he appears in this picture in a wheel-chair is as much a surprise to me as to you."

"You never told me he was delicate," Lou said.

"People have very different ideas on what constitutes someone being described in such a way," Mrs. Derange replied. "Mothers who adore their children often like to consider that they are delicate and have to be made a fuss of and cosseted. I was waiting to see the *Duc* before I expressed my own opinion of his state of health. I suggest you do likewise."

"I'm not going to marry a man who looks like that," Lou said.

"What does he look like?" Mrs. Derange asked. "Give me the newspaper."

"I don't want to look at him again," Lou said petulantly.

She threw the paper on the floor and walked across

to the window. Alloa hesitated a moment and then went forward to pick up the paper, smooth it back into shape and hand it to Mrs. Derange.

"Thank you, Alloa," Mrs. Derange said.

As she took the paper, Alloa could see that her hand was trembling. 'It means so much to her,' she thought.

She was suddenly full of compassion for both of them—the mother who wanted the best for her daughter; the daughter who didn't know yet what she really wanted from life and could therefore be swayed first in one direction and then another.

Mrs. Derange stared at the photograph.

"You know, Lou," she said slowly, "I think you're being rather hasty in your judgment. This is the face of an aristocrat. Of course, it's hard to see—newsprint can distort any features—and yet I myself feel quite sure that the *Duc* is a very good-looking man. What do you think, Alloa?"

Alloa looked at the paper which Mrs. Derange held out to her. The picture had been taken in strong sunlight. It was therefore hard to distinguish anything very clearly.

There was no doubt that the *Duc* looked frail. He was quite obviously not a man of great physique. Yet she could see that Mrs. Derange had reason for saying that he might be good-looking.

At least it was a pleasant face as he smiled at the attendants who were lifting him down from the aeroplane.

It was obvious that Mrs. Derange was waiting for her to say something and after a moment Alloa said hesitantly:

"It is . . . difficult to . . . see, but he might easily be . . . good-looking."

"It wouldn't matter if he were an Adonis if he has

164

to go about permanently in a wheel chair," Lou snapped.

"But why jump to conclusions?" Mrs. Derange asked. "The *Duchesse* said nothing to me about a wheel-chair. She said her son had been ill, he had gone to Baden-Baden to have a rest cure and he was coming home because the doctors said he was much better."

"You're very plausible, Momma," Lou said with a shrug of her shoulders. "But it certainly isn't my idea of what the *Duc* was to be like."

"People seldom look like one expects," Mrs. Derange said firmly. "Now, Lou, be sensible. You can reserve your judgment until you have met the *Duc* tomorrow evening. When you see him in his own surroundings, in that wonderful *Château*, I feel sure he will look very different."

"He'd better," Lou said snappily. "Let's make this quite clear. I'm not marrying anyone to be a nursemaid. I want somebody young and gay, who will do things with me—swim, play tennis; who can dance and ski; who likes sailing a boat, driving a car and flying an aeroplane. Do you think that little object could do any of those things?"

"Lou! Lou!" Mrs. Derange remonstrated.

"Oh, I know what you think," Lou said with a sudden passion. "You think having a coronet is worth all that. Well, I don't. Just so that I can call myself a *Duchesse* I'm not going to trail round for the rest of my life with a man who is really a hospital problem—and nothing you can say, nothing, is going to make me think differently."

Lou walked out of the room as she spoke, slamming the door behind her. The sound reverberated round the walls as Alloa and Mrs. Derange looked at each other.

"She's upset," Mrs. Derange said. "She'll think differently when she's met the *Duc* in his own surroundings."

"What is wrong with him?" Alloa asked.

Mrs. Derange shook her head.

"I don't know, and that's the truth. The *Duchesse* was very vague. It's a shock to me to think that he's bad enough to be in a wheel-chair."

"It may have been just because of the journey," Alloa suggested hopefully.

"Perhaps so," Mrs. Derange agreed. "Anyway, we can't do anything until tomorrow. Just try and soothe Lou down, there's a good girl. She'll listen to what you say."

Alloa thought privately that Lou would listen to nobody, but there was no point in depressing Mrs. Derange further by saying it.

"Is there anything I can do for you?" she asked.

"No, nothing," Mrs. Derange said. "I feel upset by what has happened. I think I'll take one of the pheno-barbitone pills the doctor gave me and lie quietly for a little while."

"Yes, I should do that," Alloa said. "Would you like me to lower the blinds?"

"No, no! I don't mind the sunshine," Mrs. Derange said.

She pulled out the drawer of her bedside table and taking a small white pill from a cardboard box slipped it on her tongue and took a drink of water from a glass standing on the table.

Alloa picked up the letters that had not yet been answered and put them on the writing-table; then without saying any more she went from the room, closing the door quietly behind her.

She hesitated as to whether she should go in to see Lou, then decided to knock gently on the door.

"Come in," Lou said sharply, and as Alloa entered the room, added: "Oh, it's you, Alloa. I hoped it was."

166

Lou was seated on her bed. Alloa crossed the room to stand beside her.

"Is there anything you want?" she asked.

"There're lots of things," Lou answered. "First of all I should like to go back to New York right now, this very moment. As I haven't got a magic carpet to take me there, I suppose I shall have to go through with this awful visit."

"You mean to the *Château*?" Alloa asked.

"Where else?" Lou enquired. "I hate the very thought of it now, and I was looking forward to it so much."

There was something plaintive and rather childish in her disappointment.

"He may be so much better than you expect," Alloa said. "He looks nice."

"I suppose I'm a fool," Lou said, "but I had really begun to believe Momma. I had imagined him tall and dark with a wonderful figure like those Frenchmen you see on the films. I lay awake last night imagining him making love to me in that little Ante-room which was all hung with rose pink brocade, do you remember?

"I thought of us dancing in the ball-room, me wearing a huge tiara and he whispering in my ears how much he loved me. I was already half in love with him—the man I imagined, of course, not that sickly creature in the newspaper."

"Perhaps you were expecting too much," Alloa said.

"What do you mean?" Lou asked.

"Well, I don't think one ever gets everything in life," Alloa said. "If folks are very rich, then they often have some disability, such as ill health or blindness, to balance their wealth; and if one finds somebody very attractive with whom one is very much in love, then perhaps he is very poor or . . . or . . . or other things."

She was thinking of Dix as she spoke, wishing with

167

all her heart not that he was rich but that he was honest.

"I see what you mean," Lou said. "What you're really suggesting is that I'm greedy."

"Well, aren't you?" Alloa enquired. "You've got so much yourself, you can't expect all that and Heaven too. I merely said it was unlikely that he would also be a duke."

She met Lou's eyes as she spoke and they knew they were both thinking the same thing. Steve Weston was young and good looking and very much in love—but he was not rich and he was not a duke.

Lou got off the bed suddenly and walked across to the dressing-table and sat down.

"Do you think that a house, however wonderful, could be enough?" she asked.

"No, of course it couldn't," Alloa said.

Her voice was positive.

Lou looked at herself in the mirror for a long time and then at length she said in a voice that was deliberately indifferent:

"Well, there's no harm in looking. We will see what tomorrow brings forth."

Alloa knew by the tone of her voice that the moment of confidence was passed. Lou had made up her mind to play the game her own way.

She was still hoping in her heart that she could bring herself to marry the *Duc* and thus be the possessor both of a title and of the *Château Pougy*. Alloa knew there was nothing else she could say.

"Will you excuse me?" she said. "I have got some letters to do in my bedroom. If your mother wants me, perhaps she will ring."

"I'll tell her when I see her," Lou said.

Alloa went back to her own room. She put Mrs. Derange's correspondence down on the writing-paper

168

and opened the drawer to look for a piece of carbon paper.

As she did so, she saw the letter addressed to Claridge's which had been written to her by Steve.

She took it out of its envelope and read it again. Then she looked at the address on the top of the writing paper and the telephone numbers which were printed beneath it.

Should she get in touch with him?

The idea leapt into her mind and yet she shrank from interfering. Suppose she wrote to him and then nothing came of it?

Suppose when Lou saw the *Duc* she decided, whatever he was like, that it was worth marrying him to obtain the great advantages he could offer her? She did not love him; she would never love him; and Steve could, if she could only see it, offer her so very much more.

"I mustn't interfere," Alloa said aloud.

Yet she was utterly convinced in her heart that this would be a tremendous opportunity for Steve to press his suit, if only he were there.

Wasn't it fair that he should have the chance to state his case? And what moment could be better than at a time when Lou was disillusioned, perhaps even repulsed, by the man she had come across the Atlantic so glibly to marry?

"She can't do it, she can't," Alloa said.

She suddenly thought of Lou, tied, as she had expressed it herself, to a wheel-chair. She would be unhappy and inevitably she would make the *Duc* unhappy too.

No money, no title, nothing could compensate for a life of frustration for two people who had nothing in common except greed for what the other possessed.

Alloa jumped to her feet. She walked across the room

and picked up the telephone. She had always heard how efficient the telephone service was in America, but she had not many illusions about the difficulties of the French exchange.

It was therefore with a feeling of surprise that she heard her bell ring twenty minutes later and learned that she was connected with New York.

She had made the call a personal one and a few seconds later she was informed that Mr. Steve Weston was on the line.

"Is that Steve Weston?"

"Hello! Who is it?"

"It's Alloa Derange."

"Why, hello! Where are you speaking from?"

"From Biarritz."

"Is Lou all right? Does she want to see me?"

"She doesn't know I'm telephoning you," Alloa said. "But I thought I must tell you what has happened."

Speaking quickly, conscious that francs must be totalling up every second, Alloa told him of what had happened that morning, of the *Duc's* picture in the paper and of Lou's reaction.

"I'll hop on the first plane I can get," Steve Weston said.

"Are you sure? I . . . I mean . . . perhaps I shouldn't have telephoned you, but somehow I thought . . ."

"Don't worry," he interrupted. "It's been swell of you to let me know. Say nothing to Lou. I'll walk in and surprise her."

"We shall be at the *Château* . . ." Alloa began, only to realise the line had gone dead.

Well, when he came to this hotel, they would tell him where he could find them, she thought, and then wondered with an almost sick feeling inside her whether she had done the right thing.

Anyway, it was too late to regret it now. Steve

Weston would, she was quite certain, keep his word; and perhaps when Lou saw him she would realise that he really loved her and that love was so much more valuable than money or position.

Alloa gave a little sigh. Lou's problems were in some ways so much easier than her own.

A letter to her father and mother had to be written; and yet, she asked herself, how could she possibly write and tell them what had happened when she did not even know the name of the man whom she was going to marry?

It was all so ridiculous, so absurd, and yet, in the excitement and thrill of last night, when she had finally promised herself to him, it had never struck her that she did not even know what name he would give her.

To anyone outside the whole situation would seem crazy.

But now, with the sunlight coming through the window, she wondered if perhaps she herself had not been a little touched the night before.

Had she really promised to marry a man who was a complete stranger? A man who was an acknowledged crook, thief and smuggler; yet a man whom she loved and who loved her.

'Why does my whole body thrill to the touch of him?' she wondered.

Why did his lips make a flame leap within her body so that she could not think coherently but only feel herself tinglingly, thrillingly alive with an ecstasy she had never known before?

'I love him,' she thought exultantly, then she felt her spirits drop at the thought of telling her parents.

She pulled a block of paper towards her and picked up her pen.

"Darling Mummy and Daddy.

"I have fallen in love with a Frenchman . . ."

171

She came to a full-stop and sat reading over and over again the words she had written.

Somehow she could see her father's face all too clearly. She could see herself standing in front of him when she was a child; she could hear her own voice saying:

"But I want to do it, Daddy, I want to do it."

"But it's wrong, my darling."

His voice was grave and yet full of understanding and pity. Why should it be wrong? He had taken her on his knee and tried to explain.

"There are certain rules that we all have to obey. If we keep them, then that is right and good. If we disobey them, then that is wrong and bad."

Alloa put her hands up to her face. Wrong and bad! That was what her father would think of Dix. And yet she knew, with a sudden irrefutable conviction, there was nothing bad about him personally.

His actions might be wrong, they might be anti-social; but in himself he was good. She was as sure of him as she was of her father and her mother, of everyone she had ever loved and trusted.

'Oh, what a muddle it is,' Alloa thought miserably, and put the letter on one side.

It was so hard to write, so hard to put into words her own feelings, when she was not even sure of them herself.

She picked up the piece of writing-paper and thrust it into a drawer.

'I'll write it tonight,' she thought, and knew she was taking the coward's way out.

She was avoiding what eventually would have to be faced.

Mrs. Derange called her to her room about four o'clock and finished off the letters which had been set on one side in the morning.

She did not make any mention of the scene that had taken place over the photograph of the *Duc*. She looked tired and she did not dictate as fluently as usual, and Alloa knew that often her thoughts wandered and her worry over Lou interfered with her concentration.

Finally Mrs. Derange dismissed Alloa, who went back to her own room. She had hardly got inside the door before the telephone rang.

She felt it must be Steve Weston and picked it up hastily, hoping that by some curious mischance this call hadn't been reported to Lou.

"Hello!" she said apprehensively.

"Hello, my darling."

It was Dix, and her heart gave a sudden leap of sheer, unutterable joy at the sound of his voice.

"I didn't think it would be you."

"Who were you expecting? Another man? I am jealous."

"No . . . I thought it was a call from America."

"Do you often have calls from across the Atlantic?"

"No, no! I can't explain now but I will tell you about it sometime."

"You can tell me tonight."

"Tonight?"

"Yes. I have rung you up to ask you to come to a party."

"A party! But, how can I?"

"It's a very special party. I didn't ask you last night because I thought they wouldn't allow you to come; but when I explained that we are going to be married they were only too delighted."

"Who are they?"

"My friends. Some people I particularly want you to meet because they mean so much to me."

"Then I should like that very much," Alloa said. "Do you think I ought to ask Mrs. Derange?"

"Does she usually want you in the evening?"

"No, I am always free after dinner."

"And what time is that?"

"They are dining with friends at nine o'clock so they will be leaving the hotel a little before half-past eight."

"Good! Then I will be waiting for you just outside the gates at eight-thirty. Look your prettiest. I want my friends to see how lucky I am."

"I will be there," Alloa said.

"I love you! Don't forget that."

He spoke softly and then there was a click.

He had not waited for her answer. She replaced the receiver slowly, feeling the thumping in her heart subside a little, the blood fade away from her cheeks.

She would see him tonight. That was all she could think about for the moment, and then she remembered what he had said. 'Look your prettiest.'

She thought with a feeling of despair that that was the hardest thing he had asked of her. She had nothing special to wear, only the little black dress that she had worn in London, that she had refurbished so often to make it look different.

She wished now she had bought another dress in London, and yet if she had done so she would not have been able to send so much money home to her mother.

"He must take me as I am," she said aloud.

But even as she said it she knew the longing which every woman feels to look lovely in the sight of the man she loves.

She took down the dress from the wardrobe. Perhaps if she wore it without the collar and cuffs, with a little bunch of artificial flowers at the neck, it would look gay enough for a party.

At any rate she could press the dress and do her best with it.

174

She put it over her arm and went along to Jeanne's room which was at the very end of the passage. Jeanne was sitting sewing by the window as she went in, and looked up with a smile.

"Can I use your iron, Jeanne?" Alloa enquired.

"But of course, *M'mselle,*" Jeanne replied. "You will find it in the cupboard."

Alloa got out the ironing board and the special travelling iron which could be adjusted to any voltage.

"You are going out tonight, *M'mselle?*" Jeanne asked.

"As a matter of fact I am going to a party," Alloa confessed. "Don't say anything to Mrs. Derange, because I wouldn't want to make a lot of explanations."

"Pouf! It's no business of hers what you do in your free time," Jeanne said. "I had an employer once who always asked questions. I said to her:

'*Madame,* you employ me to work for you; but when I am not working, when it is my time off, then I employ myself. I answer no questions, I make no explanations, you understand?' "

"And what did she say?" Alloa asked, seeing some comment was expected of her.

Jeanne smiled.

"She said nothing after that. I am a very good maid and she wished to keep me, so she was very careful not to ask questions as to what I did."

Alloa laughed.

"Well, that was certainly one way of settling the matter. But I am sure you are much braver than I should be."

"Are you going to wear that dress at the party?" Jeanne asked.

"It's the only one I've got," Alloa said.

"It is not right for you," Jeanne said. "If it is a party with French people they will be smart, very smart. You cannot wear that dress. It has no style, no *chic.*"

"I have got nothing else," Alloa said, "so they will have to put up with it."

She felt, miserably, that Jeanne had put into words what she had been feeling herself, but it was no consolation to know the truth when one could do nothing about it.

"Wait a moment," Jeanne said.

She got up and opened the cupboard in her room and brought down a dress of pale blue lace stiffened so that it swirled out in a huge skirt from a tiny waist, while the pattern was sprinkled with iridescent sequins which glittered and sparkled with every movement.

"What a lovely dress!" Alloa exclaimed.

"It is one I made for my niece," Jeanne said. "She is young and pretty like you and she works in Paris. She sent me the lace and asked me to make it up for her. It is finished and I was going to send it off to her next week, but you shall wear it for your party."

"Oh, no! No!" Alloa exclaimed. "I couldn't think of it. I might spoil it. It is far too lovely."

"You shall wear it, *M'mselle*," Jeanne said firmly. "It will fit you, I am sure. My niece is just about your size."

"But I couldn't, really," Alloa protested. "I should be too frightened. Besides, it is far too kind of you to think of anything like that when you have made it specially for your niece."

"You have been very kind to me, *M'mselle*," Jeanne said. "You have helped me; you have done lots of little things that another young lady in your position would not have done. If you want to look pretty at this party tonight, then you wear the dress."

"Oh, Jeanne, do you really mean it?" Alloa asked.

She felt fascinated by the beauty and glitter of the frock. It was just the sort of dress she had dreamed of.

She could imagine the expression on Dix's face when he saw her, and she knew that, wearing a dress like

176

that, he would not be ashamed to introduce her to his friends.

"But of course I mean it," Jeanne said. "Slip it on. If there is any little alteration needed, I will have plenty of time in which to do it."

Alloa took off her cotton dress and Jeanne helped her into the blue lace.

It fitted tightly over her breasts, showing the delicate curves of them and giving her a better figure than she had ever imagined she had.

The little short sleeves slipped off the shoulders, there was a stiffened waist-band of blue velvet embroidered with sequins and tiny diamonds.

Then the full skirt stuck out over stiffened silk underskirts to rustle seductively as Alloa tiptoed across the room to stand in front of the long mirror which was attached to the wall.

"It's lovely! Absolutely lovely!" she exclaimed. "Are you quite, quite certain, Jeanne, that you do not mind my wearing it?"

"I should like you to wear it," Jeanne said. "Now you look as you ought to look—a princess."

Alloa laughed.

"Cinderella is what you mean," she replied. "And you really are my fairy godmother. I was feeling depressed at wearing that old black, but I had nothing else. And now I feel entirely different. Quite, quite different."

"That is just what clothes do for a woman," Jeanne said. "The right clothes."

Alloa thought to herself with a feeling of fear that Dix would always expect her to have the right clothes.

He was a Frenchman. He knew what Englishmen never knew, not only how much clothes meant to a woman, but how much they could do for her.

It was no use pretending. She did look different because she was rightly dressed.

And then, even as she thought of the future, some cold, logical part of herself asked the bitter question:

'And how will you pay for these new clothes?' How would Dix pay for them? Where would the money come from?

She felt as if the questions shrieked themselves at her, as if they came from some horrible nightmare to haunt and taunt her with the innuendoes behind them.

Resolutely she refused to listen.

"Thank you, Jeanne," she said. "I can never thank you enough. And I will be careful, terribly careful, with your niece's dress."

"One day, when we have both saved a little more money, we are going to set up a shop together," Jeanne said. "And perhaps, *M'mselle*, you will come and patronise us. I should like to dress someone as pretty as you."

"You flatter me," Alloa smiled. "But if I ever have the money to afford beautiful dresses, you will find me on the doorstep."

She bent down and kissed Jeanne.

"Thank you," she said again.

"Now mind you enjoy yourself," Jeanne admonished. "And mind the lucky man who is taking you to the party appreciates what he has got."

"I think he will do that," Alloa said.

She took off the dress and put on her own cotton one again, then carried the blue lace very carefully down the passage to hang it up in her own wardrobe.

She left the door open so that she could see it, almost believing that it might disappear into smoke and that when the time came to meet Dix she would still have to wear her old, despised black.

The hours went by slowly. She could not settle to anything she was doing.

She took the letters to Mrs. Derange for signature when she came up to dress for dinner, but Lou was having her bath and so Alloa did not see her. Somehow she was thankful for that. She did not want to meet Lou at the moment and wondered if she had betrayed her by sending for Steve Weston.

Already she was feeling apprehensive and afraid of what she had done. And then she told herself that if the worst came to the worst it only meant that Steve would be no worse off than he had been before.

All the same it was worrying and only the sight of the blue dress hanging up in her wardrobe managed to waft away the worry from Alloa's mind.

She had her bath, brushed her hair until it shone like silk, and then at quarter-past eight put on the blue lace dress. Jeanne was right. Clothes did make one look different.

The evening sunshine glittered on the sequins and the diamonds on the belt and made her look as if she, too, was dressed in sunbeams.

She had no idea that her skin was so white or that her eyes could shine so brightly because she was going to see someone she loved.

She was ready five minutes before it was time to go downstairs.

She spent the time moving aimlessly about the room, tidying first this thing and then that, and then finally opening the drawer in her desk to look at the letter to her mother and father.

"I have fallen in love with a Frenchman."

That part, at least, was true enough. She loved him. She knew she loved him, and yet there was that terrible barrier of being unable to say more.

She shut the drawer with a bang, picked up her

179

handbag and ran downstairs. The porters and the door-keeper looked at her curiously as she passed through the hall.

"*Un taxi, M'mselle?*" the doorkeeper enquired.

"*Non, merci,*" Alloa replied.

She knew he was looking after her in surprise as she walked across the courtyard.

She could hear the underskirts rustling as she moved and felt they made her walk proudly, as if there was a red carpet beneath her feet.

The car was waiting. Dix sprang out and she saw his eyes narrow a little at the sight of her. Then he had raised her hands to his lips.

"You look lovely, enchanting," he said.

She felt herself quiver at the touch of his lips.

At the same time she could not help feeling triumphant because there was no disguising the admiration in his face.

He opened the door and she got into the car. He got in the other side. He did not start the engine immediately but turned to look at her.

"I never believed anyone could be as beautiful as you," he said.

There was a deep note in his voice which told her that he was speaking the truth.

"I . . . wanted to look . . . nice for . . . you and your friends," she faltered.

He took both her hands in his and turning them over buried his face in the palms.

"Oh, my darling, my sweet, I am not worthy of you," he said.

Chapter Ten

Dix raised his head.

"You look so lovely that I am almost afraid to touch you," he said hoarsely. "What have you done to yourself?"

Alloa laughed.

"I am only wearing a new dress," she said. "You see what a difference it makes; and yet people try to say that clothes don't matter!"

"You look lovely whatever you wear," he said. "But tonight there is something else, some excitement and joy about you which makes your beauty irresistible."

There was so much passion and intensity in his voice that her eyes dropped shyly.

He bent forward as if he would kiss her and then realised that people were passing along the road and looking in at them in the car.

Without another word he started up the engine and drove away.

They climbed the hill until they were out of the town and among the fir trees where Alloa had walked and seen the light of the torches which had led her to discover the smugglers.

They reached a spot where the road was very near to the sea and the pine trees silhouetted against the crimson glow of the sky. Here Dix stopped and switched off the engine.

"I want to talk to you for a little while," he said. "I hate the thought of going to a party because it means sharing you with other people."

He drew in a deep breath.

"You are so exquisite tonight that I want you all for myself."

"Jeanne lent me this dress," Alloa smiled, smoothing the lace with her hand. "She is Mrs. Derange's lady's maid and she had made it for her niece, but when she heard I was going to a party she lent it to me. People are so kind."

"Perhaps you sow what you reap," Dix suggested. "Hasn't your father told you that?"

Alloa's eyes clouded for a moment.

"Yes, often," she answered. She thought with a little pang of unhappiness that Dix was sowing something which might turn out to be a very dangerous harvest.

As if he read her thoughts, he asked:

"Have you written to your parents yet?"

Alloa turned her face away from him to look out of the window.

"I have started the letter," she answered in a low voice.

"And why haven't you finished it?" he enquired.

She hesitated for a moment and then told him the truth.

"Do you realise that I don't even know your name?" she said. "How can I write to my father and mother and say I am engaged to a man whom I know only by a nickname and who has not yet told me the truth about himself?"

"I wondered how soon you would say that to me," Dix remarked.

There was something bitter in his voice and Alloa put up her hand and laid it on his arm.

"I am not being unkind," she said. "I don't want you even to think that I'm being curious, that I'm trying to find out more than you are prepared to tell me. But you must see how difficult it is, how hard for me."

"I have told you that I'm not worthy of you," he

said. "Perhaps you would be wise to refuse to see me any more, to forget me, to throw me out of your life. That's what you really mean, isn't it?"

"No, I don't," Alloa replied. "I love you. I have told you that I love you. But I also love my father and mother. I have got to think of them and their feelings when they learn that their only child is to marry a . . ."

Alloa was about to say the word "stranger", but Dix spoke before she could enunciate it.

". . . a thief! That is what you are thinking in your heart. That is what you really feel about me inside yourself, isn't it?"

Alloa was very pale. There was both pride and dignity in the way that, holding her head high, she turned to look him straight in the eyes.

"I love you whatever you are."

Dix gave a sigh.

"If only I could be sure of that. If only I could be certain that your love is big enough to accept me as I am."

"It is impossible to measure love," Alloa said quietly.

"It is also something which changes very easily," Dix answered bitterly. "You may believe that you love somebody today, and tomorrow your feelings will be quite different."

"I have never loved anyone before," Alloa said. "But I don't believe that what I feel for you will change, except that it will deepen and become more as time goes on."

Dix said nothing and after a moment she said with a little break in her voice:

"If you won't believe me, then there's nothing I can do about it."

Almost instantly his arms went round her.

"Darling, I am a brute to you," he cried. "It is only that I want to be sure of you. I am so afraid of losing you. I can't believe that someone as lovely, as perfect and as good as you are can really love me.

"That is why I am torturing myself and you by questioning everything you say and everything you do. Forgive me and tell me once again you are mine."

His lips were very close to hers and now there was no need for words.

She surrendered herself to the ecstasy of his kisses, to the fire which awoke flickeringly within themselves to become almost immediately a consuming flame.

"I love you! I love you!" Dix was murmuring against her mouth.

He held her closer still, straining her against him until she could hardly breathe and the fierceness of his kisses bruised the softness of her mouth.

At last he let her go.

"You go to my head," he said unsteadily. "It is hard for me to control myself when I touch you. Let us get married soon, my darling, very very soon. I want you. I want to be alone with you. I want to teach you to love me as I love you."

"I want also to be married to you," Alloa replied. "But first we must tell my parents."

Despite herself she felt a little barrier fall between them and she knew that Dix was thinking of that unfinished letter.

"I will write to them tonight," she murmured.

"I expect it will be tomorrow morning," Dix smiled, "because tonight we are certain to be very late."

"Won't you tell me where we are going?" Alloa asked.

"I am going to introduce you to my friends. This is a very special party and they have only allowed me to bring you because I have told them that we are to be married."

"You told them that!" Alloa said, and there was a note of consternation in her voice.

"It is the truth, isn't it?" Dix asked quickly.

"Yes, yes, of course," Alloa answered. "It's only that I wasn't prepared for anyone to know it yet; not until we knew each other a little better."

"We know each other well enough to know that love is the only thing that matters. You've told me that in promising to marry me," he said. "You do not know who I am or what I am, and all you do know about me is to my disadvantage, but you love me. Isn't it that which counts?"

"Yes," Alloa agreed. "But I am afraid of meeting strange people. Who . . . who are they?"

"As I have already said, they are my real friends," Dix replied. "Because I want you to love them and to realise, as I do, their true worth, the warm, brave heart which beats in each one of them, I am going to tell you about them before we go there. But first, kiss me."

She turned towards him, but for a moment he did not put his arms round her.

Instead he looked down into her eyes, lit by the light of the dying sun. It shone on her hair, turning it to gold, touched her skin, too, with a faint glow.

"How can I be sure of you?" he said in a low voice almost as if he spoke to himself.

Then before she could answer he bent his head and laid his lips against hers.

Once again everything was forgotten as they clung mouth to mouth.

Alloa's head was thrown back, his arms drawing her closer and closer to him. She felt as if they shot away from the earth into the sky.

There were stars shining all round them as they moved together, glorious and inseparable, across the eternal heavens.

Then suddenly Dix released her and she was back to earth again. But in her heart, because she loved him, because his kisses brought her an ecstasy beyond words, almost beyond thought, she knew that she would never be the same again.

Each time he kissed her it seemed as if he opened out new vistas within herself, new possibilities, new wonders and unprobed depths of which previously she had had no knowledge.

And because of this her instinct told her what he needed and what he wanted of her. A little shyly she put up her hand and touched his cheek.

"I love you and I trust you," she said. "Tell me just what you want me to know. I won't ask any questions."

She knew by the sudden light within his eyes that she had said the right thing.

He took his arms from her and said:

"Then sit further away from me, otherwise I won't be able to tell you anything; I shall only want to kiss you."

She laughed softly but obeyed him, moving further along the seat of the car, then turning sideways so that she faced him.

"How old were you when the war broke out?" Dix asked unexpectedly.

"I was three in 1939," Alloa answered.

"And I was eleven," Dix said. "I can remember all the excitement there was about it. People talking of nothing else and all the men I knew in the village being called-up to join the regiments. But the war did not really touch me till 1940 when France collapsed and the Germans advanced on Paris."

He paused, drew out his cigarette case and lit a cigarette. Alloa watched him.

'He must have been a very attractive little boy,' she

thought, 'to have grown up into such a very handsome man.'

"In 1940," Dix went on, "things happened here which changed my whole life. We were, of course, under the Vichy Government and this part of France was to be unoccupied. But my friends who lived here in Biarritz and the country round about were determined to play a more active part in the war than that of collaborators."

He sighed as if at a memory.

"I suppose I must have been a very precocious child for I never seemed to associate with children of my own age, but to be permanently in the company of grown-ups I used to slip away from my home to come down and talk with the shopkeepers, make friends with the fishermen, exchange views with the waiters in the cafés.

"I soon learned what was being planned amongst a small clique of those who really loved France. They were determined, all of them, to make their way to Paris.

"They nearly all had relations or friends in the city and they thought that there they could set up a resistance group of their own, their idea being to make things as unpleasant and difficult for the Germans as was possible. I made up my mind that I would go with them."

"But you were too young!" Alloa exclaimed.

"I was only twelve years old in age, but I was much older than that in cunning and in determination to have my own way," Dix answered with a smile. "I was a friend of all who were going and so they talked openly in front of me.

"I learned which day they were setting out, how they intended to travel, where they would meet when they got to Paris. They were all aware that the sooner they put their plan into operation, the better.

"The Vichy Government was issuing new instructions every day. They all expected that in time it would be impossible to move from place to place without special permits."

"I always imagined that everything was in a wild turmoil," Alloa said.

"Naturally everything was at first," Dix answered. "But Marshal Petain was already calling for calmness, for people to remain at their posts and for passive collaboration. He was also getting ready to enforce what for the moment sounded only a request."

"What happened?" Alloa asked breathlessly.

"I ran away from home and went with my friends to Paris!" Dix said. "My parents never forgave me. I suppose in a way it was a cruel thing to do, but I was fired with a desire to do something for France, to prove my manhood and if necessary to die while fighting the enemy."

"But you were too young," Alloa repeated.

"I think it was my youth which made me brave enough," Dix answered. "I did not, of course, tell my friends that I was going with them. They wouldn't have taken me. They would have informed my parents of my intentions."

He laughed.

"I diddled them all! They set out on a cold, rather rainy evening. There was a bitter wind. I followed them. I kept out of sight until we were over fifty miles away from here, then I revealed myself and it was far too dangerous for them to take me back.

"They tried to persuade me to return of my own accord but, of course, I refused. I told them that if they would not take me with them, then I would go to Paris on my own and set up a resistance movement by myself. I convinced them that I was in earnest and so they let me join them."

"What about your parents?" Alloa asked.

"I sent word to them from time to time that I was alive. I didn't, of course, dare tell them where I was in case they made enquiries, and in searching for me incriminated my friends. It was only when the war was over that I went home."

"It must have been terrible for your mother," Alloa said.

"I suppose it was," Dix admitted. "My father died in the last year of the war and my mother told me when I returned that he had never forgiven me, not even when he knew he was dying."

"How extraordinary some people are!" Alloa exclaimed. "I can't imagine anyone not forgiving his own son once he was sorry, however bad a crime he had committed."

"I think my father had an affection for me," Dix said. "But what mattered to him far more than affection or love was propriety. Anyone who behaved in a way which he considered wrong was beyond the pale."

"Of course it was wrong of you to run away," Alloa said.

"Yes, I know," Dix admitted. "But what was the alternative? To sit in Biarritz and play no part in the war? To let the Germans tramp over the soil of France just as they wished and wait for the British and Americans to rescue us?"

"I can understand your feeling like that," Alloa sympathised. "But you were only a boy."

"That was where I was most useful," Dix answered. "A boy could do things that a man would not dare to do. I was small and quick. I could slit tyres, remove a valve, steal the key of a car or something else of value from under the Germans' very noses while they were looking for the villain in the shape of a grown man. I did a lot of damage and took from them quite a lot of things they valued."

"So that's how you began to steal," Alloa said without thinking.

Even as she said the words her fingers went up to her mouth in consternation.

"Yes, that's how I learned to steal," Dix said with a cynical smile.

"I didn't mean that," Alloa said quickly. "That was unkind of me."

"Why should you apologise?" he asked. "When you met me, you thought that I was a thief; and nothing that you have seen since has led you to think otherwise. I admit to you that the car I was driving when I rescued you from the unpleasant attentions of that man outside Alençon was a stolen vehicle. Actually I did not steal it myself, but it was stolen."

"Oh, Dix!"

Alloa hardly breathed the words and it seemed as if he did not hear them because he went on:

"You are right. I learned to steal so that I should be a nuisance to Germans. I learned how Allied airmen could escape being taken prisoner.

"I learned how to carry messages across Paris at times when no grown-up man or woman would dare have set a foot out of doors. Yes, I was useful, very useful, to our people—and a thorn in the flesh to the Germans."

"I think it was very brave of you," Alloa said.

"I think half the time I was too young to appreciate how dangerous it was," Dix answered. "I know now, and sometimes at night I wake up sweating with fright when I understand just what risks I took and what would have happened to me if I had been caught."

"They would not have spared you because you were only a boy?" Alloa asked.

"Not them!" Dix replied. "I have seen boys who were only half my age shot because they were caught spying. I have seen women after they have been tortured by the Gestapo. It is not a pleasant sight."

"And yet you went on doing it all through the war," Alloa said.

"I didn't stay in Paris all the time," Dix answered. "But our headquarters were there and I always came back. The last year—1945—I was very nearly caught. They were after me. They knew what I looked like. It was just touch and go whether they got me. Tonight you will meet the woman who saved my life."

Alloa felt a sudden pang of jealousy at the warmth in his voice, the smile on his lips. She wished she could have saved his life to make him speak of her in the same way.

"She is the only person tonight whose name you will learn," Dix went on. "She is known at *Mère Blanchard*, and when the war was over she received not only the French *Legion d'honneur*, but also a British decoration which she wears beside it very proudly."

"Do you mean that none of the other people are known by their names?" Alloa asked.

"No, only by their numbers," Dix replied.

"So that is why you are called Dix."

"That is why. From the time that I left here in 1940 until the time I returned I was known only as Dix. Can you understand that, as far as I am concerned, I have no other name that matters?"

"Yes, I can understand that," Alloa said.

"*Mère Blanchard* keeps the sweet shop here in the main street," he said. "Her sister kept one in Paris. That is where she went in 1940. It was a small, insignificant little shop in a back street; but to us it meant home, it meant comfort, it meant a moment's rest and peace from the terror and suffering outside."

"How was it they didn't suspect her?" Alloa asked.

"Because messages were brought backwards and forwards by children," Dix answered. "Even the Germans didn't suspect that a child of four or five toddling into a shop with a five *centimes* piece clutched tightly in his hand was carrying a message.

"A five *centimes* piece is quite a large coin. Information written on a piece of the thinnest paper could be stuck to the back of a coin which the child handed quite naturally over the counter.

"He would receive in return a small bag of sweets. There would seem nothing suspicious in that. Messages were written inside the bag."

"What a clever idea," Alloa said.

"We had some very narrow escapes," Dix answered. "Once a British airman lay all night on the roof during a snowstorm. He was almost frozen solid when we got him down, but he survived and a month later was back in England flying with his squadron."

"I think it was wonderful of you," Alloa exclaimed.

"Nonsense!" Dix answered. "I only helped those who were the brains of the scheme. But I wanted you to understand whom you are meeting tonight and what they have done."

"I shall be proud to meet them," Alloa said softly.

"They have a party once a year," Dix told her. "On that occasion we become exactly as we were in the war—just comrades; all of us equal, all of us joined by a common cause. We have no identity outside, we are just numbers. Only *Mère Blanchard* remains *Mère Blanchard*. For the rest, we are *Un, Deux, Trois . . . Dix . . . Cinquante*, and so on. There are many gaps in our numbers of those who died for the cause."

"You make me feel ashamed that I have done so little in my life," Alloa said.

"To me you have done the biggest thing that anyone could do, in loving me," Dix answered.

He bent to kiss her cheek and then he started up the car.

"We shall be late," he said. "But I wanted to explain to you in case, when we arrived, you got the wrong impression."

"Where is the party?" Alloa asked.

"It takes place where we met here originally," Dix answered. "In the cellar of a house on the outskirts of the town. For obvious reasons no one mentions the name of the owner; but he, too, is one of us."

They drove away from the pinewoods and struck inland and then came down on to the town of Biarritz by a different way.

It was growing dark, but Alloa had a glimpse of a large, imposing *château* built in grey stone with pointed turrets on either side of the building.

Dix left the car in the drive and then, turning away from the house, drew Alloa by the hand through some shrubs which were planted on one side of the building.

They made, she noted, a small tunnel-like entrance to where eventually some steps went straight down into the earth, through an open hatch which was un-latched and supported by wooden props.

"This wasn't open in the war-time," Dix told her. "We used to have to knock and then someone opened it from the inside."

The steps down into the cellar were dark, but im-mediately they reached the bottom there were lanterns hung on the ceiling of a stone passage which led to a lighted door through which came the sound of laughter and voices.

Alloa felt suddenly shy; but Dix, taking her by the arm, led her forward.

Suddenly she found herself in a large, lighted cavern beyond which were archways leading into the cellars.

The whole place had been decorated in gay colours and there were comfortable chairs, tables and people sitting around beneath hanging lanterns of polished brass which looked like lights which had come from an old ship.

As Dix and Alloa appeared, a cry went up.

"Dix! Dix! Welcome! We have been waiting for you."

There was a sudden surge forward, the chatter of voices, and for a moment Alloa's impressions were chaotic. She felt her hand being shaken warmly, while Dix was being thumped on the back and being congratulated again and again.

Then at last Alloa was able to look around her and see Dix's friends. They were a very strange lot.

There were fishermen wearing their high-necked jerseys and rough trousers; there were several neat little, bald-headed men with waxed moustaches who were obviously shopkeepers, barbers or apothecaries.

There were women with black shawls over their shoulders, and others who were dressed in the very latest fashion and whose diamonds sparkling round their necks were quite obviously real.

In the centre of the room, enthroned as it were in a high-backed chair, was a woman whom Alloa knew at once must be *Mère Blanchard*.

She was just what she expected—very fat with twinkling eyes, white hair and a warm, deep-throated laugh which seemed to start everyone laughing as if to keep her company.

"So this is your bride-to-be, my dear little Dix," she said in a deep throated patois. "Does she realise what a bad boy she is getting for a husband?"

"I have warned her," Dix answered, his eyes twinkling.

"He is a bad boy, but we all love him," *Mère Blanchard* said, turning to Alloa. "I am glad he is being married. Perhaps he will settle down and behave himself."

"You are not to frighten her," Dix said.

"It is you who should be frightened," *Mère Blanchard* retorted. "A wife will make you behave yourself. It will be very good for you to give up your naughty ways."

"You see how severe she is with me," Dix said to Alloa. "She was always the same. When I went back to her in the war, I was never quite certain whether I should get a kiss or a spanking."

"You usually deserved both," *Mère Blanchard* laughed.

Someone pressed a glass of wine into Alloa's hand.

There were perhaps thirty people present, and all of them so different that it was hard to believe they could have so close a link in common.

One man, Alloa thought, was quite obviously an aristocrat and perhaps the owner of the cellar.

He was tall and thin with pointed features and the most beautiful hands she had ever seen on anyone. She was not surprised when later in the evening he sat down at the piano and played so beautifully that many of the listeners were near to tears.

But there was other music besides his. There was a thin young man with red hair who beat the drums so that everybody felt their feet itching to dance.

There was another who played the piano and obeyed requests for songs which had been popular in the war and which obviously had special memories for those who asked for them.

"He played in one of the bars most patronised by

the Germans," Dix told Alloa. "They checked up on him over and over again and never discovered that he understood German as well as he understood French."

"That was my accomplishment, too," a voice said.

Alloa looked up to see a very beautiful woman, with dark seductive eyes, smiling up at Dix.

"You had so many accomplishments, *Sept*," he said quietly.

"How sweet of you to remember," she answered.

She looked at him as she spoke, her red lips pouting a little, and Alloa suddenly understood that there had been something between them.

It was nothing she could put into words, she just sensed it instinctively and could not help comparing herself with this attractive, beautifully dressed woman. And everything she saw was to her own disadvantage.

"Do you remember," *Sept* asked softly, "that night in Chantilly?"

"I remember at the moment that I have not introduced you to my future wife," Dix answered. "Alloa, this is *Madame Sept*. She is a very charming person and the Germans enjoyed her hospitality and never realised how much they gave away as they drank the delicious wine she offered them and ate the exquisite meals prepared by one of the most notable chefs in all France."

"You make my achievements sound so banal, Dix," *Madame Sept* complained.

"I hope I am making you sound as generous as you were—and still are," Dix replied.

He met her eyes and there was a challenge in them and perhaps something else which Alloa did not understand. *Madame Sept* sighed.

"I would rather have been generous only to those I liked and loved," she said. "But we all had our duty to perform."

"We did our best," Dix answered. "None of us could do more."

"No, none of us could do more," she answered.

She put out her hand and he raised it perfunctorily to his lips.

"I shall always be grateful to you," he said.

"That is poor comfort," she answered.

Without another word she turned away and crossed the room to join a group of people standing by the piano.

Alloa watched her go and then she turned to Dix.

"She loved you once, didn't she?" she said.

He glanced at her quickly.

"Is that an accusation?"

Alloa shook her head.

"No, only a statement," she answered. "I think I am beginning to understand things I never understood before."

"Such as?" he enquired.

"It is difficult to put into words," she said. "But perhaps a man must try many things before he finds what he really wants, before he is sure, quite sure, what is the best life can hold for him."

"You are growing very wise," Dix said softly. "It is another reason why I love you."

"You are quite sure now about me though, aren't you?" Alloa asked.

"Quite, quite sure," he answered steadily. "You are the best for which I have been looking all my life."

She felt his words reassure her; and then, as someone claimed his attention and they drank together to some memory of the days that were past, Alloa walked across the room to where *Mère Blanchard* was still sitting.

She looked up as Alloa approached and held out her hand.

"Come and talk to me, my little one," she said. "You

are British. Do you think you will be happy to live in France?"

"I think I shall be happy to live anywhere so long as I can be with Dix," Alloa answered.

"That is good, very good!" *Mère Blanchard* cried with delight. "That is the answer I would want you to make. You are young, but you have learned already that it is not where we are that matters, but whom we are with."

"Dix has told me," Alloa said, "how he ran away from home when he was a boy and went with you to Paris. I am glad that you were there to look after him."

"He wanted a lot of looking after," *Mère Blanchard* said with a smile. "He was very naughty and quite uncontrollable. He took risks which no one in their senses would have taken. Because he was *Dix* he got away with them. He always does what he wants to do. You will find that when you marry him."

Alloa felt a little chill in her heart.

She knew that she was still hoping that she would change Dix and make him give up the life he was leading, make him see that honesty and security, however humdrum, however badly paid, were better than the life he lived now.

"But do not worry yourself," *Mère Blanchard* was saying. "He has a heart of gold and he has always wanted to help people. No one has ever turned to Dix for help in vain. We all love him. Perhaps also we spoiled him a little—but we love him all the same."

"I want to help him," Alloa said.

Mère Blanchard looked at her.

"You will be able to do that if you love him enough," she said. "He loves you now. You can keep that love only by loving him in return and by giving him something he has always lacked."

"What is that?" Alloa asked.

"A home," *Mère Blanchard* said.

"But he had one," Alloa answered. "At least, he ran away from one to be with you."

"I mean a real home," *Mère Blanchard* said. "Oh, bricks and mortar do not make a home, don't run away with that idea. It is the love that one finds in it that matters. Dix's mother and father never loved him and they never tried to understand him.

"They wanted him to obey them, they wanted him to grow up in the ways they had chosen for him, in the manner they had decreed was right and proper."

She sighed so deeply that it shook the whole of her fat soft body.

"He was a rebel—he has always been a rebel," she went on. "You cannot fit him into a square hole and tell him that is the shape he has got to be. Dix will always be himself. I still say that he needs a home and that the right type of home will be his salvation."

"Thank you for telling me," Alloa said softly.

She looked across the room. Dix was searching for her.

She could see his face as he wondered where she had gone, and then as his eyes found her, there was a sudden light in them.

She got to her feet, forgetful of *Mère Blanchard,* of everyone except Dix. He wanted her—that was enough. She went to his side and he slipped his arm through hers.

"Shall we go now?" he asked.

"Without saying goodbye?" Alloa enquired.

"We don't want to make our departure obvious," he said. "It always breaks up a party."

He helped her up the steps and through the darkness of the shrubbery to where their car was waiting.

Only when they had reached it and were inside together did he pull her into his arms, roughly and passionately.

"It is too long since I kissed you," he said. "I couldn't wait any longer. What have you done to me that even my friends seem a waste of time when I might be with you? Alone with you, Alloa. That means my whole life to me now."

He kissed her again, but after a moment she drew away from him.

"I have got something to tell you," she said. "We are going away tomorrow. We are going to stay in the country."

"But how shall I see you?" he asked.

"I don't know," Alloa said. "I don't know what to do. I thought of refusing to go, but apparently the *Duchesse* made a point of asking me."

"The Duchesse?"

She thought in the semi-darkness of the car that Dix's eyebrows were raised.

"Yes, the *Duchess de Rangé-Pougy*," she said. "I haven't told you the reason why we are here in Biarritz."

"I was quite certain there was a reason," he said with a faint smile.

"I tell you about it now," Alloa went on, "because I know that I can trust you to say nothing to anyone else. It wouldn't be fair. But I am worried, terribly worried, because of something I have done."

"Something wrong?"

She heard the laughter in his voice.

"I do not know, that is the whole point," she said. "Is it wrong to interfere with other people's lives?"

"Not the way you do it," he said and raised her fingers to his lips.

"Please, I want you to tell me if you think I have done the wrong thing," Alloa said. "It has been worry-

200

ing me all day, all this evening. It has nearly been impossible for me to think of anything else."

"Even me?" Dix asked.

"You know I can't help thinking about you," Alloa smiled. "At the same time I have been thinking about Steve Weston coming across the Atlantic, getting nearer to us every hour, and wondering if I should meet him at the airport and send him straight back again."

"And who is Steve Weston?" Dix asked, making a little gesture of helplessness. "Suppose, darling, you start from the beginning. You're being quite incomprehensible."

"Very well, I'll tell you," Alloa said. "It all began in London when I learned that Mrs. Derange was planning for Lou to marry the *Duc de Rangé-Pougy*. You can understand, in a way, how keen she is on it, because the *Duc* is the head of the family—both Lou's and, of course, mine."

"And Miss Lou is entirely in agreement with this arrangement?" Dix asked.

"That's the whole point," Alloa said with a sigh. "She was very keen about it when we were in London, but she learned today for the first time that the *Duc* is a cripple."

"She didn't know about it before?" Dix enquired.

"No, of course not. Mrs. Derange had told her all sorts of lies, saying how handsome and attractive he was; and then Lou opened a French newspaper this morning and saw a picture of him getting out of an aeroplane."

"And what did she say?" Dix asked.

"She was somewhat hysterical and furious with her mother. She swears that she won't go through with this arrangement. A marriage of convenience, of course, but one in which she would have gained a title and a wonderful *château*. I hadn't told you about that. We went over to see it yesterday."

"And how does Steve Weston come into all this?" Dix enquired.

"He was in love with Lou before she came to England, and I think she was in love with him, too. In fact, I think she is still in love with him and . . . and, oh, this is what frightens me. I telephoned him and told him to come here."

Dix put back his head and laughed.

"You are not to laugh at me," Alloa protested hotly.

He put his arms round her.

"Darling, I'm not laughing at you, only at the tragic note in your voice. Of course you've done the right thing. Steve Weston will arrive, sweep Lou into his arms, and love's young dream will triumph once again."

"Do you really think so?" Alloa said. "Suppose she's furious at the sight of him? Supposing she sends him away again as she did in London?"

"It's a risk that any man in love would be prepared to take," Dix said. "You see, I know what I'm talking about because I, too, am in love."

He looked down at her tenderly.

"You're so sweet," he said. "So utterly, adorably sweet and serious."

She stirred a little in his arms and turned her head away.

"What about us?" she said.

"Us?" he queried.

"We are going away tomorrow to the *Château*. I shan't be able to see you again."

"But, of course you will," he said. "Do you think the walls of any *Château* would keep me away from you?"

"But, you mustn't come there," Alloa said quickly.

"Why not?"

"Because it would be dangerous. They might find out. It would be difficult for me to creep out of a house like that and meet you in the garden."

"Why?" he enquired. "Is it different from any other house? It must have doors and the bolts will be on the inside."

"Oh, don't you understand?" Alloa said. "It would be so difficult. It's so big and I shan't be able to find my way about."

"I will find out where your bedroom is and you will hear me whistling beneath," Dix laughed.

"I don't think . . . we ought to . . . do that," Alloa answered hesitantly, but it was quite obvious that she was weakening.

"And the *Château*?" Dix enquired. "Did you find it very awe-inspiring?"

"It's the most beautiful place I've ever seen," Alloa answered.

"Tell me about it," he commanded.

"I can't begin to describe it," Alloa replied. "I've never seen tapestries, pictures and furniture, which all individually should be in a museum, seem so exactly right in a private house."

"It sounds pompous," Dix said.

"No, it isn't—at least, it didn't seem so to me," Alloa contradicted. "There was something about the house which made me feel as if I, too, belonged to it; a sort of atmosphere as if, despite all its grandeur, its age and its luxury, it was really a home, a place where people have lived and loved and died."

She paused for a moment and drew a little sigh as if remembering something utterly wonderful. And then she went on:

"The pictures in the *Grand Salon,* the collection of snuff boxes in the Ante-room leading to it; they were quite exquisite, set with miniatures and diamonds and all of them with a history."

"You'll have to tell me about them," Dix said. "Perhaps you could even show them to me."

"But, how could I . . . ?" Alloa began, then stopped suddenly.

The dark suspicion seemed to come into her mind, why was he so interested?

Why did he want to know about the *Château*? Why was he quite happy for her to go there, so far away from Biarritz?

Perhaps she stiffened as the thoughts came to her. Perhaps his intuition was so strong where she was concerned that he knew what she was thinking almost before she thought it herself.

As he spoke, she turned to look at him and saw the dark expression on his face.

"So that is what you are suspecting me of now," he said.

His voice was low and unexpectedly harsh.

"No! No!" she cried, putting out her hands towards him.

"That is what you are thinking," he said, inexorably. "You know it. You don't trust me. You don't love me enough even to know that I love you."

"It isn't true," Alloa said.

"Yes, it is," he went on. "Do you really think that my love is so debased that I would involve you in something like that? Oh, Alloa, and I thought you were different."

"I am. I mean . . . Oh, Dix, why do you look at me like that? What are you saying to me? I don't understand."

"I think you do," he said.

He started up the car and they drove off, and she realised with despair that he was taking her the quickest and shortest way back to the hotel. It would only be a few minutes before they were outside the gates and she must leave him.

"Please, Dix," she pleaded. "Please understand."

"I do," he retorted.

He drew up in the roadway outside the entrance to the courtyard.

The lights of the cars coming up the hill, carrying people home from the Casino and the gala dances, were full in their faces. Alloa turned towards Dix.

"Dix, please don't be cross with me," she pleaded.

"I am not cross," he answered.

"Then you're hurt, which is worse," Alloa said. "Oh, Dix! Don't you understand? I want to trust you. I do trust you, and yet . . ."

"And yet," he said, "your mind pulls you one way and your heart another. Poor little Alloa. You can't help yourself, and I can't help you either."

"What do you mean?" she asked in sudden fear.

"I mean," he answered, "you haven't yet written that letter to your parents."

He got out of the car as he spoke and coming round, opened the door for Alloa.

There was nothing she could do but get out. She felt the night wind on her neck and on her hair. She looked up at him beseechingly.

He did not take her in his arms; instead he raised her hand to his lips, and then, before she could beg him to stay and talk further, he had got back into the car.

"Go in, Alloa, you will get cold," he said.

"Dix! Wait a minute! Please . . . Dix . . ."

But before she had finished speaking he had driven away. She saw the car slide past her, watched it gradually gathering speed, and then there was only the dark red glow of its tail light as it disappeared down the hill.

Alloa felt the tears welling up in her eyes, and because she knew she could not cry here, outside in the road, she turned and ran towards the hotel, knowing as she went that the evening was spoilt.

There was within her an aching emptiness which made her feel more alone than she had ever been in her life before.

Chapter Eleven

Alloa awoke feeling tired and dispirited.

She had wept herself to sleep, and the dark lines under her eyes and her pale face were evidence of her miserable night.

"How could I have been so stupid?" she asked herself for the thousandth time. How could she have let Dix see or guess at her thoughts? And why had she been fool enough to think such things of him?

It seemed to her as if her suspicions of him were quite separate from herself. They were merely devils which came tempting her and trying their best to dispossess her of her happiness and her faith.

"I love him! I love him!" she murmured over and over again, and yet she knew that last night he had been right when he said she did not love him enough.

Why could she not trust him? Why could she not believe that, though he might be a smuggler of cars, a crook in many ways, he would not use her as an accessory to his dishonesty?

Yet his face had been dark with anger as he drove away. She could still feel the stiffness of his fingers as he held her hand, could still feel the very light brush of his lips.

So different from the hot, passionate kisses he had

206

rained on her palm at other times, and the gentle and sweeter touch of his mouth when, as he did so often, he kissed her hand just because he loved her.

"Oh, Dix! Dix!" she cried, and felt the tears welling again into her eyes.

There was a knock at the door and her breakfast was brought in and set down beside her.

For the first time since she had come to France the sight of fresh crisp *croissants* gave her no pleasure, and not even the fragrant smell of the coffee made her want to raise her head from the pillow.

Instead, she lay going over once again the adventures of the night before.

She could still see that red tail light disappearing down the hill, she could still feel that agony of helplessness, of watching something wonderful slip away from her, leaving her alone.

How hopeless it all was, she thought now. She could not ring him up; she did not know where he was—she did not even know his name.

It was as if he were not even real, but was just a mirage, a figment of her own imagination who had never really existed.

Suppose she never saw him again? She knew now that this was the terror that had been haunting her all through the night. Had he really left her? Had he vanished for ever?

How could he question her love, she asked herself, when her whole body throbbed and ached with misery because she had offended him?

If only she could get hold of him to tell him how sorry she was, how bitterly she regretted her disloyalty.

Again and again she asked herself why she had not denied it, why she had acquiesced in what was, after all, only a guess on his part. And yet she knew she could never lie to Dix.

Because she loved him she must tell him the truth. She was not subtle or clever, she was just someone who, having given her heart, gave everything.

She gave a little sob and as she did so the telephone rang.

For one moment she was very still and then, with a wild leap of her heart, she ran across the room to pick up the receiver.

"Hello!"

She could hardly say the word. It was a woman's voice who answered.

"Is that you, Alloa?"

"Oh, hello, Lou!"

"Come along will you? I'm awake and I want to talk to you."

"Very well."

Alloa put down the receiver.

She had hoped it might be Dix; but she knew now that all day, and perhaps for ever, every time the telephone rang, she would hope it would be him. And suppose he never rang her?

She dared not face the answer to that; and so instead, with a feeling of sheer desperation, she picked up her notebook and pencil and went along the corridor to Lou's room.

Lou was lying back against the lace pillows on her bed, wearing a dressing-jacket of peach-coloured chiffon.

"Have I called you too early?" she asked as Alloa came into the room.

"No," Alloa answered.

"I wanted to talk to someone," Lou said. "And you know I'm not really speaking to Momma at the moment."

"Poor Mrs. Derange!"

Alloa could feel almost a sympathy with her.

"It's no use being sorry for her," Lou said. "She's behaved abominably and she knows it. She's still hoping that when I see the *Duc* I'll think he's a pill worth swallowing for the sake of the *Château*."

"And will you?" Alloa asked.

"Do you mean will I marry him?" Lou enquired. "That, of course, depends."

"On him?" Alloa enquired.

"I suppose so," Lou said. "After all, he may not be so bad as he looks in that picture. He may have great charm and tremendous brains and he need not be a permanent invalid. There are a lot of possibilities, aren't there?"

She spoke in a hard, brittle voice which told Alloa all too clearly that she didn't mean a word of what she was saying.

"Oh, Lou," she said. "Don't do anything stupid. After all, you're young and it's your whole life that's at stake."

Lou looked at her and suddenly she smiled.

"I know, Alloa, and I'm not going to do anything really until I've thought it over, discussed it and, in fact, chewed the whole thing into a wet rag. Momma's trying to rush me, I'm well aware of that; but I'm not going to be rushed."

"Good for you!" Alloa exclaimed. "But be careful."

"What do you mean, be careful?"

"I don't know quite what I do mean," Alloa said, "except that I can't help feeling that you may get embroiled in all this and not be able to back out."

"I know what you mean," Lou said seriously. "If the worst comes to the worst, I can always run away, can't I? I can always go back to America."

"To your friends," Alloa said.

"Exactly! To my friends," Lou agreed.

Alloa dared not say anything more definite.

She only looked out of the window at the great expanse of blue sky, at the Atlantic rollers splashing on the beach, and thought of Steve Weston.

He would be on his way by now. Perhaps already he had reached England. He would have to come either to London and get a plane from there to Biarritz, or to Paris.

She felt herself tremble and wished she hadn't sent for him. It did not seem to her that, however worried Lou might be about the *Duc*, she was pining for Steve's company.

"What are we going to do today?" she asked, to change the subject.

"Well, as far as I can make out, we are going over to the *Château* in the evening. Momma's idea is that we should arrive in time to change for dinner. Someone told her once that that was the correct time for guests to make their appearance, and so she is sticking to her book of etiquette."

"What are you going to do till then?" Alloa enquired.

"Well, I thought of having a bathe this morning," Lou replied. "If I've got the energy. There's just a chance that I might be asked out to lunch by a rather fascinating Frenchman I met last night. He said he would try to call me, but he might be too busy."

"He sounds rather rude," Alloa suggested.

"Not really," Lou said. "You see, he is down here from Paris on a job. As a matter of fact it's very exciting. He told me all about it. He's in the *Sûreté* and they have sent him here to round up a gang of smugglers. It sounds quite eighteenth century, doesn't it?"

"A gang of smugglers!"

The words came from between Alloa's lips almost in a whisper.

"Yes. He told me not to say anything, but it won't

210

matter my telling you," Lou said. "It's just like a film. Apparently there has been a lot of car smuggling going on here."

"And the police know about it?" Alloa asked.

"Yes. They have been trying to find out about it for some time," Lou went on. "You remember when they said I couldn't drive in Spain because the *Triptique* was in your name? Well, that was because they have been having an awful lot of trouble with cars being smuggled over the frontier."

Alloa made a little sound, but Lou did not hear it.

"This Frenchman told me all about it," she continued. "There's a gang which have been operating for months and making an absolute packet out of it."

"Does . . . your friend . . . know who they are?" Alloa asked.

"Well, I think so. He didn't tell me names, of course, but apparently they have got the whole thing tied up and they are waiting to make an arrest at any moment."

"Did he say where?"

"Well, I gathered it was here in Biarritz," Lou said. "Apparently there are quite a gang of them and they are going to get the whole lot. It's a real round-up. I do wish I could see it, don't you?"

"What else did he say?" Alloa asked.

"Oh, I think that was all," Lou answered. "He just said they had been waiting for some time—playing with them like a cat plays with a mouse. That was his very metaphor. And now they will get them red-handed—the whole lot."

"The whole lot," Alloa repeated in a whisper.

"Why, Alloa, what's the matter?" Lou asked. "You look as if you're going to faint. Shall I get you something?"

"No, no, it's all right," Alloa answered. "I'm quite all right."

"Well, you look absolutely rotten," Lou said. "Do you think you'd better go and lie down?"

"Yes, if you'll forgive me I will go to my own room."

"Of course. Shall I come with you or can you manage by yourself?"

"I'm quite all right, thank you," Alloa answered. "I will go and . . . lie down."

She reached the door and turned the handle.

"I do hope you'll be all right," she heard Lou saying, and then the door closed behind her and she was running as hard as she could down the corridor.

She reached her own room to stand there with her hands to her face, thinking, 'Dix! Dix!'

She must save him. She must warn him.

She thought wildly of going to the place on the cliff where she had seen the car being loaded in the fishing boat, but she knew that was ridiculous.

He wouldn't be there at this time of day.

The police must have found out their headquarters where they were all staying. It was somewhere in Biarritz, but Biarritz was a big town. How could she find him? How could she?

It was then that she remembered something—*Mère Blanchard* had a shop in the town. Dix had said so last night. A shop in the town!

Alloa ran from her room and downstairs.

She did not even wait for the lift. It was quicker to hurry down the two flights into the lofty quietness of the big hall. She ran across it and out through the revolving door and into the courtyard. The porter was standing under the portico.

"Please tell me where there is a sweet shop kept by someone called *Mère Blanchard*," Alloa said in French.

He looked at her for a moment in surprise and then his face broke into a wide smile.

"*Mère Blanchard*!" he said. "Ah, she is a great character. Everybody in Biarritz knows *Mère Blanchard*."

"Where is her shop?" Alloa said.

He explained to her that it was in the second turning past the Casino, down a narrow roadway which led to the sea.

"You cannot miss it, *M'mselle*," he said. "And if you do, anyone will tell you. There's no one in Biarritz who doesn't know *Mère Blanchard*."

Alloa had gone almost as he finished speaking.

It was hot in the sunshine, but she did not feel hot as she raced down the hill past the Casino and through the crowd of people loitering along the pavements or staring at the shop windows.

She found the small, narrow roadway which led down to the sea. *Mère Blanchard's* shop was almost at the bottom. The window was filled with brightly coloured sweets and delectable *pâtisseries* thick with cream.

Alloa pushed open the shop door.

There was only a small girl behind the counter— a child of about eleven years old.

"Is *Mère Blanchard* here?" Alloa panted.

"I will call her, *M'mselle*," the child answered.

"No, I want to speak to her. Let me come with you," Alloa said.

She glanced over her shoulder and saw a woman staring into the window, obviously about to enter the shop.

"I will come with you," she repeated.

She pushed her way behind the counter, following the child through the door at the back of the shop.

"I had better tell my *grandmère* you are here," the child said as they came into a small, dark room which was piled with boxes.

"Please tell her quickly. It is very urgent," Alloa said.

The child hurried away. Alloa moved restlessly around the small room, staring at the boxes of sweets with unseeing eyes, hearing only Lou's voice saying,

"They are going to get the whole lot. It's a real round-up."

"*Grandmère* says will you please come into the kitchen," the child said from behind her, in a high voice.

Alloa followed her down a passage and into a large kitchen which obviously stood at the back of the house. *Mère Blanchard* was making pastry on the table in the centre of the room.

It was a kitchen which might have been depicted in an old French painting.

There were the cross beams in the ceiling, the huge range set in one wall, the dresser with its brightly coloured plates and brass saucepans shining so that they acted like strangely distorted mirrors in which one could see reflected the whole kitchen and its occupants.

Mère Blanchard looked up with a smile.

Her sleeves were turned up above her fat elbows and she wore an apron which seemed to accentuate the mountainous size of her heavy body.

"Good morning, *M'mselle*! This is a surprise. I had not expected to see you so early."

"*Madame*, I must speak to you alone. It is very important," Alloa said.

Mère Blanchard looked at her small grand-daughter.

"Run back to the shop, Louise," she said. "And don't forget, when *Madame Lisard* comes, her cakes are on the shelf ready for her."

"I won't forget, *Grandmère*," the child said and went from the kitchen.

Alloa went up to the table.

"*Madame Blanchard*," she said, "where is Dix? You must tell me where he is."

214

Mère Blanchard put down her rolling-pin.

"He has not told you?" she said.

"No, but I must get to him."

"If he has not told you," *Mère Blanchard* said, "then he does not wish you to know."

"But, I must find him," Alloa said desperately. "You do not understand. *Madame*, he is in great danger."

Mère Blanchard's eyebrows went up.

"In danger! You are sure of it?"

"I am quite, quite sure of it," Alloa said. "And I must warn him. I must tell him and he must get away at once."

Mère Blanchard looked at her in what Alloa thought was a strange manner.

"Please," she said quickly. "Please, please believe me. Dix is in danger. I know you helped him during the war, and now you must help him again. I must go to him. There is no time to be lost."

Mère Blanchard seemed to be thinking. After a moment she said:

"Listen, *M'mselle*. You must wait for him here. I will send for him."

"But, surely it would be quicker if I went to him myself," Alloa said. "If you know where he is, please tell me."

"If he has not told you himself, then it would not be right for me to do so," *Mère Blanchard* said. "Come! It is quite simple. I will send for him and then you can tell him what is in your mind."

She opened another door of the kitchen as she spoke and beckoned Alloa to follow her. Feeling as if every moment that passed added new dangers to Dix's freedom, Alloa went with *Mère Blanchard*.

There was a short passage and then a room which looked out over a small back-garden. It was a very stiff, conventional sitting-room. The windows were shrouded in lace curtains; the furniture was arranged stiffly against the walls, and in the centre of the room there was a round table on which reposed some wax flowers covered by glass.

"Wait here," *Mère Blanchard* said, "and I will send a message."

"I wish you would let me go to him myself," Alloa said.

"You must trust me," *Mère Blanchard* said.

She shut the door behind her.

"Trust me!"

The words seemed to echo round the room after she had gone.

"Trust me! Trust me!"

It was what Dix had said. And yet, Alloa thought, she had not been able to trust him, and because of that she had failed him. And yet was there any reason why she should trust him when even at this moment he was in such a desperate predicament?

She was terrified lest she should be too late to warn him. It was impossible for her to sit down on one of the stiff sofas or chairs.

Instead she walked about the room.

The minutes seemed to pass by like hours. Alloa walked up and down the room; her whole mind was a turmoil of terror and suspense.

Why did Dix not come? Was he far away? Was it sheer madness to wait here for him when she might be warning him, telling him to get away?

Perhaps at this very moment he was being arrested. Perhaps the police had broken down the door before the men had time to get up and leave their lodgings or their hiding place.

Perhaps Dix was already in prison.

She wanted to cry out at the sheer horror of it, when suddenly the door opened. She whirled round.

Dix stood there in the doorway.

He was wearing only an open-necked shirt and rough trousers such as the fishermen wore. There was sand on his canvas shoes and his hair looked a little untidy as if he had run quickly to get here.

"Alloa!"

He said her name and then suddenly she was close against him, her arms were round his neck and he held her to him.

"Darling, what is it?"

"Oh, Dix! Thank God you've come! You've got to get away at once; now; quickly."

"What do you mean? What is the matter?"

"They have found out. They are going to arrest you this morning."

"Who are 'they'?"

"The police, of course. Oh, don't ask me how I've heard about it. There isn't time. Just go—go quickly. You've got a car."

Dix held her closely to him and bent down very slowly and kissed her mouth.

"I love you," he said.

"Oh, Dix, don't waste time," Alloa begged. "I love you, too. I am sorry about last night, terribly sorry. There's not time to talk about that now. You have got to get out of here. Don't you understand? You're going to be arrested."

"Darling, you're trembling," he said, "and your hands are cold, too. You are frightened, aren't you? Frightened for me."

"You know I am," Alloa said. "Do listen to me, Dix. It is no use standing here talking. You've got to get away."

"Tell me about it," he commanded.

"Lou told me," Alloa said, trying to speak quickly and clearly. "She met a man last night. He is in the

Sûreté and he told her he had been sent down here especially from Paris to arrest a gang of smugglers. They have been watching them for some time but have been wanting to get them all together. They are going to round them up today—all of them."

"Darling, what a very indiscreet person this gentleman in the *Sûreté* must be," Dix said.

"We ought to be grateful," Alloa said. "Terribly grateful. It has given me time to warn you. I couldn't think at first how to get hold of you, and then I remembered that you said *Mère Blanchard* had a shop in Biarritz."

"That was clever of you to remember that," Dix said.

"She wouldn't let me come to you. She said if you hadn't told me where you were, you didn't want me to know."

"She was right. I didn't," Dix said.

"I was so afraid she wouldn't get to you in time, but now you are here it's all right. She can hide you, and then as soon as you can you must slip out of the town. You must be careful of the roads though. Perhaps they will be watched. Will it be possible to go by sea?"

"You're thinking of everything, aren't you?" Dix said. "But you've forgotten one thing."

"What is that?" Alloa asked.

"That I won't go without you."

She stared at him for a moment as if she couldn't believe that she had heard him aright.

"What do you mean?" she asked at last.

"What I say," he answered. "Do you think I want to run away and live in obscurity without you? Better go to prison than that; better be with my friends than alone with nobody at all."

"Do you really mean that?" Alloa asked.

"You know I mean it," he said. "I want you! I love you! If I run away, then I want you to come with me."

"Where would we go?"

Dix held wide his arms.

"Anywhere," he said. "The world is big. What does it matter as long as we're together? The French may be seeking for us in France, but what is wrong with Africa, with South America, the Caribbean or the West Indies? And any of them, Alloa, will seem like paradise with you."

"But we should be fugitives," she said softly.

"Yes, fugitives," he answered. "But together."

She took a deep breath.

"Won't it make it worse for you if you have me with you?" she asked. "You might be able to travel swifter alone. But hampered with . . . with someone else it might make it twice as dangerous."

"It would be worth it," he said. "Worth anything to know that you were with me, that you belonged to me."

"And if I don't come?"

He shrugged his shoulders.

"Then I shall let things take their course," he said. "I ought to be loyal and stand by my friends."

"They are not your friends," Alloa said hotly. "You may work with them, you may be linked with them because of the things that you do, but they are not really your friends. The people you met last night are your friends, not those horrible men who threatened me, who tied me up and frightened me because I knew that they would stick at nothing."

Dix smiled.

"Very well then, they are not my friends. What do you want me to do?"

"To get away," Alloa said. "Oh, please try and understand. Every moment is precious. The police will not take this lightly. If they are going to trap you, they will have it all worked out. You must get away now."

"And you will come with me?"

Alloa knew then the answer she must give him.

She knew then that everything she had done and everything she had been feeling had been working up to this moment.

This was what was so important—her answer now.

She had one last thought of her father and mother. She loved them, but somehow even her love for them was not as important or as vital as her love for Dix.

"I love you!" she said very quietly. "And I will come with you."

He looked at her for a moment incredulously, as if he hardly believed he could have heard aright. And then with a little inarticulate cry of joy he put his arms around her.

"Do you mean that?" he asked. "Do you really mean it? I want you to say it again. I want to be certain I heard you aright."

"I will come with you," she said.

"You know what it means," he said. "We shall be outcasts; we shall be running away from justice; we shall be afraid of our own shadows. Are you quite certain you know what you are taking on?"

"I know," she said, "but I am still prepared to come if you want me."

"If I want you!"

It was almost a cry and his arms tightened round her until they hurt.

"If I want you!" He looked down into her face. "You haven't any idea how much I do want you. If you come with me now, I will devote my whole life to trying to make you happy.

"At the same time you will belong to me and to me alone. Do you understand what that means? I shall be jealous of everyone and everything. I want you completely and absolutely. Mine! My love, my life!"

He held her so closely to him that Alloa could hardly breathe.

"Look at me, Alloa," he went on. "Look into my eyes and tell me that you really mean it, that it is not just a trick to get me to go away, it is not just a despairing effort to save me from myself."

"You know it is not that," Alloa said.

"Then why are you coming? Why? Tell me why? So that I can no longer have any doubts of it."

"Because I love you," Alloa said. "Don't you understand, Dix, that I love you so much that I have discovered that nothing else matters. I am yours to do what you want with me. I will follow you wherever you go, even to the ends of the world."

He bent his head as she said that last word and his lips met hers in a long, passionate kiss which seemed to burn its way down through her lips to her very soul.

Then as she clung to him, as she felt her heart fill with ecstasy by the fire and wonder of his passion, suddenly he took his arms from her and dropped down on his knees at her side.

"I love you, Alloa!" he said. "And so I am kneeling to you. I am kneeling to tell you that I am always at your feet, that I worship you because of your love for me, that I shall serve you, in my own way—nevertheless as your slave—for the rest of my life."

He pressed his lips, hot and burning, against the palms of both her hands.

Then he rose to his feet and swept her once again into his arms.

"I love you! Oh, darling, how I love you!"

She wanted to surrender herself to him, but instead she fought herself free.

"We have got to go, Dix. Please understand, we have got to go."

He shook his head.

"I can't go yet," he said. "I have got to stay here today. I have got to warn my confederates. I have got to help them. You understand that, don't you?"

Alloa gave a cry.

"No, I don't," she said. "If you go back now, they will catch you. They will put you in prison. Can't you understand that you are not invincible or omnipotent? You are a man and you are pitting your brains against the law.

"You will never win, never, because right always triumphs in the end. Come away now. I will come with you. This moment; this second. It is no use wasting time."

He put his hand under her chin and turned her face up to his.

"I never thought I should hear you say that to me," he said.

"But I am saying it," Alloa answered. "And now you won't listen. You are being so foolhardy, so stupid. You have got to save yourself."

"I can't go now," he said. "There are things I have got to do, people I have got to help. But I promise you one thing. They shan't catch me."

"But, if they do . . ."

"They won't," he said. "You have got to trust me."

"You are crazy," Alloa said. "What more can I do to make you see that this is not a game?"

"You have done everything there is to do," Dix said. "You promised to come with me. You are still certain you want to do that? What will you say to your father and mother?"

The flush of excitement faded a little from Alloa's cheeks, but her eyes were quite steady as she looked up into his.

"I have thought of that," she said. "It will hurt them, but one day perhaps we will make them understand."

"Do you think they will ever accept me as your husband? The man I am."

"They will understand when they know how much I love you," Alloa said.

"Oh, darling, you are so sweet," he cried. "I told you that I was unworthy of you and I mean that. One day, perhaps, I will make you proud of me."

"I want to be proud of you now," Alloa said. "I want you to be sensible and come away, this very minute."

"Do you think you would be proud of me if I deserted my friends—or, if not my friends, the people who have trusted me? No! There are things I must do first. Go back to the hotel. If you have not heard from me by this evening, go with Mrs. Derange and her daughter to the *Château*. I will get in touch with you there tonight."

"But, Dix, you can't do that. I have tried to save you. I have offered to go with you. You can't send me back now. You can't risk being arrested, being thrown into prison."

"You have got to trust me," Dix said obstinately. "I can't explain. I only know that I can't come with you now. There are too many things involved, too many things that I have to do because my honour is concerned."

"Your honour!" Alloa said incredulously.

"Yes, my honour. Even thieves have honour, you know, and I want you to believe in mine."

"I do believe in it," Alloa said. "I believe in you now as I never believed in you before. But . . . oh, Dix, I'm afraid."

He held her close to him.

"Afraid for me?" he asked.

"Afraid of losing you," she said. "We are too happy."

"So the gods might be jealous," he said with a little smile. "I never thought to find you superstitious."

"I don't think it is being superstitious," Alloa said. "I think it is because I have just woken up to the fact that I have been so smug, so sure of myself. My world all fitted into nice neat little compartments. It was all so tidy, so easy; and suddenly I find that it is not a bit like that, it is entirely different."

"And now what is it?" Dix enquired.

"It is frightening; it is insecure; and it is wildly, crazily wonderful," Alloa said, and her voice broke.

"Oh, you darling," he said. "Only you could have said a thing like that and only you could have made me believe it."

He kissed her mouth again and then drew away.

"I have got a lot to do," he said. "But I promise you that I will do nothing stupid, nothing that imperils our happiness together. If it is possible, I will come for you at the hotel before you leave. If not, I will get in touch with you some time tonight. Don't be surprised at anything—how I appear, in what way or at what time. Just be expecting me, because I love you."

"You will take care of yourself?"

Alloa was very pale and her voice shook a little, but her eyes were brave.

"I will take care of myself because you have asked it of me," Dix replied.

"I shall be praying," Alloa said, a little catch in her voice. "Praying all the time."

He kissed her forehead, her eyes and last of all her mouth.

"I shall be thinking of you," he said. "Every moment, every second until we meet again. *Au revoir*, my darling, my perfect love, my future wife."

She tried to cling to him, but quite suddenly he had slipped from her arms.

He opened the door which led into the passage, blew her a kiss from the doorway and then was gone. She heard his footsteps for just a moment and then there was only silence and the song of the birds outside in the garden.

She walked across to the window and stood there feeling the elation and the excitement and the rapture of his kisses die away from her.

Now fear was returning, fear of what would happen to him.

She knew, even as she trembled for him, that he had been right to go.

Although she would have gone with him willingly if he would have taken her at that very moment, there would always have been the feeling that he had taken the coward's way out, that he had run away from what was going to happen and abandoned everyone to his own interests, his own desires.

"I respect him," she whispered, and knew that for the first time that was true.

She had loved him for what seemed to her a long time, but she had neither trusted nor respected him; and now both those things unexpectedly were there.

It was then she realised to what she had committed herself—to a life without anything that had been hers in the past.

They would not be able to go to Scotland, because if the police were looking for him that was the most likely place where they would wait.

They would be outcasts, without home, without family, without background.

Alloa wondered where they would wander, where they would find a resting place; and suddenly she knew none of it mattered. Love conquered all things!

That was the real answer.

Love mattered more than security, more than respectability, more than anything, so long as it was real enough and true love.

She thought then that her life would not be easy.

There would be difficulties and dangers, there would even be differences between her and Dix; but everything was surmountable, everything was possible so long as they kept their love for each other the glorious and shining thing it was at the moment.

She felt herself tremble again as she had trembled in his arms, felt the warmth of her mouth that had been soft and passionate beneath his kisses.

She knew that this was the man whom she had been meant to find, who had been waiting for her somewhere in the world.

He was not what she had expected, was not at all the sort of hero husband she had dreamed of in her girlish dreams.

But he was the man who was meant for her, the man to whom she belonged and who would possess not only her body but her mind and her heart for all time, for eternity.

"I love him!" Alloa whispered. "Oh, thank you, God, for letting me find him."

Chapter Twelve

"Now, Lou, don't be in a hurry to make up your mind. Don't say anything or do anything until you've had time to consider it carefully. That's what your father always used to say—everything is worth considering carefully."

Mrs. Derange's rather high, nasal voice harmonised with the purr of the car engine so that both noises to

Alloa were continuous, as they drove towards the *Château*.

Lou said nothing.

She sat staring over the countryside, a rather fixed look in her eyes as if she were divorced from reality and living in a world of her own imagination.

"What I feel," Mrs. Derange went on, "is that you are standing at the cross-roads. It is of the utmost importance for you to make the right decision. Young people think only of what is happening at the moment. They forget that the future lies ahead of them; years and years when love will often seem an empty dream and more tangible things are very much more important. I want you to visualize yourself when you're forty, fifty, sixty; to think what will matter to you then."

Lou shrugged her shoulders with a weary gesture and said in a tired voice:

"All right, Momma, I get your point. You want me to be a Duchess and that's that."

"I want you to be happy, dear," Mrs. Derange corrected. "But happiness doesn't always mean dancing cheek to cheek with some young man whose only asset is that he's got a handsome profile."

"Oh, scrap it!" Lou exclaimed. "I know whom you're talking about. Why not give the profile a name?"

"I'm not speaking of anyone in particular," Mrs. Derange said. "All I'm asking you to do is not to be hasty."

"We're certainly not being very hasty at the moment," Lou said. "Alloa's driving like a funeral procession."

Alloa started.

"I'm sorry," she apologised. "I thought there was no hurry."

Her thoughts having been on Dix, she was hardly conscious of what she was doing. She just drove automatically along the long, tree-bordered road that led inland.

Where was Dix now? she wondered. What was happening? What was he doing? Was he safe?

She had found it almost more than she could bear to leave Biarritz, to come away from the hotel, to remember all the things she had to do for Mrs. Derange, such as tipping the staff, paying the bill, checking out the luggage.

It had been the greatest effort for her to perform her duties when all the time she was longing to run down to *Mère Blanchard* to ask her if she had any news, to beg her for information about Dix.

It was only pride which prevented her from doing this even though she knew it would be useless. *Mère Blanchard* would not, or could not, tell her any more than she knew already.

Dix would not be there, because he was risking his liberty and perhaps his life.

All through the afternoon Alloa kept remembering the man who had threatened to cut her throat, and she shivered at the thought of him.

If the police tried to arrest men like that, there was certain to be a fight; knives would be used and guns. More than once she found herself listening and knew she was waiting for the sound of shots.

At last all the luggage had been piled somehow into the car, filling the back seat as well as the boot so that Mrs. Derange and Lou could sit in the front beside Alloa.

"Do you want to drive today?" Alloa had asked Lou before they left the hotel.

The latter had shaken her head.

"If I try to drive towards the *Château*, I shall very

likely find myself going in the opposite direction," she said. "And then what will Momma do?"

The two girls were alone in Lou's bedroom and instinctively Alloa's hand had gone out towards her.

"Don't go if you feel like that," she said. "Stay here."

"What for?" Lou had asked. "I might as well go and look-see."

It was on the tip of Alloa's tongue to tell her that Steve Weston was on his way over, and then she had bitten back the words even as they moved her lips. Let Lou see the *Duc* first. If she liked him, then Steve could go back to where he had come from. If she didn't, then he would have more chance if his arrival was unexpected.

Lou walked across to the window and looked out over the sea.

"What would you do if you were in my place, Alloa?" she asked. And then added before Alloa could speak: "Don't tell me, I know. You'd plump for love, wouldn't you?"

"Yes, I would," Alloa replied. "Love is the thing that matters most in the world."

"Only to some people," Lou said. "And perhaps I'm not the right type."

She turned away almost petulantly from the window and walked across to the mirror.

"I'd look charming in a coronet, wouldn't I?" she asked mockingly.

"You'd look lovely whatever you wore," Alloa answered. "But I think it is happiness that makes one look one's best and not jewellery, however expensive."

"You've always got the right answer, haven't you?" Lou said mockingly. "By the way, are you feeling better? You still look pale."

"I'm all right," Alloa answered quickly.

"What upset you?" Lou asked, suddenly curious. "Don't say that you're in love with someone."

She had spoken without thinking. The flush that flamed into Alloa's pale face was a surprising answer to her question.

"Alloa!" she said incredulously. "You're in love! But who with?"

"I don't want to talk about it. Please leave me alone," Alloa said.

She spoke without thinking and her words sounded brusque, almost rude, and yet she could not help it.

She could not bear that her love for Dix should be talked about or exclaimed over at this moment.

Every nerve in her body was quivering with fear for him, she felt almost distraught with anxiety, and she would, if it had been possible, have stood by his side and faced whatever might be waiting for him, even if it were death itself.

What did Lou know about love, if she could even consider for one moment marrying a man whom she had never seen and whom she believed to be a cripple and an invalid?

If she had ever experienced the ecstasy, the glory and the wonder of being in the arms of a man whom she loved and who loved her, then there would never be any hesitation, never any question of what she should do.

Alloa went from the bedroom.

She heard Lou call after her, but she did not go back. Until it was time to leave the hotel, she took good care not to be alone with either Lou or Mrs. Derange.

She bustled around, seeing to the luggage, consulting Jeanne and doing a thousand and one things which kept her busy and at least one part of her mind occupied.

When everything was packed it was discovered that

there was too much for one car if four people were to travel in it, and a taxi was therefore hired to take Jeanne and several of the larger boxes.

"She can get off at once," Mrs. Derange said. "If she's there before us, all the better. She can start unpacking and pressing what we shall wear tonight. I've told her, Lou, that you will wear your red satin. It will look magnificent in those enormous rooms and I want you to make a good impression."

"Like a lamb being led to the slaughter," Lou said, only to receive a quick frown from her mother.

"Being sarcastic was never becoming to you, dear," she reproved her. "If you don't want to go, of course we can always call the visit off."

It was an idle suggestion, as both Lou and Mrs. Derange knew. Nothing at that moment would have prevented the older woman from going to the *Château*.

There was no doubting the excitement in her voice and the glint in her eye as finally they set off from the hotel.

Even Lou seemed in a good temper as they swung out of the courtyard on to the main road; but as soon as they got out of Biarritz Mrs. Derange made the fatal mistake of starting to talk.

It was obvious that her remarks soon put Lou in a bad temper. She slumped lower in the seat, her mouth drooping at the corners. She made little or no effort to answer her mother.

'Leave her alone,' Alloa longed to say. 'Let things work out without so much chatter about them.'

But soon Mrs. Derange's monotonous voice ceased to affect her.

She was thinking her own thoughts, remembering only Dix, praying for him, willing him to come through this safely and return to her.

"There's the *Château!*" Mrs. Derange exclaimed suddenly.

They had a sudden glimpse of towers and roofs shining through the encircling protection of green trees and a high wall.

A few moments later they came to the lodges. Two huge ornamental iron gates surmounted by coronets were opened by a lodge-keeper.

Now, as the *Château* in the warm glow of the evening sun, came slowly into view, Alloa forgot her own troubles in the wonder and the beauty of it.

It was like a fairy palace, so delicately conceived and built with all the brilliance of the seventeenth-century craftsman. The bridges which spanned the moat, the great lakes sweeping out on one side, the gardens, formal and yet miracles of horticulture—they were all like pieces of some exquisite tapestry wrought with loving hands.

And yet once again Alloa had the feeling that it was not awe inspiring, not frightening, but welcoming. There was something intimate and sympathetic about it all which pleased not only her mind but her heart.

She drove carefully up to the wide stone steps which led up to the front door. The footmen in their velvet livery enriched with silver braid came hurrying down to open the doors.

"Shall I take the car round to the garage?" Alloa asked.

Mrs. Derange looked shocked.

"No, of course not. I am sure they'll send someone for it. You must come in with us. You're a guest just as we are."

Alloa was a little surprised.

It was not like Mrs. Derange to be so effusive; and then, with a little inward smile, she remembered that she bore the same name and therefore, on this occasion, she was to be one of the family.

A butler led them through the hall, which smelt of beeswax and carnations, into the *Grand Salon* where the *Duchesse* was waiting for them.

She put down her embroidery as they entered, rose from the sofa and came gracefully across the room, her white hair silhouetted against the painted walls, her feet moving silently over the exquisite Aubusson carpet.

"I am so glad to welcome you to the *Château*," she smiled.

She shook hands with Mrs. Derange, then with Lou and lastly with Alloa.

"You must look on this visit as coming home," she said. "For the *Château* is, indeed, the home of everyone who bears the family name. Won't you come and sit down?"

As she spoke, she indicated the tapestry-covered sofa and chairs which were arranged a little formally around a low table on which were some exquisite specimens of *Sèvres* china.

"I have arranged a dinner party tomorrow night," she said, "at which you will meet some other members of the family—cousins who live in the vicinity and also one or two of our most intimate friends."

"That is very kind of you," Mrs. Derange said. "But we shall be perfectly happy with you and . . . your son."

She hesitated a little before she mentioned the *Duc*. Alloa watched the *Duchesse* to see her reaction. Her face was entirely expressionless.

"My son will be here shortly," she said. "He regrets that he was not able to meet you, but having been away so long he had matters of business to attend to. A vast estate like this entails a lot of work."

"I can understand that," Mrs. Derange said. "When

233

my late husband, Mr. Derange, bought a place in Florida, he often said it was more trouble to look after than all his other businesses put together."

"My son, of course, has many experts to help him," the *Duchesse* said. "But he likes to do things for himself."

There was a rather uncomfortable pause, but Alloa was no longer listening.

Once again she was thinking of Dix. Would he come to her tonight as he had promised? She had not yet seen her room.

She wondered if he had really meant it when he said he would whistle under her window. Supposing a house like this had a night watchman. Supposing there were dogs patrolling the grounds?

There were so many dangerous possibilities, and yet Dix had seemed so light-hearted about it.

She wished he was more serious; and then she thought that she would not have him altered in any way. She loved him as he was.

Bad, crooked, a smuggler or a thief—she still loved him.

Yet there was an ache in her heart as she thought of her parents, of the letter they would receive in two days' time. She had finished her letter to them and posted it before she left the hotel.

It had not been easy to write and she did not have time to say all she had wanted. She had only told them how much in love she was and how nothing else in life was of any consequence.

"*We are going away*," she wrote, "*but where I do not know. When I do, I will try to write to you; but it may not be easy. He is wanted by the police. He has done things which are wrong, but which he could not help. Whatever happens, I must be with him, I must stand by him. I do not even know where we shall be*" married or when. I will try to tell you all this, but it may not be safe to say too much."

She felt her eyes fill with tears before she finished writing the letter.

She knew what unhappiness and anxiety it would bring to her father and mother, and yet she had known she must tell them the whole truth.

She could not pretend, could not lie to them.

She knew that when they read it they would feel distraught and at the same time would know, despairingly, that while she had said so much, she had told them so little.

She had not been able to tell them even the name of the man she was marrying.

She hoped they would think it an oversight, but she was well aware that it would seem to them ominous and even terrifying that she had taken such a decisive step while they were still left in the dark.

Finally she had added a postscript.

"Please, please forgive me if this makes you unhappy. Try and understand that I have all the happiness in the world because I love him."

Seated now in the *Grand Salon* Alloa tried to calculate how long it would be before her father and mother received the letter. She had played with the thought of telephoning them and then realised it was impossible.

How could she explain all that on the telephone? Besides, she knew that, if she talked to them, they would beg her to wait, beg her to come home first before she did anything decisive.

There was no time for that. She had to leave with Dix tonight at the very latest.

She hoped that there would be a chance of going upstairs soon. She had tried to put all the things she was likely to want with her in one small suitcase.

She wondered if she would have to lower it out of

the window to Dix or if she would carry it downstairs herself and slip out to him by some side door.

It was all so difficult to know what to plan, what to think.

She half expected that when the time came she would have to go to him with nothing. If that was necessary, she would do so without question. She was past troubling over trivialities.

"Don't you think so, Alloa?" Lou asked suddenly.

Alloa jumped.

She realised that Lou had asked her a question and saw that the *Duchesse* and Mrs. Derange were waiting for her answer. She had no idea what they had said.

"I am . . . sorry," she stammered. "I was thinking of . . . something else. What was it you asked me?"

"I asked you . . ." Lou began.

At that moment there was an interruption. The door of the *Salon* was opened and a footman appeared.

"*Monsieur le Duc!*" he announced.

Alloa felt her heart give a little thump. She saw Lou turn her head quickly, saw Mrs. Derange's eyes fixed on the door. The *Duchesse* moved forward graciously.

The *Duc* was wheeled into the room. He was even smaller and frailer than he had seemed in the press photograph. A very little man with a face lined with suffering and dark eyes set deep on either side of a thin aristocratic nose.

It was obvious to Alloa that he had little strength. The hand he held out in greeting seemed almost transparent, the blue veins prominent against the whiteness of his skin.

He stopped his chair beside Mrs. Derange.

"I am so sorry not to have been here to meet you," he said in a low voice speaking precise and almost perfect English. "We were not certain what time you were

236

to arrive and I had certain formal matters to attend to with my notary."

Mrs. Derange shook him by the hand.

"We quite understand," she said. "You have such a very beautiful place here that it must demand a lot of your time and your attention."

"Too much, I am afraid, for my health," the *Duc* said.

He held out his hand to Lou. She took it tentatively as if she were afraid that a hard hand-shake might hurt him.

"I have heard so much about you from my mother, *M'mselle*," he said.

Lou said nothing. She opened her lips as if to speak and then closed them again.

"And this is Alloa Derange," the *Duchesse* said. "Another member of the family, this time of the British branch."

The *Duc* smiled at Alloa in a very friendly manner.

"I must show you the family tree," he said.

"I should love to see it," Alloa answered.

The *Duc* looked round.

"Where are the cocktails, Mother?" he asked. "I told you that our American guests would expect them."

"I ordered them," the *Duchesse* said briefly.

She touched a little gold bell which was on the table. The door opened immediately and a footman stood there.

"The cocktails, please," the *Duchesse* said, speaking in French.

Almost immediately two footmen entered the room with silver trays on which were a variety of bottles, ice and glasses.

"You shouldn't have bothered for us," Mrs. Derange said. "I am sure you don't usually have cocktails."

"My mother has always refused to taste one," the

Duc said. "Now is the right occasion for us to overcome her prejudice. I personally enjoy a Dry Martini, although when we are alone here I find it somewhat depressing to drink by myself. What are you going to have? There is everything, even a Mint Julep if you prefer it."

"I call it very considerate of you to think of our tastes in this matter," Mrs. Derange said. "I would love a Mint Julep, but I expect Lou, like you, would prefer a Martini."

"If I am allowed to express my own preference," Lou said in rather a rude voice, "I should like a Scotch on the Rocks."

She was being deliberately defiant, Alloa knew that.

Lou very seldom drank whisky. For some reason of her own she wished to annoy her mother and perhaps shock the *Duchesse*.

Neither the *Duchesse* nor the *Duc*, however, seemed to think the request in the least extraordinary. The footman brought round the drinks.

Alloa asked shyly for a tomato juice and was rewarded with what appeared to her to be a glance of approval from the *Duchesse*.

The *Duc* raised his glass.

"And now we must have a toast," he said. "To our American cousins, and may their visit here be one of many."

Alloa was somewhat startled by his words. It did not appear as if he expected Lou's stay to be permanent. Mrs. Derange did not look disconcerted. In reply she raised her own glass.

"To you, *Duc*," she said. "And may you soon be quite well."

"That is what we all wish," the *Duchesse* said in a low voice. "I am convinced that in a month or so he will no longer need a chair."

238

The *Duc* smiled at her.

"Your faith, *ma Mère,* is unquenchable," he said softly.

"I went to *Lourdes* while you were away," she said quietly.

He smiled at her again and bent forward to touch her hand. For a moment there was a suspicion of tears in the *Duchesse's* eyes. She rose to her feet.

"And now, if you have finished, I will show you to your rooms," she said. "Dinner is at eight o'clock. I expect you would like to have an hour in which to bathe and change."

"That will be very nice," Mrs. Derange said, putting down her glass.

A little awkwardly, because the *Duc* could not accompany them, they filed from the room, the *Duchesse* leading the way up the grand staircase to the huge, luxurious bedrooms to which they had been allotted.

Mrs. Derange and Lou were in one suite with a boudoir and a bathroom on their own; Alloa was next door in what seemed to her an equally magnificent room with her own bathroom and a little balcony overlooking the flower garden.

"It's lovely; thank you so much," she said to the *Duchesse*. The moment the door closed behind her hostess, she ran to the window.

Would Dix be able to reach her from the garden? And if he was there, how would she be able to get to him? She stood on the balcony and looked down.

He would be very conspicuous, she thought, if he made a noise on this side of the house, and she could only hope that neither the *Duc* nor the *Duchesse* had bedrooms looking this way.

She decided that as soon as dinner was over she would try to discover if there was a side door opening on to the garden. Frantically she tried to make a map of the house in her mind—the hall and the *Grand Salon*, the Dining-room, the Library which they had seen on their first visit.

It was too complicated for her to remember or to visualise. There were so many rooms, each more magnificent than the last.

The house had been built almost in a square. She began to calculate that there must be more than one staircase by which one could reach the ground floor.

She stood so long at the window trying to make up her mind in which direction Dix would come and how he would find her room that it was only the clock on the mantelpiece which made her conscious that time was passing.

The evening sunshine glinted on the huge, square crystals which surrounded its face and recalled her wandering senses to the fact that she had to have a suit-case ready so that she could go with him.

It was then, in horror, that she discovered that her clothes had been unpacked.

Everything that she possessed was hanging in the wardrobes or arranged neatly in the beautiful inlaid chest-of-drawers which stood against the pale peach-coloured walls of the room.

What was more, her suit-cases had disappeared. She searched for them frantically, looking in the cupboards, going even into the little tiled bathroom to see if she could discover them there.

This was a blow she had not anticipated, and she wondered desperately what she should do. To ring the bell and ask for her suit-case would seem a strange action on the part of a guest who had just arrived.

Why, why, she asked herself, could not Dix have taken her away this morning when she had begged him to do so?

Everything was getting more complicated hour by

hour and she knew now that the only thing she could do was to take a bundle with her.

'Like a gypsy,' she told herself with a slight smile.

She put some of her things together—a night-gown, change of underclothes, face powder, stockings and handkerchiefs—and wrapped them round with a light shawl which she sometimes wore in the evenings.

Then she hid them in the cupboard and started to change.

After a bath she felt somehow less agitated. Why did she worry? Of one thing she could be certain, she could rely on Dix. If he had said he would come to her, he would do so.

Perhaps he would bribe one of the servants who would escort her downstairs and out through a back door to where he could be waiting for her. Perhaps he would himself enter the house and come to her room.

She remembered how easily he had got into Claridge's and been in Lou's bedroom without any conscious effort, without anybody suspecting that he should not be there.

Why should he not do the same thing here?

Alloa took up her plain black evening dress and slipped it over her head. Last night, she thought, she had looked radiant in the dress that Jeanne had lent her. Tonight Cinderella was back in her rags, looking very plain and unobtrusive.

She was just wondering whether to wear a coloured belt or a plain black velvet one when there came a knock on the door.

"Come in," she called.

A maid wearing a lace cap and an apron to match came into the room.

"I have brought you this, *M'mselle*," she said, holding out a silver salver on which reposed a beautiful corsage of pink roses.

241

"For me?" Alloa asked. "Are you quite certain it is not for Miss Lou Derange?"

"No, for you, *M'mselle*," the maid smiled.

"Oh, thank you," Alloa said.

The roses were wired and their stems covered with silver paper. Alloa held it against her dress and realised that it transformed the plain severity of it into something gay and festive.

"It is just what I wanted," she said aloud, and realised that the maid had gone and she was talking to herself.

She pinned the corsage in place, gave a last brush to her fair hair as it fell softly against her shoulders, then went along to Lou's bedroom.

She knocked on the door, dreading what Lou would say, dreading this moment when she felt that Lou would confide in her what she felt about the *Duc*. And then with relief she realised that both mother and daughter were emerging from another door of the suite.

"Oh, there you are, Alloa!" Mrs. Derange exclaimed. "I think we ought to go down. The *Duchesse* told me they meet in the *Grand Salon* before dinner."

Lou was wearing a magnificent red satin dress which had come from one of the famous French *couturiers*. She looked, Alloa thought, as if she had stepped from some eighteenth-century picture on the walls.

She might have been one of her own ancestors, with the great, billowing skirts of her dress rustling against the banisters as they walked slowly down the wide staircase to the ground floor.

Lou wore no flowers. Mrs. Derange had an orchid on her shoulder, and Alloa supposed that flowers were always sent to the guests before dinner. It was a nice touch, she thought, but wondered if the *Duc* would be offended that Lou had not appreciated the gesture.

The *Duchesse* was already in the *Grand Salon,* the

Duc beside her in his wheel-chair. Mother and son seemed to have been talking earnestly as they came in, and Alloa had the idea that the *Duchesse* was a little agitated.

She had, however, been trained not to show her emotions. She rose and came towards them.

"I do hope you found everything you wanted," she said, "and that your maid is being looked after."

"Everything was perfect," Mrs. Derange said, "and Jeanne is in the seventh heaven to be staying in a private mansion again. She has spoken to me so often of the glories of French houses. Nothing we can offer her in America is anything like as good as what she has enjoyed at home."

The *Duc* laughed.

"That's typical, I am afraid. Our people grumble when they are at home, but when they are abroad their memories are entirely golden."

He turned to Alloa as he spoke and said:

"Do you find that you, too, only remember the pleasant things and forget those that are unpleasant?"

"I think when one is homesick everything seems much better than it ever was in actual fact," Alloa replied.

"And are you homesick?" he asked.

"Not at the moment," Alloa answered. "I am so thrilled to be here. I only wish my father could see the *Château*—he has spoken of it so often."

"You must bring him here," the *Duc* said. "I should like him to feel proud of what I have done to preserve the family treasures."

Alloa wondered if he would give her the same invitation after she had run away. What would he say tomorrow when her bedroom was found empty? When they learned that she had disappeared with a man who was wanted by the police?

243

She gave a little sigh. The *Duc* looked up at her.

"Are you unhappy?" he said.

He spoke in a low voice so that the others would not hear and there was something in his eyes which compelled the truth.

Alloa nodded.

"Don't be," he said. "Happiness is always waiting where you least expect it, and it's always worth waiting for."

He spoke with some deep and inner conviction that left Alloa speechless, and yet his words had released within her the sudden tempest of apprehension and fear.

Suppose happiness was not waiting for her round the corner?

Suppose Dix was dead or wounded or in prison? Suppose she waited all night for him and he never came? What would she do? What could she do?

She felt then as if everything that was happening was like some horrible and uneasy dream—the beauty of the room, the people sitting in it, even herself, were all unreal, all without substance.

It was only Dix who mattered, only Dix and his problems which filled the whole world to the exclusion of everything else.

As if it came from a very far distance she heard the *Duchesse's* voice.

"I am so sorry if dinner is delayed," she said. "But we are waiting for our other guests."

"Pierre is always late," the *Duc* murmured.

The *Duchesse* turned to Mrs. Derange.

"I am afraid my younger son is notoriously unpunctual," she said. "And he is bringing a friend with him."

Even as she finished speaking the door opened.

"*Le Comte Pierre, Madame!*" the footman announced.

Alloa glanced indifferently towards the door; and then, as she did so, her heart seemed to stop beating.

She would have got to her feet, only she could not move; she could only sit paralysed in her chair, her fingers gripping each other and the blood receding slowly from her face and leaving her deadly pale.

It was Dix who stood there!

Dix, smiling, his dark eyes glancing round the assembled company, his hair shining in the sunlight from the windows.

Someone else was with him, too. A tall man, square shouldered, wearing a loose, grey suit.

"You must forgive us being late, *ma Mère,*" Dix said to the *Duchesse,* "but the aeroplane was delayed. May I introduce Mr. Steve Weston?"

It was Lou who broke the spell which seemed to have gripped both her and Mrs. Derange. With a cry that was almost a shriek she rose to her feet and ran across the room.

"Steve! Steve!" she cried.

And then without pause and without thought she flung her arms round his neck.

"Hello, Lou! Are you glad to see me?" Steve asked needlessly.

Then he bent his head and kissed her.

"May I introduce my youngest son, Pierre?" the *Duchesse* said in her gentle way.

Apparently quite oblivious of what was happening between Lou and the strange young man who had just entered the room, she was patiently introducing her son to the assembled guests.

Alloa looked up into Dix's eyes.

"We know each other already," he said.

He bent down and took Alloa's hands in his. They were cold and her fingers fluttered like captured birds.

Very gently he drew her to her feet.

"I told you to trust me," he said. "I said I would come for you."

"But, . . . I don't . . . understand."

The words came stammeringly from between her lips. Her eyes, looking up to his, were like the eyes of a frightened child.

"I will explain everything," he said. "But at the moment I am ravenously hungry. I've had nothing to eat all day."

"Dinner is served!" boomed a butler from the doorway.

"Shall we go in?" the *Duchesse* said to Mrs. Derange.

For a moment Mrs. Derange did not hear her. With an expression almost of stupefaction on her face she was looking at Lou. Steve Weston's arm was round her and she was transformed from a rather sulky, indifferent girl into a radiant, glowing creature whose whole face was alight with happiness.

"I am sure we are all looking forward to our dinner," the *Duc* said.

With an effort Mrs. Derange forced herself to answer him.

"Yes, I am sure we are."

It was a conventional, unimportant reply, but it prevented her from making a scene, from trying to force Lou and Steve Weston apart from each other.

She was defeated and she knew it; but as she walked towards the dining-room she held her head high, her mind already busy with the plans for the wedding.

Dix had slipped Alloa's arm through his.

"Why didn't you tell me?" she asked.

"I have got so much to tell you now that I don't know where to begin," she replied.

"But you pretended . . . you lied . . ." she said incoherently.

"Not really," he answered. "And if I did, you have to forgive me."

They were the last of the procession moving towards the dining-room and, oblivious of the footmen who stood in the doorway, he bent his head and kissed her forehead.

"I love you," he whispered.

Somehow it was all she wanted to hear.

She felt bewildered, astounded and puzzled, and yet at the same time nothing mattered because Dix had said, "I love you."

Dinner should have been a difficult meal because Lou and Steve Weston sat staring at each other, having apparently nothing to say either to themselves or to anyone else.

Mrs. Derange was obviously pre-occupied with her own thoughts, and Alloa felt it impossible either to eat or to speak.

But despite this it was a gay hour that they all spent in the great painted Banqueting hall.

It was Dix who kept them laughing, telling them of some absurd adventures he had had the year before in a fishing boat off Capri; he teased his brother about his recent visit to Baden-Baden; and made even the *Duchesse* unbend as he chaffed her about the alterations to the garden and the present that he had brought her from Paris.

He was a host in himself, and the *Duc*, laughing at his jokes and watching him with a twinkle in his eyes, was a very willing foil to his wit.

'He loves him,' Alloa thought, watching the *Duc's* eyes upon his younger brother.

Then she turned to see a very different expression on the *Duchesse's* face. Alloa was not quite certain what it was.

Was it disapproval or was it resentment because Dix

looked so strong and well while his elder brother was so frail and ill.

She could not analyse the difference in her own mind, and it only added one more to the many other questions which besieged her mind as dinner finished and Dix, instead of remaining in the dining-room with the *Duc* and Steve, followed the ladies from the room.

"Come with me, I have something to show you," he said, taking Alloa by the arm.

Before she knew what was happening he had drawn her into a doorway leading to a small ante-room and from there into the garden.

The sun had just set. The sky was a blaze of crimson and gold in the west, while high in the sky the first evening stars were twinkling.

In silence he led her down through the rose garden and then they turned along a little paved path and came to an arbour covered with orange blossom beside a stone fountain.

There Dix stopped and turned to face Alloa, one hand tipping her chin upwards so that he could look down into her eyes.

"Oh, Alloa!" he said.

It was just her name spoken in a deep voice, but it had the power to move her immeasurably. She felt herself quiver, and then, because she was longing so desperately for him to kiss her, she put out her hands to hold him from her.

"No, not yet. Not until you have given me an explanation."

"I love you," he said, "isn't that all you want to hear?"

"It is all that matters," she answered. "But I have got to know the rest."

"Are you so curious?" he smiled.

248

"Curious and angry," she replied. "Why did you lie to me? Why did you let me believe you were a thief?"

"Because I am one," he assented. "I have stolen your love, haven't I? You tried so hard not to let me have it but it is mine. I knew that when you came to me this morning, when you were ready to run away with me, to go into exile, to face an utterly foreign and alien future so long as we could be together."

Alloa felt herself blushing.

"I thought you were in danger," she said. "I would not have said what I did if I had not believed that."

"Darling, I adore you for it. It was what I wanted you to say."

"But, why? Why?" Alloa asked.

"Can I kiss you before I begin my explanations?" he enquired, his voice deep and passionate.

She shook her head, glorying for the moment in her power over him, seeing the desire in his eyes, the eagerness with which his hands went out towards her.

"No," she answered. "Tell me what you have to tell me first. I am not certain that I am going to forgive you."

He smiled at that and lifting her hand kissed the palm so that she felt herself tremble and longed, with an almost overwhelming intensity, to throw herself into his arms.

Then she checked herself.

He must be punished a little for what he had made her suffer. She drew her hand away from him.

"Tell me from the very beginning," she said.

He gave a little sigh as if in impatience and drew her into the arbour where there was a comfortable seat arranged beneath the fragrant blossom.

"I told you what happened to me in the war," he said. "That was the truth, all of it. I ran away and my father and mother never really forgave me. One cannot blame them. I caused them a great deal of anxiety.

"But when the war was over, I had to come home again; and I found myself bored with the very restricted life at the *Château*. I had a lot of education to make up. My parents procured tutors for me and I went, for a short time, to one of our universities.

"Having tasted excitement and liberty I did not take well to restrictions. I was what you call very wild. I got, also, an extremely bad reputation. I was sent down from the university. I was involved in several very notorious love affairs.

"I did all sorts of very reprehensible things and, as I told you in all truthfulness, I am looked on as the black sheep of the family.

"I suppose it was my fault, but my mother got it into her head that, whatever happened, my brother must produce an heir. I think she was filled with horror at the idea of my inheriting the title and the estate. She wanted to do anything, however desperate, to prevent that happening.

"There had never been any question of my brother marrying. He has always been an invalid. He was a sickly child, and though he has been to every possible specialist they all said the same thing—there is no hope of his ever being cured.

"But my mother was determined that a miracle should happen. He would get well, he would get married and he would produce an heir.

"It was while she was thinking in these terms that she had a letter from Mrs. Derange. It seemed to her that here was a Heaven-sent opportunity.

"An American girl who wanted a title and who was, in a sense, a relation, was exactly the sort of bride my mother was looking for."

Alloa stirred and Dix put out his hand and took hers.

250

Alloa did not repulse him. There was something infinitely comforting in feeling the strength and warmth of his fingers.

"You know what happened. The two older women arranged it amongst themselves and my mother tentatively spoke of the idea to my brother. He told her the whole thing was ridiculous and she promised to forget it. It was only because he was not certain that she had really dropped the idea that he told me about it.

"I was in London when I got his letter; and as I was staying at Claridge's, I thought I would have a look at this Miss Lou Derange who was being very much written up in the newspapers."

"You were staying at Claridge's!" Alloa ejaculated. "So that was why . . ."

"I saw the door of the suite open," Dix said, "and so I walked in. It was just on an impulse. I thought perhaps I should find out something about this girl who was willing to marry my brother because he had a title.

"I saw the miniature on the dressing-table and I picked it up. I guessed it was of her, and while I was looking at it you came into the room."

"So you weren't thinking of stealing it," Alloa said. "Oh, what a fool you must have thought me!"

His hand tightened on hers.

"Shall I tell you what I thought?" he said. "I thought you were the most adorable person I had ever seen in my life. You also astonished me. No one had ever tried to reform me before."

"You must have been laughing at me all the time," Alloa said miserably.

"Not laughing," he corrected. "Loving you."

"That's not true," Alloa murmured.

"Yes it is," he answered. "I loved you from that moment, but I had a great many things to do in Lon-

251

don and I was not able to see you again. I sent you the flowers and I hoped you would not forget me."

"You realised then that we were coming to Biarritz?"

"I realised it two days later when I got a letter from my brother saying that my mother was still persisting in her idea of marriage. He asked me what he should do and I telegraphed him to do nothing, but to let things take their course. I said that because I knew that it would mean I should see you again."

"But if you hadn't rescued me . . ." Alloa asked.

"I should still have come in search of you at Biarritz," Dix replied. "It was just luck that we met when we did. It merely confirmed what I thought the first time I had seen you, that you were the loveliest and most adorable person in the whole world."

"But the smuggling? When I found you with the car, and those men?" Alloa said.

"I am coming to that," Dix went on. "The car you saw me in was stolen, but not by me. I had been on the wrong side of the law for such a long time that when I was invited by the Chief of the *Sûreté* to help them in a very difficult job, I accepted. I should not have done so if the original request had not come from my friends in Biarritz."

"Your friends?" Alloa questioned.

"Yes, my friends! *Mère Blanchard* and some of the others whom you met at that party," Dix said. "They told me that while they were prepared to shut their eyes to a little inoffensive smuggling over the Spanish frontier—it always has been done all through the centuries—they were becoming alarmed by the gang that was operating the smuggling of cars."

"The men I saw?" Alloa questioned.

"Yes, the men you saw," Dix told her. "They were a real rough lot; bad men, men who would stick at nothing, not even murder."

Alloa shivered.

"That is what I felt when that man threatened to cut my throat."

"You will never know how frightened I was for you that night," Dix said. "If they had thought you were really dangerous, if they had not believed me when I said that you were my friend, you would not be alive at this moment."

He put out his arms and drew her close to him.

"Think what that would have meant," he said. "That I should not have been holding you here at this moment; I should never have known that you love me."

"Go on. Please go on," Alloa pleaded.

"That is the whole story," Dix said. "Because my friends begged me to help them, I worked with the Sûreté to bring this gang to justice. To do so I had to join them.

"They knew my record; they knew the trouble I had been in on one account or another, and so they accepted me. I took over their cars once they had stolen them. I brought them down to Biarritz. I helped ship them to Spain."

"But why didn't the police catch them the night that I was there?" Alloa asked.

"Because two of the main organisers of the gang were in Paris. They had their own hideaways there which even I did not know—hideaways which would have enabled them to avoid arrest if there had been the slightest suspicion of French interference.

"We had to get them down here to Biarritz. We had to arrange that they would all be present before the police could do the final round-up."

"Then Lou's friend was speaking the truth," Alloa said.

"He is an extremely stupid young man who has been

talking far too much," Dix said grimly. "He will be dealt with at headquarters, I promise you that."

"And the men have been caught?" Alloa asked.

"They were all arrested this afternoon," Dix replied, "with the exception of two."

"Two?" she queried.

He nodded.

"Myself and one other. A young man whom I wanted to save. It was not his fault he had got caught up in this gang. He is a decent boy who will go straight now he has the chance of getting a decent job, of being able to make money without resorting to crime."

"A job you have found for him?"

Dix nodded.

"He was worth saving."

"And the rest?"

"The rest will be locked up for a number of years. Two of them at least will go to the *guillotine*. They are charged not only with smuggling, but with murder."

"And they didn't suspect you?" Alloa said, a little breathlessly.

"Not until the last moment," Dix said. "And then a bullet missed me by less than an inch. I think darling, fate was preserving me for you."

"Oh, Dix!" She gave a little shudder. "That was what I was afraid of, only I thought it would be a police bullet that might hit you."

"When that happens, it doesn't exactly matter who fires it," he said with a twist of his lips.

"But you are safe."

"I am safe," he told her gravely.

"And that's all," she said with a little sigh.

"Not quite," he answered. "When you told me about Steve Weston, I was determined to wait at the aerodrome and bring him straight to the *Château*. I wanted

Lou to be happy, as we are going to be happy. Besides, my brother had a long talk with me last night."

"What about?" Alloa said.

"He told me," Dix said, and his voice was very serious, "that he has not long to live. The specialist whom he saw in Germany has given him perhaps six months at the outside.

"He wants me to get married as soon as possible, to stay here with him and take over the estate.

"There is a great deal to be done from the legal point of view, and also it would give him very great happiness to know that the *Château* will still go on being a private residence, that a *de Rangé* will still be living here for at least another generation."

There was a little silence and then Dix added:

"Shall we do that and make him happy?"

Alloa looked up at him.

"Is that what you want?" she asked.

Dix turned towards her.

"I want it more than anything else in the world," he said. "Oh, my darling! Perhaps I have been cruel to you. Perhaps I should have given you a hint that things were not what you thought. But I wanted you to love me for myself.

"I have made love to so many women, I'm not pretending to you that I haven't.

"But always I've had the feeling that it was not only me they loved, but the position I held, perhaps the position I might hold in the future.

"I wanted to be loved just because I was myself, despite my bad character, despite all the wrong things I have done and maybe will go on doing. I wanted love as it was meant to be, love as you have given it to me."

His voice seemed to vibrate round the little arbour, and then, very slowly and gently he drew Alloa closer to him.

255

"I will try and alter myself," he said. "But somehow I don't think it will be difficult to be good with you to help me, with you to guide me."

"I love you as you are," she answered. "Oh, Dix! I can't believe all this is happening. I am so happy, so utterly, madly happy."

"And that is what I want," he said. "Not only now, but forever."

He looked across the arbour and his voice was very solemn as he added:

"You have prayed for me. I pray to God that he will help me to be worthy of you."

"Oh, Dix! I have been such a fool about many things," Alloa whispered.

He laughed at that and she felt the solemnity vanish as he drew her masterfully so close to him that she could hardly breathe.

Then she felt his lips, first on her forehead, then on her eyes, and then at last, passionately and possessively on her mouth.

"You are mine," he said. "We belong to each other and there is no escape for either of us ever again. After all, I don't think I will change. I will remain as I am—a thief who has stolen your love and who will hold it for all time."

Alloa put up her hand shyly and touched his cheek.

"A thief," she said. "But my thief. The thief I have loved from the very first moment I saw him."

He kissed her hand and then once again his lips were seeking hers.

"Love does conquer all things—doesn't it, my darling?" he asked.